THE
BROADWAY
MURDERS

THE
BROADWAY
MURDERS

Agata Stanford

Second Edition

A Jenevacris Press Publication

THE BROADWAY MURDERS
A Dorothy Parker Mystery / June 2010
Second Edition March 2011

Published by
Jenevacris Press
New York

This is a work of fiction. Names, characters, places, and incidents
either are the product of the author's imagination or are used
fictitiously. Any resemblance to actual persons, living or dead,
events, or locales is entirely coincidental.

———◆———

ISBN 978-0-9827542-0-7

Printed in the United States of America

www.dorothyparkermysteries.com

for Serena

Acknowledgments

I thank a number of people for their encouragement and support throughout the process of writing the books of my Dorothy Parker Mysteries series. An author needs resources, feedback, and sounding boards as well as emotional support from family, friends, and colleagues. So it is with gratitude that I mention, here, the names of those wonderful people who have provided their time and love and assistance: Rosaria and Anatole Konstantin, who read everything I sent to them and let me know if I was on track; Mary Rose Greer, who has listened to my ideas over the years, and has been an invaluable "sounding board," allowing me to find my own way; Brenda Bright, my very good friend, who encourages me, and whose opinion I value; Lisa Green, good friend and avid reader of all my work; the lovely librarians of the Richard's Library in Warrensburg, New York, Sarah, Linda, and Lynn, who always greet me with a smile and who ordered whatever I needed for research; the research staff at The Baseball Hall of Fame, who kindly answered all of my questions about the 1926 World Series for *Mystic Mah Jong*; Jerome Cortellesi, for taking me on a personal tour of the University Club; Amanda Mecke, my agent; and Eric Conover, without whose talent these books would not look nearly so good. And, going way back, to when I first took an interest in the Theatre and writing, I must thank Mrs. Kominars, my 7th- and 8th-grade English teacher at P.S. 185 in Queens, New York. She encouraged me and always said I should become a writer.

Contents

Cast of Characters ... ... *Page xi*

Chapter One ... ... *Page 1*

Chapter Two ... ... *Page 43*

Chapter Three ... ... *Page 59*

Chapter Four ... ... *Page 89*

Chapter Five ... ... *Page 111*

Chapter Six ... ... *Page 137*

Chapter Seven ... ... *Page 155*

Chapter Eight ... ... *Page 189*

Chapter Nine ... ... *Page 203*

Chapter Ten ... ... *Page 221*

Chapter Eleven ... ... *Page 249*

Chapter Twelve ... ... *Page 261*

The Final Chapter ... ... *Page 283*

Poetic License ... ... *Page 297*

About the Author ... ... *Page 301*

Who's Who in the Cast of Dorothy Parker Mysteries

The Algonquin Round Table was the famous assemblage of writers, artists, actors, musicians, newspaper and magazine reporters, columnists, and critics who met for luncheon at 1:00 P.M. most days, for a period of about ten years, starting in 1919, in the Rose Room of the Algonquin Hotel on West 44th Street in Manhattan. The unwritten test for membership was wit, brilliance, and likeability. It was an informal gathering ranging from ten to fifteen regulars, although many peripheral characters who arrived for lunch only once might later claim they were part of the "Vicious Circle," broadening the number to thirty, forty, and more. Once taken into the fold, one was expected to indulge in witty repartee and humorous observations during the meal, and then follow along to the Theatre, or a speakeasy, or Harlem for a night of jazz. Gertrude Stein dubbed the Round Tablers "The Lost Generation." The joyous, if sardonic, reply that rose with a laugh from Dorothy Parker was, "*Wheeee! We're lost!*"

Dorothy Parker set the style and attitude for modern women of America to emulate during the 1920s and 1930s. Through her pointed poetry, cutting theatrical reviews, brilliant commentary, bittersweet short stories, and much-quoted rejoinders, Mrs. Parker was the embodiment of the soulful pathos of the "Ain't We Got Fun" generation of the Roaring Twenties.

Robert Benchley: Writer, humorist, boulevardier, and bon vivant, editor of *Vanity Fair* and *Life Magazine,* and drama critic of *The New Yorker,* he may accidentally have been the very first standup comedian. His original and skewed sense of humor made him a star on Broadway, and later, in the movies. What man didn't want to *be* Bob Benchley?

Alexander Woollcott was the most famous man in America—or so he said. As drama critic for the *New York Times,* he was the star-maker, discovering and promoting the careers of Helen Hayes, Katherine Cornell, Alfred Lunt and Lynn Fontanne, and the Marx Brothers, to name but a few. Larger than life and possessing a rapier wit, he was a force to be reckoned with. When someone asked a friend of his to describe Woollcott, the answer was, "Improbable."

Frank Pierce Adams (FPA) was a self-proclaimed modern-day Samuel Pepys, whose newspaper column, "The Conning Tower," was a widely read daily diary of how, where, and with whom he spent his days while gallivanting about New York City. Thanks to him, every witty retort, clever comment, and one-liner uttered by the Round Tablers at luncheon was in print the next day for millions of readers to chuckle over at the breakfast table.

Harold Ross wrote for *Stars and Stripes* during the War, where he first met fellow newspapermen Woollcott and Adams. The rumpled, "clipped woodchuck" (as described by Edna Ferber) was one of the most brilliant editors of his time. His magazine, *The New Yorker*, which he started in 1925, has enriched the lives of everyone who has ever had a subscription. His hypochondria was legendary, and his the-world-is-out-to-get-me outlook was often comical.

Jane Grant married Harold Ross but kept her maiden name, cut her hair shorter than her husband's, and viewed domesticity with disdain. A society columnist for the *New York Times*, Jane was the very chic model of modernity during the 1920s. Having worked hard for women's suffrage, Jane continued in her cause while serving meals and emptying ashtrays during all-night sessions of the Thanatopsis Literary and Inside Straight Club.

Heywood Broun began his career at numerous newspapers throughout the country before landing a spot on the *World*. Sportswriter and Harlem Renaissance jazz fiend, he was to become the social conscience of America during the 1920s and beyond through his column, "As I See It." His insight and commentary made him a champion of the labor movement, as did his fight for justice during and after the seven years of the Sacco and Vanzetti trials and execution.

Edmund "Bunny" Wilson: Writer, editor, and critic of American literature, he first came to work at *Vanity Fair* after Mrs. Parker pulled his short story out from under the slush-pile and found it interesting.

Robert E. Sherwood came to work on the editorial staff at *Vanity Fair* alongside Parker and Benchley. The six-foot-six Sherwood was often tormented by the dwarfs performing—whatever it was they did—at the Hippodrome on his way to and from work at the magazine's 44th Street offices, but that didn't stop him from becoming one of the twentieth-century Theatre's greatest playwrights.

Marc Connelly began his career as a reporter but found his true calling as a playwright. Short and bald, he co-authored his first hit play with the tall and pompadoured *George S. Kaufman.*

Edna Ferber racked up Pulitzer Prizes by writing bestselling potboilers set against America's sweeping vistas, most notably, *So Big, Showboat, Cimarron,* and *Giant.* She, too, collaborated with George S. on several successful Broadway shows. A spinster, she was a formidable personality and wit and a much-coveted member of the Algonquin Round Table.

John Barrymore was a member of the Royal Family of the American Stage, which included *John Drew* and *Ethel* and *Lionel Barrymore*. John Barrymore was famous not only for his stage portrayals, but for his majestic profile, which was captured in all its splendor on celluloid.

The Marx Brothers: First there were five, then there were four, then there were three Marx Brothers — *awww, heck,* if you don't know who these crazy, zany men are, it's time to hit the video store or tune into Turner Classic Movies!

Also mentioned: *Neysa McMein,* artist and illustrator, whose studio door was open all hours of the day and night for anyone who wished to pay a call; *Grace Moore*, Broadway and opera star, and later a movie star; Broadway and radio star *Fanny Brice* — think Streisand in *Funny Girl*; *Noel Coward*, English star and playwright who took America by storm with his classy comedies and bright musical offerings; *Condé Nast,* publisher of numerous magazines including *Vogue*, *Vanity Fair,* and *House and Garden; Florenz Zeigfeld* — of *"Follies"* fame — big-time producer of the extravaganza stage revue; *The Lunts*, husband-and-wife stars of the London and Broadway stages, individually known as Alfred Lunt and Lynn Fontanne; *Tallulah Bankhead* — irreverent, though beautiful, southern-born actress with the foghorn drawl, who later made a successful transition from the stage to film—the life of any party, she often perked up the waning festivities performing cartwheels sans bloomers; *Irving Berlin, George Gershwin,* and *Jascha Heifetz*—famous for "God Bless America" and hundreds more hit songs; composer of *Rhapsody in Blue* and *Porgy and Bess* and many more great works; and the violin virtuoso, respectively.

THE
BROADWAY
MURDERS

Chapter One

"Woodrow Wilson," I ordered, "sit there and don't say a word. If Aleck suspects, the Wit will throw a fit!"

I spooned out a small helping from the rounded hill of pâté de foie gras, and then, with my fingers and a butter knife, filled in the unsightly crater. I admired my handiwork, and then peeked over my shoulder for witnesses to my thievery, as I fed the chopped liver to Woodrow Wilson, my co-conspirator.

"Too much garlic, don't you think?" I asked Woodrow as I licked my fingers.

Garlic or not, he wanted more.

It is the fall of 1924. Manhattan. We're sitting at the table waiting for the others, and this room, a hotel dining room on West 44th Street, is the heart of my world.

A couple blocks away is Broadway. Alfred Lunt and Lynn Fontanne are making their first big splash in *The Guardsman*, and *Desire Under the Elms* promises fame for its playwright, Eugene O'Neill. The ubiquitous Barrymores dominate the stage for yet another season. George S. Kaufman has two shows running, one written with Edna Ferber, the other penned with Marc Connelly, and Sam Harris's and Irving Berlin's *Music Box Revue* (starring my closest friend and confidant, Robert Benchley) has recently closed after a lengthy run. These glorious people are just a few of my friends, people I've broken bread with and washed down the crumbs with innumerable bottles of hooch, here in this dining room, the Rose Room of the Algonquin Hotel, the heart of my world.

While the Gershwin boys are hacking away at words and music, and gin is distilling in bathtubs throughout the country, political dramas (demanding suspension of disbelief) play out on the world stage: Calvin Coolidge is running for president against J.W. Davis; a smug bullyboy named J. Edgar Hoover just got appointed director of the Bureau of Investigation; and Woodrow Wilson, a man of great insight, integrity, and intelligence (unusual qualities in a politician) has died. To honor the great man I've named my Boston terrier puppy after him.

On the other side of the pond, in Germany, a nasty little upstart with a Little Tramp mustache has been sentenced to jail, an uncouth braggart named Mussolini grips power in Italy's first Fascist election, while philosophical infighting among the Reds is causing havoc in Russia. Had I to review such melodrama, top-heavy with villainous protagonists and shakily supported by an incompetent cast, I'd've asked, "What fresh hell is this?" and advised an absinthe chaser after swallowing such swill!

As these great and inconsequential events pass through my life, resulting in little more emotional reaction than a head-shake and a mindless tongue-cluck, I am unexpectedly knocked for a loop when Reginald Ignatius Pierce, Broadway producer, man-about-town, bon vivant, general swell, and pain-in-the-ass, is found dead in his 46th Street apartment, saving anyone the bother of pulling a trigger, plunging a dagger, or poisoning his highball. It was generally known in Theatre circles that there were numerous people who would have gladly wielded an ax, tightened a rope, bloodied their hands, but for fear of persecution, if not lack of nerve to live out their dreams of murdering Reginald. Not to sound hard-hearted, but for me and my friends, the surprise is not that he is dead, but that he had not been murdered.

The news of his sudden death came as we were lunching at our usual haunt, the Rose Room of the Algonquin Hotel. Frank Case, the hotel manager, had called Aleck Woollcott away to the telephone, putting an end, if only temporarily, to Aleck's vitriolic remarks concerning Condé Nast's latest sexual transgressions.

All of the kids were arriving; the scrape of chairs and shuffling feet were reminiscent of the game of musical chairs at children's parties.

Alexander Woollcott and I had been the first

to arrive. George (S. Kaufman) and Edna (Ferber) were taking a break from yet another collaboration, arriving in time to scoop up and devour most of the popovers. Charlie (MacArthur) bounded in with Harold Ross, who grabbed the remaining stalk of celery and crunched a fervent plea in my left ear for the short story I had promised to deliver a week ago last Thursday. Ross is all worked up about a new magazine he is about to publish, which we'd all agreed should wear the moniker, *The New Yorker*, if he ever got it off the ground.

Columnist FPA — Frank Pierce Adams — and sports journalist Heywood Broun beat my friend and neighbor, artist Neysa McMein, who ambled in with Irving Berlin, to the last sorry pickles, and wouldn't you know that Harpo (Marx) flew into the room and used the art of distraction by kissing my right shoulder to help himself to a handful of pâté at my left, which I had been diligently guarding, like a dodo bird her newly laid eggs, for Aleck. I couldn't sculpt over the devastation, so I popped the garnish of parsley into my mouth and offered the smattering that remained to a grateful Woodrow Wilson, before signaling our waiter, Luigi, to bring another portion.

We are all a little crazy. The War made us this way. Artistic temperament and youthful energy, too. Reckless pride brought Europe to war, and America jumped in to end it. The often frenzied exuberance of my generation is just our juvenile insistence that we return to a happier time: before loss, before senselessness. Senseless death inspires in some people a quest for meaningful living; for others, senseless death gives rise to senseless living. (How else does one explain the song lyrics, "Diga-Diga-Doo, Diga-Doo-Doo"?) I live in a place somewhere between the Sublime and the Ridiculous.

As in a well-directed farce, Aleck bounced back into the room with the authority of a school headmaster, and an unprecedented silence fell over the table. Except for celery chewing that crunched a beat not unlike the tick-tock of a time bomb, *no one spoke!* Such a thing had never happened before. We are a circle of friends whose rapid-fire conversation could send a stenographer off for an extended stay at Bellevue.

All eyes were drawn toward Aleck's sizable form. His triple chins quivered in rotation, sunlight reflected off one of the lenses of his heavy spectacles, and he was solemnly wiping sweat from his brow with his kerchief. Our silent expectancy did not escape his notice. He milked the moment, relishing the rare, undivided attention for a few dramatic seconds, almost overlooking the fact that the plate of pâté was gone. I thought he was about to make comment of it, when, with dour expression, his hands resting on the back of his chair, he stared down at the expanse of white cloth, and announced solemnly, "Pierce, Reggie Pierce is dead!"

"Well, we know that, darling; his last show bombed—dead in the water," I jumped in, relieved that Luigi had arrived with the new plate of chopped liver.

"Not finished, Dottie, but dead."

"*Holy moly!*" squeaked FPA.

"What a scoop!" yelled Harold Ross.

"*Awww, shit!*" I added.

It was just then that Bob Benchley arrived, scanned the table for something edible, and settled on the very last, forlorn-looking cherry tomato on the pickle dish, which he tossed into the air and caught in his mouth. "How'd he kick off?" he asked.

"Choked on a cherry tomato."

Like the newfangled machine that spits out tennis balls, Mr. Benchley ejected the murderous fruit for a high velocity flight across the table, only to be caught by an ever-ready, ever-scavenging Harpo, who donned it like a clown's nose.

"Natural causes? Who'd have thunk it?"

"He was found in his apartment just a little while ago."

"How come I didn't hear about it?" asked George Kaufman, who still works at the *New York Times* for seventy-five dollars a week, even though he's made a fortune as a playwright.

"I have a friend at the *Morning Telegraph* who has a friend whose brother has a friend whose sister's husband has a friend on the police force," said Aleck.

"Aleck, you mean your Cousin Joe up at the 20th Precinct," piped in Ross.

"I guess we have to scribble a piece on Pierce for tonight's editions," said Heywood.

"I rather like that alliteration," considered Marc Connelly.

"Can't somebody who didn't know him write it?" asked George. "How about you, Ross?"

"Afraid?" challenged Aleck.

"You betcha! If I had to write it, they'd suspect he was murdered and that I'd've done him in."

"I can see the headline now: 'Stage Star Tomatoed!'" chimed in Harpo.

———————

Autumn in New York is a truly glorious time of year. The days are cool and crisp and usually a welcomed relief after summer's deep-fry heat rising off the streets.

A couple hours after lunching at the Gonk and hearing the news about Reggie Pierce, Woodrow Wilson and I took a long walk around the neighborhood. We walked through Bryant Park, behind the New York Public Library. Construction on the new American Radiator Company Building was nearing completion. Thirty-six stories high, its black brick and four-storied pyramidal step-back tower stood like a dark imposing guard over the park, library, and 40th Street. Such feats of human ingenuity amaze me.

An hour later, Woodrow Wilson and I were window-shopping fifteen blocks north along Fifth Avenue, when my attention was called by the very chic moss-green silk Charmeuse little number, draped over one shoulder with a lace reveal at the bodice, in one of Bergdorf's windows. The gown would go very nicely with the bracelet I'd just admired at Tiffany's, and wouldn't you know, I had the perfect little pumps at home to complete the look. I was contemplating how I might justify such purchases, had I the cash in the first place, when I was heralded by a sound, like a deep and raspy foghorn, wafting on a breeze of Bal au Versailles. Without needing to turn my head I knew who'd addressed me.

"Dottie, *dahhhling*," drawled the star, "any designs you may have on that dress must never be realized, you know that, don't you? It screams 'Hippodrome Chorus Girl.'"

"Tallulah, dear," I said, turning to greet the glamorous creature. Her honey-colored hair lashed my cheek as she leaned in for an airy kiss. "Those are Worth Paris gowns, and 'darling' yourself. You were planning on buying it for yourself, of course. And ravishing you will be in it."

Woodrow Wilson barked agreement.

"I wouldn't be caught dead in it!"

Woodrow Wilson chimed in with a whine.

"Good, because Marilyn Miller purchased that one this morning. She didn't know that Helen Hayes had bought one yesterday. One more girl wearing that dress at the Actors Equity Ball— why, the three of you'd be mistaken as a triplet vaudeville act brought in for after-dinner entertainment."

Once again Woodrow Wilson barked.

"Does he always agree with you?" Tallulah looked

at me and then down at Woodrow with a suspiciously raised pencil brow. "How do you know such things? Do you bribe the store clerks to ring you up after they've rung up their cash registers?"

"I have my sources." I knew for certain that neither Marilyn nor Helen had purchased a frock. My friend, Jane Grant, had seen the ad in yesterday's *Tribune*, cut it out, and slipped it to me this morning. Jane knew I was looking for a new dress and suggested I stop by the store to check it out. I really couldn't afford such a gown, but I made up the tale about the Broadway stars' purchasing the dress because I could read Tallulah like a cheap novel, and I thought I'd have a little fun playing with her. I've found that all really beautiful and accomplished women are riddled with self-doubt. Everything this actress did bordered on the outrageous, and I suspected most of her escapades were born from her fear of being perceived as normal and boring. As if she could ever be boring! Tedious at times, but never boring. We've been friends for several years, since she first arrived in town. Every day during her first year in New York, before she got steady work on the Broadway stage, Tallulah Bankhead would bound into the Algonquin at lunchtime, wearing the same sorry black dress, and pick at the food from our plates. She was clever and funny and wild, so we rarely slapped her hand. And, now, she was doing well enough to buy most any dress in Bergdorf's windows. She was welcome to the dress, really. I just didn't want to be rushed out of my fantasy of buying it just yet.

"Did you hear about Reginald Pierce?" she

asked, pushing a Marcel wave under her hat, while checking her reflection in the window glass. "Alas, we won't have Old Reg to sling mud at anymore."

"There's always Billie Burke," I reassured her. She gave me a sly smile, then threw back her head and let out a hearty, throaty laugh.

You see, a couple of years ago, while working at my first job as an arts editor at *Vanity Fair*, Frank Crowninshield, the magazine's editor-in-chief, took me out to lunch at the Tea Court of the Plaza Hotel, and while sipping cocktails and slurping down oysters—actually we were slurping down cocktails as well as the oysters—Frank fired me after four years in his employ. He explained I was not being let go because I didn't know how to change the typewriter ribbon (as was my usual quip for not handing in copy in a timely manner), but because of my review of Miss Billie Burke's performance on Broadway in *Caesar's Wife*. I made note that Miss Burke was far too "mature" at thirty-five to be playing the ingénue role in the play. Actually, I think she was miffed because I insinuated that she had thick ankles. Had the review been about anyone else, or had Miss Burke not been the wife of the great Florenz Ziegfeld, one of the most powerful Broadway producers as well as the magazine's biggest advertiser, my comment that Miss Burke's impersonation of Eva Tanguay (the *I Don't Care* Girl) had been an unfortunate artistic choice might have merely elicited chuckles of agreement and kudos for my cutting wit.

"Poor old Reggie," moaned Tallulah, slipping

a hankie from her purse. She was dabbing dry eyes when an idea suddenly dawned to light up her face. "I must be off, Dottie, *dahhhling*."

"You're running off! Well, I thought, since we're here, we'd go in the store and look around, 'Lulla, and then slink on over to Tony Soma's for a drink," I pouted with disappointment. I liked Tallulah, and I was glad she'd stopped me on the street. Here was an opportunity to catch up with some long-neglected gossip. She was as serious a drinking woman as I, and lots of fun. "Why the bum's rush?"

"*Dahhhling* Dottie, you're no bum, *dahhhling*. It's just—I realized Reggie's apartment must be available, now he's dead and all. . . . I've got to find out if it's available to rent before anyone else leases it!"

"'Lulla, dearest, unless you wish to purchase the Reginald Pierce Theatre on West 46th, you can't get the apartment." Her frowning stare informed me she hadn't a clue about what I was talking about. "Reggie lived in the apartment above his new theatre. You'd have to buy the entire building."

"Rats!" she said, her hopes dashed. "I thought he had an apartment at the Dakota."

"*Ahh*, I see. No, dearest, his wife threw him out last winter, so he made himself a gorgeous pied-à-terre on the top floor of the theatre."

"That's right, he was married. I forgot he was married."

"Reggie forgot he was married, too; that's why Myrtle threw him out."

We walked into Bergdorf Goodman's, where

Tallulah drove a salesgirl to the brink of insanity while deciding which of four hats she should buy, before rejecting all and insisting we make a stop at Henri Bendel's, just up the street along 57th, to check out their haberdashery.

The streets were teal blue and the street lamps alight when we walked out of Bendel's. Rectangles of yellow light stacked vertically into the darkening sky, lending warmth to the dimming geometry of New York's cityscape. It was rush hour, and the hum and honking of traffic and the murmur of humanity bustling along the sidewalks on a million journeys brought a new rhythm to the music of my Manhattan. I love New York. It all happens here, and I never know, upon waking in the morning, what my day will bring.

All's fair in love, war, and, in Manhattan, securing a taxi. We managed to snag a cab out from under the grasp of two very determined businessmen with the help of Woodrow Wilson and a much-rehearsed trick. I said, "Hail a cab, Woodrow!" With his teeth gently pulling the cuff of one gentleman's trouser leg, before moving on to the cuff of the other fellow's, he succeeded in causing just enough distraction for us to hop into the cab before the boys realized they had been bamboozled.

"Good boy, Woodrow!" I laughed as he leaped onto my lap and licked my face.

"I have to get me one of those," said Tallulah.

"Woodrow is a very special puppy dog," I cooed, rustling his wiry fur.

It was only a dozen blocks to Tony Soma's, my

favorite watering hole. We got out on 49th Street before what appeared a brownstone whose residents were not at home. The ground-floor windows were shuttered, and those who didn't know better would never guess at the action happening within. The peephole isn't even a giveaway. Tony's establishment is only one of dozens of places like this along 49th Street.

My knock was answered, and I gave the password. Not that I had to; Buddy, the doorkeeper, knew me well. Metal rasped against metal as the slide bolt released and the door swung open. We entered the secret world of Tony Soma's Speakeasy.

At Tony's you can be assured that the liquor is safe and won't make you sick, as in some less salubrious establishments around the city, and the clientele includes lots of my friends in the Theatre and publishing. Best of all, Tony's doesn't close until the last customer has gone home.

A homey haze of cigarette smoke mingled with the aroma of frying steak and tomato sauce. There was the promise of a T-bone in Woodrow's near future, and he sat, expectantly, while we checked our coats and bags before we were shown to a checker-clothed table.

Maurice, our waiter, took our order: an orange blossom for me, a gin-fizz for Tallulah, and a bowl of water for Woodrow. It wasn't long before we were joined by Bunny Wilson and Heywood Broun, who had spotted us from the bar. No girl-talk tonight,

I realized, when Johnny Barrymore, still high from last -year's brilliant portrayal of Hamlet, moved in on us. An hour later he and Tallulah ordered dinner in time to leave for their respective stage shows.

Aleck Woollcott walked in with Mr. Benchley, and as none of us had a show to review this evening, we were all free to relax into an evening of good food, great conversation, and if not quality liquor, at least decent booze.

Under the table, Woodrow Wilson was snoozing in postprandial splendor, several steak bones nibbled clean at his paws, as we drank from heavy white "coffee" cups. The sudden death of Reginald Pierce was among the various topics of discussion, and there was wild speculation about what would happen now that his empire had been dealt such a blow. Rumor had it the divorce from wife Myrtle had not been finalized, although there were rumors that it had been. If he and Myrtle had still been married when he died, would she cancel the evening's performances of his three Broadway shows, or would the curtains go up? Would, because of the publicity and perhaps a macabre interest, his shows sell out, even though two were just hanging in there by threads and the third was set to close any day now, after a shaky opening and bad reviews? Three-hundred-and-fifty-six people might either be out of work soon, or enjoy a reprieve from joblessness. And then there was the real estate, the vast art collection, the many stockholdings, as well as the production companies. Who, if the divorce had been finalized, would inherit? All I can say is that there had been a lot of scrambling around the past nine hours since the discovery of Reginald's dead body, and along with the disingenuous whispers and long faces there existed a good smattering of glee that he'd finally got his comeuppance. Just as soon as the topic had made a full circle, people moved on to the next pain-in-the-neck of local gossip: Lee Shubert and his new theatre, which was built without stage access from the dressing rooms and without hot water!

Bunny and Heywood got into enthusiastic conversation with a couple of editors from the *Times*, who sat at the next table, about the elections in Italy, and by eight o'clock, Aleck, Mr. Benchley, and I, pulling along a very reluctant Boston terrier, bid all a good-night and bustled out into the street.

The evening was pleasantly cool as we sauntered along toward Sixth Avenue. We were only a couple of avenues from Broadway and Times Square. Curtains would rise soon, and the streets became brighter and busier with automobile, streetcar, and pedestrian traffic as we neared the Great White Way.

Fur-wrapped and chiffon-gowned women, their jewels sparkling, and men in shiny black top hats and tails spilled out of Silver Ghosts, Duesenberg touring cars, Packards, and Stutzes at the prompting of liveried chauffeurs. And mingling with the swells were modestly attired office girls and stock clerks arriving in cabs and trolleys and rising from the steps of the subways to fill the cheap seats of the balconies.

Marquees were lit with the names of our friends.

On 47th Street alone, Katherine Cornell was appearing in *The Outsider*, Helen Hayes in *Dancing Mothers*, Ethel Barrymore in *The Second Mrs. Tanqueray*, and Marilyn Miller in a revival of *Peter Pan*, with Leslie Banks playing Captain Hook! We were stopped numerous times, much to Aleck's pleasure—he is a ham and likes to be fawned over—by many friends and acquaintances, as we strolled through the crowds of theatregoers who were eagerly anticipating the exciting spectacles of the Stage. Not only were the marquees lit up with electricity, so were the people.

On our way to Aleck's new residence, which he had purchased with Jane Grant and Harold Ross on West 46th Street, it came at us like a surprise to find ourselves approaching the Reginald Pierce Theatre. It looked like the curtain was going to go up in spite of the producer's death and the show's God-awful reviews. Aleck's critique for the *New York Times* was hysterical, if brutal, if deserving. The play received only one good notice, and that was from the *Tribune's* Ralph (pronounced *Rafe*) Chittenham, in which he praised the show, calling Lucille's Montaine's performance "inspiration in touching understatement," whatever the hell that means!

"See what the right kind of publicity can do?" I said.

"Murder the producer and you've got a hit," agreed Mr. Benchley.

"Better to have murdered the star, of course," said Aleck. "Lucille Montaine's performance will most definitely clear the house—if not tonight, then eventually."

"I agree with you, Aleck. After this mob endures Lucille's mumbling, bumbling, and stumbling, my review for the *Saturday Evening Post* will seem kind."

This is where I should enlighten those who do not know me—people living in Saskatchewan or the sparsely populated regions of these United States that receive no postal delivery for subscriptions of the *Saturday Evening Post* or *Vanity Fair* or the *Bookman*. For those who might chance upon this journal, unwittingly tossed aside by a camper from the city during an exploratory expedition, when, while relaxing with one of the aforementioned journals by the evening campfire, said camper was rudely interrupted by a black bear demanding more than the fellow's marshmallows: My "celebrity," for I would not be so presumptuous as to call it "fame," aside from my very fresh, honest, and often self-deriding poetic verses, arose from my natural talent of cutting to the quick in a fashion that is humorous. Sometimes, I flip the viewpoint, as in my review for this, Reginald Pierce's new show, which was such an abomination that I couldn't find a way to begin to tell my readers just how bad it was without using the word "shit." So rather than deal with the censors, I concentrated my critique on the very fine performances of the theatre ushers, the doormen, the house manager, and the box office staff, and the exceptional debut of the ladies' lounge attendant, a newcomer in black dress and starched white pinafore and cap, agile in sensible shoes, who delivered her line, "Good-evening, Madame!," with aplomb, while at the same time handing over a crisp, white towel. I rested all my criticism on the audience: their failure to applaud, stomp, and whistle at the appropriate times. I love the Theatre and the people who are part of making *great* Theatre. It's true that my readers expect me to write with clever, entertaining insight, but why be mean when I can get the point across by being droll? And here's a secret: I actually liked Reginald Pierce. Others may have seen him as a rat, but he always behaved gentlemanly toward me. Aside from the fact that he'd suffered more than his fair share of flops in recent years, he'd also brought to the Stage many successes, many works of high quality. I think people didn't like him because, like me, he didn't suffer fools easily. And the Theatre is full of fools, let me tell you. In this business, too, as in any other, success *does* breed contempt. People relish the downfall of the rich, the powerful, and the accomplished.

"Aleck, have you ever been to Reggie's apartment?" I asked, picking up Woodrow Wilson, who was dragging from fatigue.

"Only been to the Dakota apartment with Edna Ferber, to a party for Myrtle, her birthday or something-or-other...."

"Is the entrance to the apartment from inside the theatre's lobby?"

"How the hell should I know! I've never been here, I say!"

"Stop being such a crank," I chided. He was obviously more upset by Reggie's death than he had been letting on. "I only thought we might go on up and pay our respects, and maybe drink a toast to him; I hear Reggie imported the very best Scotch, so they say."

That lightened his mood.

We inquired within the lobby for the entrance to the apartment, but were told we needed to walk around past the stage-door entrance where another door, further along, led to an elevator that would take us up to the top floor.

Easily found, but the door was locked. I rang the bell. No one answered after a second and third try. Finally, disgruntled once more, but this time at the disappointing possibility of really fine Scotch whiskey being beyond his reach, Aleck took my purse and riffled through, looking for an appropriately sharp and pointed object. Failing that, Mr. Benchley took out his penknife and told us to step aside. A couple of precise twists and we were in.

"Mr. Benchley, I'm pleased to inform you that you are now among the rank-and-file of New York's criminal element," I applauded him.

"But, I deplore politics!"

We entered the elevator, and soon found ourselves arrived at a small foyer, walls painted blood-red, and facing an elaborately decorated door. We knocked and waited, and knocked again. It never dawned on me that there would be no staff to welcome us. When

I turned the knob as a last resort, it turned without resistance.

We located a switch and the room that lay before us came alive with light. And what a room it was! No luxury had been spared in its décor, and one would never guess this had once been an empty space above a theatre. It was as architecturally detailed as any Beaux Arts building on Central Park West, and the soft pools of lamplight accentuated the sleek, curved lines of modern sofas, banquettes, and upholstered silk chairs in the latest Art Deco style. Wall sconces sent inverted triangles of light toward the ceiling, and scattered about with deliberation among the furnishings were sculptures by leading artists of the day. We crossed the thick white carpet toward the blond-birch mirrored bar.

"This is some joint!" I said, as Mr. Benchley poured neat whiskies into three crystal tumblers. I looked over the bar's shelves and found a box of pretzels. I fed one to Woodrow Wilson, and offered the box to Aleck.

"Odd," I said, looking around the vast expanse, "for a man with an extensive collection of Impressionist Art, the walls are blank."

"Maybe Myrtle nabbed them in the divorce settlement," said Mr. Benchley.

"Perhaps. . ."

Aleck handed me a drink, and we sipped in silence.

"Heavenly," I cooed, enjoying the smooth, warm

ribbon of liquid as it made its way down my throat. The boys hummed agreement.

"Let's find something to eat," said Aleck, looking around for the entrance to a kitchen. There were several doors to choose from, but like a boar rooting out truffles, Aleck opened the door leading to the kitchen and butler's pantry on his first try. Mr. Benchley and I followed, and as if he hadn't eaten less than an hour before, Aleck attacked the icebox. His huge figure blocked our view to its contents, but a moment later he turned to face us with a gleeful chirp, holding up a turkey drumstick.

"What?" he asked, mouth full, as we looked on with disapproval. "Want a bite?"

"Thank you, no. And don't you dare give that bone to Woodrow Wilson. Please move aside, now."

I peered inside to see a wheel of Stilton alongside the remains of the bird, a couple bottles of Taittinger, but little else, not even a stalk of celery.

I thought Mr. Benchley was at my side, but I heard him call to me from a distance. Returning to the salon, I followed a narrow rectangle of lamplight through the opened door of Reginald Pierce's library.

Here was the marvelous art collection, and I was immediately drawn to the little Renoir.

"So here is my pastel."

"What's this?" said Aleck. "A portrait of our Mrs. Parker?"

"This is the Renoir he bought out from under me. It really does look a little like me!"

"Spitting image," said Mr. Benchley, before losing interest and walking away to peruse other objets d'art.

"Yes, me wearing a bonnet I'd never be caught alive in, wearing too much Coty lipstick and rouge...." I considered it for another moment. "I do love it, though."

Mr. Benchley said, "I see Reginald lived with his 'Mummy.'"

"Whatever are you babbling about?" I asked.

"Come and see this sarcophagus coffin."

"From some play—last season's *Anthony and Cleopatra* no doubt; Jane Cowl was indeed marvelous as the Egyptian Queen," said Aleck through his food.

"Not on your life, Aleck. This is the real deal."

"'Lot of junk in here."

I turned away from the Renoir to join Mr. Benchley. I said to Aleck, "That piece of junk you're looking at is an altar triptych from the 13th century."

"Refill?" asked Aleck, leaving the room to fetch the bottle from the bar.

"Shit, Mr. Benchley," I said as I approached the huge coffin. "It looks like the one at the Metropolitan. Open it up!"

Just then, Woodrow Wilson yelped, and Aleck came bounding back in from the salon, decanter in hand. "Someone's coming up the elevator!"

We searched the room for a hole of escape, like mice who'd stolen the cheese when the cat fell asleep

THE BROADWAY MURDERS 23

in a dish of cream. The cat was opening one angry green eye, and there was nowhere, no closet, no sofa, big enough to conceal us.

The curtains were drawn closed and extended the entire exterior wall of the room. We killed the lights and dashed behind the drapery, Aleck, decanter in hand. If someone entered, we wouldn't be seen right away—that is, as long as no one looked toward the floor, where they'd see two pairs of size-tens flanking size-five pumps.

The door creaked open and there was the *woosh* of footsteps rushing across the Persian carpet; a pull of the lamp chain and a column of light came through the break in the curtain panels. As I was advantageously placed near that opening, I looked out to see the figure of a man lifting the seat cushion of the desk chair. Light from the desk lamp glinted off an object he retrieved: a key. With it, the man opened the front panel of the desk and began riffling through its contents. Then, the releasing *pop* of a metal spring, after which a panel opened to reveal a secret cubbyhole. The man removed something, which he placed into his pocket before shutting the small compartment. And then, oddly, he stood bolt-upright, frozen, as if listening, fearing he might be caught. Could he have heard us? Had Aleck belched? *We were done for, now,* I feared, for he turned in our direction. I held my breath, pulling back from the break in the curtain, and gripped the arms of the two men flanking me.

But I had seen the man's face: He was young,

Asian, and of small and slim stature. Suddenly the light was dashed, putting all of us in darkness. I heard the scattering of feet, and then, a *thump*, as if he had knocked into furniture in the scurry. After the brief moments of darkness, the pull of the light chain sounded once again.

I peeked out, but instead of the Asian there stood a woman, late twenties, early thirties, and dressed to the teeth in Chanel. The little Chinaman was nowhere to be seen, and I wondered where on earth he could have hidden himself?

The woman appeared to search the room with her eyes, walked over to the bookcases, changed her mind and returned to the desk. But, she didn't stop there; rather, she moved toward us. Adrenalin sobered me quickly. I was sure she had heard my knees knocking, if not Woodrow Wilson's panting.

She hesitated, and then, as if struck by a sudden revelation, spun on her heels and headed toward the refectory table.

Reaching inside a Ming Dynasty vase, she pulled out a fabric-wrapped item; after she removed the cloth, she was left holding the figurine sculpture of a duck—no, it was a falcon; well, it looked like some kind of bird, anyway. A smile crossed her lips, and it was uncanny how much she reminded me of Mary Astor, the actress, but for this girl's blonde hair. Satisfied with her find, she threw the room into darkness and was gone.

I was afraid to move, but Woodrow Wilson squirmed in my arms, demanding freedom. The boys stood in their places, but the clink of decanter to glass as Aleck refilled his glass rang out. I'd had enough cloak-and-dagger for one evening, and as Woodrow Wilson made his break, so did I.

"You two can come out, now," I said, walking over to the vase to peer into its dark interior. The smell of cigarette smoke and the faint scent of shoe polish lingered about the room and then was gone.

"But it's quite cozy here, and somebody else may chance by," said Mr. Benchley.

"So, we'll say hello and offer him a drink. By the way, either of you see a little Oriental man standing behind the curtain with us?"

Aleck stepped forth and looked around the room. From the blank look on both their faces, I realized neither had been in a position to see all I had witnessed through the break of the curtain panels. I replayed for them the past couple of minutes.

"Strange, though, I can't figure out how the Asian got out of here before the Mary Astor look-a-like came in."

"Did you say 'Mary Astor'?"

"Her blonde double."

"Sounds like you saw Marion Fields, Reggie's girlfriend," said Aleck.

"Oh, I remember her," said Mr. Benchley. "Pretty thing."

I asked, "You've met Marion Fields?"

"No, Mary Astor."

Aleck rolled his eyes, and I grabbed the hand of a slightly inebriated Mr. Benchley, to lead him out of the apartment before more people descended on us.

The wake for Reginald Ignatius Pierce was held at Campbell's Funeral Home on Manhattan's East Side. Hundreds poured in to pay their respects and offer condolences to his widow, Myrtle, and his two sons, Richard and Raymond.

Held on a Sunday evening before the Monday funeral service and burial, the royalty of Broadway were in attendance, as most theatres were dark this evening. However you felt about Reggie, whether you loved, hated, or were disinterested, it was a stellar event for even the peripheral court members to be seen attending.

All the friends of our luncheon club, which had in recent years been dubbed the "Round Table," came to the viewing. Groucho Marx said that he wanted to see for himself that Reggie was indeed dead, and that the whole thing was not some sort of practical joke. But, the truth was that a Broadway King was dead, and however much at odds many people had been in their dealings with Reggie, he was respected for his many talents. And even more, they came out of great admiration for his wife, Myrtle, who was, before retiring from the stage, not only a great dramatic actress, but instrumental in organizing the union, Actors Equity

Association. Her involvement may have caused tension in their marriage, for she was, after all, married to a producer; it is common knowledge that there isn't a producer out there who was ever willing pay an actor more than coolie wages if he could get away with it. But, Reggie didn't try to stand in her way. He came around to the idea of fair pay in his later years, once he had built his great fortune from the sweat of underpaid performers. His disputes were with those from whom he demanded impossible deadlines; his fights were with temperamental playwrights, directors, and set and costume designers. And critics!

Outside the funeral home, those hoping to catch a glimpse of the stars lined the canopied entrance ten deep. More people were wearing black than all the widows of Greece. And it was raining, to boot, so the smell of wet wool predominated and mingled with the lavender fragrance that lay heavy over the viewing parlor. There were scores of black umbrellas dripping onto the entry carpet. No one in his right mind could possibly sort out his own umbrella from that sea of black!

Aleck Woollcott, Robert Benchley, and I were joined by George and Bea Kaufman; Edna Ferber (with whom we would have dinner afterward at her apartment) arrived with Irving Berlin. It was a veritable Broadway *Who's Who* that greeted us: Jane Cowl, George Arliss, Irene Dunne, and Will Rogers; the Barrymore and Drew clans; the Astaires—brother and sister, Fred and Adele; all the Marx Brothers (for their show, *I'll Say She Is,* was dark that evening); and Ed Wynn, W.C. Fields, and Gertie Lawrence were in town, as all had shows running, so they were there, too. There was Beatrice Lillie and Marilyn Miller, and then a commotion as Marie Dressler and Eleanora Duse bounded in off the street dripping wet after their shared umbrella was ripped by a fierce gale. Oh, my, I could go on! But I won't.

We signed the guestbook and made our way through the crowd and into the parlor. There was a queue of people wrapped around the room, like a stalled conga line, to view the body. From where we stood, I could see little beyond the black-suited backs of those on line, and as I am a small cluck, an inch under five feet tall, I had to rely on the observations of my friends for any sense of what was going on around the room.

"George White and Flo Zeigfeld are actually talking to each other," said Mr. Benchley, referring to the biggest producers of musical extravaganzas.

"*Hot dog!* Sam Harris just joined in. Wish I were a flea in David Belasco's ear, because he and Lee Shubert's just joined the poker game. Shall I lift you up on my shoulders to see the spectacle, Mrs. Parker?"

"Thank you, no; people already think me lofty."

"Then you won't be able to see your favorite critic and sewer-dweller, Ralph Chittenham."

"Oh, 'Shit-in-head' is here?"

"Yes, and he's got some nice little chorus girl cornered . . . in the corner."

"Do you think there are refreshments?" Aleck asked, while waving hello to young Walter Huston.

"What do you think this is? A cocktail party?"

"Feels like we're on line for the buffet."

There are advantages to being of small stature in a tight crowd. As you're rarely eye-level with anyone else it's easy to go unnoticed. And this night, wedged between Aleck and Mr. Benchley, who fell into discussion with the promising young actress, Eva La Gallienne and our Round Table friend, newspaper columnist Frank Pierce Adams, who would undoubtedly mention our names in his column tomorrow as having attended RIP's wake, I could do little but listen to the conversations around me, unable, due to my odd positioning, to easily identify the speakers. But I recognized the distinctive voices of a man and woman in conversation, so I leaned in closer to listen.

"Have you seen Lucille Montaine? She's nowhere to be found. She doesn't answer her telephone, and I stopped by her apartment, but she wasn't there, and her neighbors haven't seen her in days."

The deep, distinctive British bell tones identified Evelyn Woods, the director of Reginald Pierce's awful new play (which I panned), *Trees in the Forest*, starring the missing actress.

"I haven't seen her here. Do you think she's so upset about RIP kicking off that she's gone off her rocker someplace, grieving?"

I had to laugh, inwardly, at the unfortunate monogram Reginald Ignatius Pierce had had to live with all of his life. I pictured sweaters, towels, bed sheets, and handkerchiefs embroidered with his initials. Undoubtedly, he'd received many such gag gifts for Christmas and birthdays.

"If she's grieving anything, it's her reviews. Did you read Dottie Parker's? If I hadn't been laughing so hard, I would have cried. At least Parker didn't mention my name; one can be thankful for that. Maybe people will take Ralph Chittenham's review to heart. I don't know why that old bastard was so nice. All I can say is, thank God there's Rosemary Willard to understudy for Lucille. She was marvelous last night. She should have had the part from the start, had I had my way."

"I don't get it. Why didn't she get the role in the first place, if she was so good?"

"RIP. He wanted Lucille. Nothing I could do would convince him."

"Maybe Lucille is so distraught she's taken her own life."

"That's not nice of you, Maddie, but from your lips to God's ears!"

"Well, it's one way to save the show. With Lucille in it, it will close as soon as interest in RIP's death lessens."

The woman speaking was costume designer Madison. She spoke with that affected New England twang that so many young actors were wearing these days.

The line was moving forward, and as we neared,

I was able to glimpse, through a break in black, members of RIP's family seated opposite the casket.

Two young men, of similar, but rather sullen features and build as the man lying prone in his coffin, sat to the right of Reggie's wife, Myrtle. To her left sat Gerald Saches, Reggie's business manager.

Both Reggie and Gerald were the children of immigrants, and from the same Lower East Side neighborhood. Both were adolescents when their fathers, who had become friendly while working as laborers digging in the tunnels of the New York City subway system, were killed in an explosion and cave-in. As each was the eldest son, each had to go out to work to support his family.

Green-grocer Robert Saches long had eyes for Gerry's mother, and offered the boy a job delivering groceries and stocking and sweeping out the store. Gerry was a clever boy and saw the grocer's interest in his mother. He was also a loyal friend to Reggie, who had few prospects for finding work, so he refused the offer from the storekeeper unless he hired his friend Reggie as well. A couple of years later, Gerry's mother married the grocer, who adopted her children before promptly dying of an aneurysm.

Gerry, at sixteen, took over the store. Reggie continued to work there, but he had big ideas for expanding the business. Gerry listened to those ideas, and although he was of a cautious nature, he was easily convinced by his outgoing and charismatic friend to take the leap. And a very successful leap it was.

Thirty years later, their frozen-food company supplied a great share of the city's restaurants, and they had discovered other markets in which to invest their money. The men had little other than their businesses in common, but for two things: Gerry's middle name, Aaron, after his maternal grandfather, also gave him an unfortunate monogram, and both men had, at one time or another, been in love with Myrtle.

It was no secret that Gerald had pursued the young Myrtle Price, after seeing her photograph in an advertisement for Milton's Castile Soap, and for a time, he believed she might agree to become his wife. Myrtle found Gerry a congenial young man, if rather conservative and plain in dress and demeanor. But, as their friendship grew, she realized that she could never think of Gerry as more than a precious and faithful friend, especially after being introduced to his business partner, Reginald Pierce. It wasn't simply that Reginald was handsome and immaculately turned out. Myrtle was not a shallow woman; she had been wooed by many good-looking fellows dressed to impress. But Reginald excited her imagination with the zest with which he lived his life. She was swept into the gravity of the planet Pierce, and Gerald, gracious and understanding, if quietly broken-hearted, toasted the couple on their wedding day.

Now, as I observed Myrtle and Gerald, I could see what anyone but an idiot could see: Gerald was still in love with the wife of his closest friend.

I felt like a voyeur, watching his tender leanings,

the way he took her hand in his own, the expression of pain that hung over his fair features as he spoke to her between interruptions of those offering condolences. There was such gentle intimacy there, and out of decency I turned away, my eyes taking in the lifeless mask of Reginald Pierce.

The usually high-colored countenance that was Reggie alive was paled by death. The bright, compelling green eyes were shut and sunken under papery lids. The Max Factor pancake makeup looked false and powdery. The big, powerfully built body was shrunken, having exhausted all earthly energy. I was struck, suddenly reminded of the finality of death; my lofty attitude toward my own mortality frightened me. I shivered. I am loath to admit that bad times have recently sent me to the brink of death, most ashamedly by my own hand!

As I stood contemplating the meaninglessness of human existence, I felt a hand on my shoulder, drawing me back into the crowded room. Expecting Mr. Benchley or Aleck at my side, I was taken aback by a devastatingly handsome face that proceeded to address me. I must have appeared peculiar, because he smiled, divinely, I must say, and cautiously backed away.

"Mrs. Parker."

"Yes."

"My name is Wilfred Harrison."

He reached to shake my hand.

My usual firm handshake melted to a limp

lump, giving meaning to the expression, "putty in his hands."

"I am the attorney for the Reginald Pierce family, and the executor of Mr. Pierce's estate."

He must have thought me daffy, as my jaw dropped and my head bobbed inanely, as all reasonable thoughts were purged from my brain, along with the flow of blood, which rushed to other organs of my body. My silence prompted him to continue.

"Mrs. Parker?"

I blinked assent.

I guess that egged him on, for he offered, "As you have been named in Mr. Pierce's will, I am inviting you to attend its reading after the interment tomorrow morning."

Key words crank-started my brain once again.

"Wait, let me understand this," I said, in recovery. "I'm in Reginald's will?"

"Yes, that's right. The burial is at ten o'clock, followed by a reception at the Dakota apartment of Mrs. Pierce. The reading of the will is at three o'clock, at Mr. Pierce's apartment above the Reginald Pierce Theatre."

"*Ahhh*," I gurgled.

"Will you attend?"

"Yes . . . I mean, yes . . . I didn't say no, did I?" I babbled.

He squinted, turned his head a little as if scrutinizing me with his best eye. And then, "Then we'll expect to see you tomorrow."

"I'd be delighted. I mean, thank you for inviting—"

An amused expression confirmed I was making a damned fool of myself. I pulled my groveling self up from his feet, lifted my chin (and jaw) in an effort to regain my dignity, and said, quite competently, "I shall be there, at three o'clock, Mister—?"

"Harrison. Wilfred Harrison."

"Mr. Harrison."

"Call me 'Will,' Mrs. Parker."

"Yes. 'Will,' then, Mr. Harrison."

He released my cranking handshake. I sighed a huge breath of relief as he moved away. I hadn't breathed since his approach, I don't think; his animal magnetism was so strong, I felt unstrung and embarrassingly overheated.

Aleck and Mr. Benchley were at my side, and by the way they looked at me I knew that they had witnessed my shameful behavior.

"I'm jealous, Mrs. Parker," said Mr. Benchley.

"You, my darling Mr. Benchley, are in no danger of losing your place in my heart."

"I'm sure Mrs. Benchley will be happy to know that," said Aleck, with sardonic glee, referring to Gertrude, Mr. Benchley's wife, tucked away with the kiddies in the suburban bliss of Timbuktu, and to the close, but platonic, relationship Mr. Benchley and I enjoyed.

It has been rumored that we are more than just the very best of friends. The truth is that our deep love and respect for one another has never breached the bedroom door. Our mutual affection developed while working together, dining and drinking together, bucking each other up when one felt low, standing tall together in friendship (Mr. Benchley, so loyal a friend, had handed in his resignation when I was fired from *Vanity Fair*), and in sharing the sharp wit and humor that we have become famous for. We are very much on the same plane, our bantering dialogue almost an extension of each other's, if differing in style. In fact, our celebrity is a result of our having set the style for our generation. I am willingly Mr. Benchley's straight man, and he is often mine. We, along with Aleck and others of our Round Table Club, set a standard, unwittingly (excuse the pun!), but a standard, nonetheless, of all that is clever and fun and exciting in 1920s New York City. I can honestly say that in many respects Mr. Benchley might be dubbed the masculine side of Mrs. Parker. So maybe we *are* having an affair of sorts, an intellectual and emotional one, but certainly with no threat to either of our spouses.

Aleck, on the other hand, is all things clever and bright and perfectly in tune with raising the bar to new heights, but sexually speaking, well, it is speculated that he has no sex life, as far as anyone knows. But, that is a story for another time. For now we had to face the widow and sons of Reginald Pierce.

Gerald rose to his feet to greet us, and I leaned in to speak comforting words to Myrtle, who graciously, and I'm sure, for the thousandth time, gave her thanks for our attending.

The sons, whom I had never seen before, appeared more interested in our celebrity than in the reason for our presence, and I got the very distinct impression that they'd had a few conflicts with the man in the box. They seemed impatient; not with their mother; with her they appeared protective. I can't tell you why I felt an undercurrent of *something* not quite right, but I did, and I would soon discover the answer.

We left a few minutes later to join Edna at her apartment across town for dinner, after which, it being two in the morning, we three piled into a cab and returned downtown to our respective apartments.

———◆———

I have recently moved into the Algonquin Hotel, on West 44th Street. Not only are my rooms convenient—I can roll out of bed around noon and simply take the elevator down to the lobby and stroll a couple of yards into the Rose Room for one o'clock luncheon with my friends. Better yet, if I've imbibed a bit too much, I can retreat back to my room on the aforementioned lift. I have room service, which is convenient, occasional dog-walking services, and the management doesn't press too hard for my rent when I am short of cash, which is often. In spite of my various demands, they are thrilled to have me, a celebrity, in their midst.

In truth, the reason for my move from uptown was not really for the Gonk's convenient location, but because my husband of seven years and I have parted ways. To best alleviate my sadness, I sought new surroundings.

When Eddie had returned from the War in Europe he was a changed man, and because of his war wounds, both emotional and physical, he found great solace in morphine and alcohol. He gave up his position at Paine Webber and returned home to the family manse in Hartford, Connecticut, and to the bosom of his family. We each had, in our own ways, tried to make our marriage work, but the demands of my career and his disinterest in his own future fractured our union. He wanted to leave New York, which he compared, unkindly, to Gomorrah, and I knew, deep in my heart, it was really for the best that we part ways. No rancor; we parted friends, and there is no reason to divorce as neither one of us has plans to wed anyone else. I needed to make a new start, and the rooms at the Algonquin suit me very well. Nothing fancy; I have never coveted possessions. All I've ever needed were three or four well-cut suits, my typewriter, Woodrow Wilson, and "a place to lay my hat and a few friends."

When I arrived home at 2:15 A.M., I stopped at the front desk to ask for an eight o'clock wake-up call, and then took Woodrow Wilson out for a quick pee. I was settled under the covers and just falling off to sleep when I was shaken from imminent slumber by the oddest thought, one so unexpected that I bolted upright and turned on the light. I had come to the realization that Reginald Pierce did not die from choking on a cherry tomato. He was murdered!

The King and Queen of Broadway—the Lunts.

Times Tower overlooking the Square

The Algonquin— Where I live and lunch.

Worth Gowns— Tallulah and
I admired the one on the right in
Bergdorf's window.

Two Girls and a Man—
A couple of swells between acts.

Ziegfeld Follies— *Billie Burke, Flo Ziegfeld's wife, didn't like the review I wrote of her performance.* She got me fired from Vanity Fair.

The Reginald Pierce Theatre— *You can see Reggie's pied-à-terre, the bank of windows on the left behind whose curtains Mr. Benchley and I spent several hours.*

MARY ASTOR

*Mary Astor— Marion is the spitting image of
Mary Astor, but blonde.*

Chapter Two

Wearing a black wool suit, pink shirt, and satin-bowed patent-leather pumps, I put the final touches on my dressing. I fastened a brooch at the neck of my shirt, engulfed myself in a cloud of Coty's Chypre, arranged my hair under my hat, and chose gloves, purse, and scarf, all while thoughts of murder raced through my head.

I hadn't slept since the light-bulb moment of the night before, and spent the remainder of the night tossing about in my bed while considering all the implications of RIP's death. His *murder*. Because that is how he died—I had no doubt. Someone deliberately killed Reginald Pierce.

While I tossed about I thrashed around all the possible suspects. After an hour of trying to sort it out, I realized I was only getting more and more confused. As his personality and success had bred the animosity of so many people, it would be impossible to point a finger at any one individual, at least not until I knew more about the complex relationships of his life.

So I threw off the covers, grabbed a pencil and notebook, and began making lists: (1) Who hated RIP? (2) Who stood to gain by his death? (3) Were any of the individuals in columns 1 and 2 capable (in my opinion) of committing murder? There were many people who stood to gain by his death, but as I was ignorant of the dynamics of their dealings with Reggie, I was running blind. But for now I could stand by my belief that Reginald Pierce was murdered. For whatever reason, I might never know, but murdered he was.

Mr. Benchley rang from the lobby to let me know that Aleck was outside waiting in a cab. We were all going to the funeral this morning. Mr. Benchley had rooms across the street at the Hotel Royalton, an exclusively male residence of the old bachelor style of the previous century. He'd taken the rooms in the city during the run of his Broadway show, as commuting home to Tipperary each evening at midnight after the final curtain proved difficult and began affecting his health. So, in Manhattan during the weekdays, he returns home by train to the hinterlands on weekends to be with Gertrude and the children. As for the big man, Aleck lives just a few blocks away, close to the offices of the *New York Times* and the Algonquin's dining room, where he holds court.

I whispered comforting words to Woodrow Wilson, whom I would be leaving at home, and he made that pathetic, forlorn doggie face that was intended to spread enough guilt throughout my day that I'd be loath to leave him behind ever again.

In the cab I dropped my bombshell.

Aleck ejaculated, "I knew it! The irony of RIP just popping-off so benignly tested credulity! Reggie was a man of *The Theatre*, after all."

"What the hell does that mean?" I said, a little annoyed at his upbeat response. I had to stop myself from lashing out at Aleck. I was one of the few people who felt saddened by Reggie's death. I looked at Aleck, who was in turn looking at me with expectation. And I realized that it wasn't joy at Reggie's passing that Aleck had expressed, but more a vindication that a man he respected (if he hadn't liked him particularly) hadn't passed from this earth undramatically. A skewed point of view, perhaps, but in the Theatre an actor always tries to make a memorable exit from the stage. "Oh, I see," I said. "Where's the drama in gagging and dropping dead via cherry tomato?"

Mr. Benchley was quietly taking in our conversation, while looking out the cab window at the passing parade of traffic, as we rode uptown to the service.

"And how did you arrive at what should have been obvious to all of us?"

"Aleck," I began, saying his name sternly as cue that what I was about to say was serious. "Do you remember when we were at the opening-night party for one of Reggie's shows a couple seasons back? You were with me. It was the one that Myra Sandstone debuted in—*Reckless Love?*"

"Henry Thompson play, marvelous theatre! Yes, I remember. I wrote my review in record time, praising play and cast. Then I went off to join the party. I recall RIP's expression when I entered through the doors, applause filled the air—"

"Well, yes, all right; they were happy to see you," I said, a bit impatiently, because Aleck does have a tendency to elaborate freely his recollections of self-aggrandizement. "Do you remember a story that was told that night? It was about Reggie, as told by Myrtle. You were sitting right there, at the table with us, picking from a bowl of strawberries."

"Strawberries?" An eyebrow shot up, making one eye look bigger than the other behind his thick glasses. "One or two, only, surely. You know I'm allergic to strawberries, Dottie."

"Yes, of course you are, and although they are marvelous with champagne, which we happened to be drinking at the time, I asked the waiter to remove the bowl and bring back some grapes, or whatever else was to be had."

"Terrible hives! Since I was a little boy I—"

"Yes, yes, of course you cannot eat more than one or two—"

"Just a taste doesn't hurt, but I think I've become more sensitive—"

"—*and* that is my *point*. I move now from strawberries to tomatoes."

"Not so good with champagne."

"The point, my dear, idiot Aleck, is that, as we sat at the table that night, allergies became the subject of discussion. A rather pedestrian topic for a festive celebration, rather like displaying for amusement's sake one another's surgical scars, but discussed, nonetheless. And amazingly, I did not snooze through the chatter because it was a story that involved a doggie, my most favorite of creatures on earth, next to you two dears, of course," I assured them.

"Myrtle told us about it, and I remember the tale vividly for another reason, for practical purposes, should my dear Woodrow Wilson ever run into a skunk while chasing squirrels in Central Park: tomato juice!"

"I haven't the foggiest notion what you are getting at, Dottie."

"Reginald and Myrtle gave their sons puppies as gifts. The dogs were of a herding breed, and chased anything that passed their way, or popped its unfortunate head out of the ground: automobiles, squirrels, rabbits, and skunks!"

"Sweet," said Aleck, smiling. "Country living is—"

"Not so sweet, Aleck; rather a nasty stink, I should say."

"*Ahhh*, yes, skunks . . ."

"Well, the tonic, the cure, the magic formula to eliminate the smell, once a dog has been sprayed, is a bath of tomato juice, a fact that I filed away for possible future use, knowing Woodrow Wilson's propensity for chasing Central Park wildlife. Well, one day, you see, Reginald was caught between the dog and a skunk, and it was necessary for him to experience the delights of a sponge bath of tomato juice."

"He broke out in hives!"

"You remember! But no one realized it was anything more than skin irritation caused by the assault of the skunk juice and the acidity of the tomato juice combined.

"It was later in the summer at their Long Island estate, when the tomatoes were ripe on the vine, Myrtle told us, and Reggie, having salted and bitten into the first fruit to be picked, a great big juicy one, had a distinct and brutal reaction to the fruit, and had to be rushed to the hospital. So, I know he was murdered because Myrtle said that the doctor warned that the next time he ate anything made with tomatoes he might not survive the allergic reaction."

Our cab was nearing the synagogue where the funeral service was to be held, when I looked across at Mr. Benchley. "You are very quiet, very unlike the Fred I know." (I often call him "Fred," usually after a few too many, or when he is, or I am, in a blue mood. His name is Robert, Bob to the rest of the world, but almost always do we call each other by our surnames, as when we worked in the offices of *Vanity Fair*, and where our boss, Frank Crowninshield, first introduced us to each other: "Mrs. Parker, meet Mr. Benchley." That silly and deliberate formality stuck, a joke, you see. But I sometimes choose to call him "Fred," a name so comforting and secure in its homely, friendly sound.)

"The other night, when we were at RIP's apartment, we thought Confucius and the Mistress Marion were stealing valuables, but they weren't really. They would have taken a few of the paintings, or the little Degas statuette, or the Ming vase, if they had been thieving."

"Yes, I suppose you're right . . . . They were removing evidence, perhaps?"

"That's what I'm thinking. Of course, it could be they knew where the really valuable coins were, or diamonds, perhaps that sort of thing."

"Well, we'll have to find out, won't we?"

"We?" asked Aleck, paying our taxi fare.

"But, we can't just go and tell the police, don't you see?"

"Of course we can; if Myrtle hasn't already told them of his allergy by now, I'd be surprised."

"Well," I said, "it's obvious she hasn't told the police or it would be common knowledge by now that he was murdered."

"Enough people know he had a tomato allergy," said Mr. Benchley. "It's not a secret, really."

"That's just it," I said. "People know he was allergic, and for some reason, for fear of being suspected, or fear of being picked-off by the murderer for having suspicions, people in the know are pretending they don't know."

Aleck said, as we moved through the crowds of spectators and attendees gathered at the entry of the synagogue, "After it's all over today, we'll have to have a sit-down talk about this. But for now, if what you're saying is true, that there's a murderer around, let's keep our eyes open and our mouths shut."

———◆———

". . . And to my wife of 27 years, Myrtle Price Pierce, I leave the balance of my estate."

Wilfred Harrison moved aside the document that was the last will and testament of Reginald Ignatius Pierce, and then removed his glasses. I noted in the natural light pouring through the windows that his eyes were blue and his hair was so black that it had a bluish sheen. Actually, I had paid attention to little more than the man's physical attributes. It's just that his very presence kept distracting me.

We were gathered together in Reggie's apartment above the theatre that bore his name, in the very room, the library-slash-office, where my friends and I had recently found refuge behind blue velvet curtain panels. The half-dozen of us who had been named in the will, or had an interest in the disposing of his estate, were scattered around the room, and the principal players—Myrtle, the sons, Robert and Raymond, and Gerald A. Saches—were seated before Wilfred Harrison at the refectory table.

Myrtle rose from her chair, quite shaken, her expression dour, and requiring the assistance of her sons to walk from the room. Once she had risen, it was a cue for all to follow.

But I didn't want to leave just yet. I wanted to snoop around a little, see what I might find, as I sensed that in this room there might be answers to identifying Reggie's murderer. And, to be completely truthful, I wanted to see if I might turn Wilfred's interest toward me, now that the business of the day had been set aside. I remained quietly seated in the wing chair beside the huge fireplace mantle as the others filed out of the room, watching as Wilfred filled his briefcase with the many documents that littered the table. When the last stragglers retreated through the open door to the salon, I made my move.

"Mr. Harrison," I purred, gliding to his side as he prepared to leave. I shined my best smile in his direction, but he was certainly not blinded, for he hummed, "*hmmm?*"

"I was wondering . . ."

"Oh, yes, Mrs. Parker. Dorothy," he said, looking up, while patting the breast of his suit jacket for the various tools of his profession—pen, eyeglasses, and so on. He came around the table on his journey toward the door.

"Yes, I do prefer being called 'Dorothy,' Will. How do I . . .? What I mean to ask is, will the . . .bequest be sent to me at my residence, or should I take it with me now?"

"Oh, no," he said, halting his progress toward the door. "You can't take it now. Although there is no law that says you can't. But you'll want to have it insured and have professional movers come to crate it properly and deliver it to you. I'll make the arrangements."

He continued toward the door, but then stopped

and turned to address me. "After all, Dorothy, it could get damaged if you took it home now in a cab." As I wasn't budging, he said, "Are you coming?"

"Where? What do you have in mind?" I said.

"Out of the room."

He *wasn't* asking me out for a drink, *damn!* Probably had women waiting for him all over town.

"Ah, yes, in a minute," I said, defeated so soon. "I just want to look at it before I go," referring to the lovely Renoir pastel of a girl who looked very much like me. I was thrilled that Reggie remembered how much I'd wanted the painting and touched that he had been generous enough to leave it to me. Ours had been a casual acquaintanceship, and it was because of the Renoir that we had met.

Several years ago I attended an auction, and with money I had scraped together, along with a loan from my sister, Helen, I had hoped to bid on and buy back the picture that had once belonged to my Uncle Martin and Aunt Lizzie Rothschild, but that had been sold by my aunt soon after a tragic event.

In 1912, while sailing home from England on the Titanic, the ship hit an iceberg, and the rest is history. Aunt Lizzie was put into a lifeboat by her husband, my Uncle Martin, who remained aboard the sinking vessel. She watched in horror as the ship nosed under the icy waters. Not long after returning home, she sold off parts of his estate. Why she sold the Renoir, I'll never really know. I recall something about Uncle Martin buying it, not so much because he liked it very much, but because it was part of a deal in the purchase of a Manet that Lizzie adored and had hung in their parlor. Six years after my aunt had sold the painting, its new owner liquidated his assets, and the Renoir was again put up for sale at auction.

The bidding reached the sky soon after the auction began, and I was way out of my league. Reggie was bidding furiously against several others for the picture, and finally won with his last bid of twenty-three-hundred dollars!

After the auction we spoke, but I was shy about telling him of my personal family interest in the picture, so I didn't. I said, if he ever wanted to sell it, and I was flush, to let me know (such bravado!). He was very gentlemanly in not alluding to my reputation for rarely being able to pay the rent, much less ever having the cash to buy such a work of art, but nodded assent before taking a good look at me and saying, "By God, Dottie, you're the girl in the picture!"

Not long after that day, as he later told me, he was discussing the Renoir's provenance with Bernard Berenson. "It had once belonged to the Rothschilds," boasted Reggie.

"Oh, not *those* Rothschilds," said the art expert. "The Rothschilds from the Upper West Side, the coat manufacturers, *you know*, Dorothy Parker's family."

So I was touched that he should think to leave me the picture. Now, not only did I have something back that had belonged to my mostly dead family, but besides Woodrow Wilson, it would be the most valuable thing I owned.

But I digress, and now go back to Wilfred Harrison.

As he appeared to have no interest in getting to know me as more than a bequest in a will, I wanted to take the opportunity of looking more closely at different items in the room. He left the room and the door ajar. I idled up and gently closed it against possible witnesses, before making a bee-line for the desk. I found the key under the cushion of the chair and unlocked the desk. It took me a couple of minutes to find the secret cabinet at the back. The door swung open when I pressed a metal lever, so small and inconspicuous that I only found it by running my hand along the smooth wooden edge before being stopped by a protrusion embedded in the wood. And it was in that cubbyhole that I found the little gun with the mother-of-pearl handle. It was small but weighty; I wondered if it was loaded. Knowing nothing about handling firearms, except what I'd learned from crime novels, or from melodramas I'd seen played out on stage, I knew enough not to look down its barrel. Holding it at arm's length I saw where the chamber could be opened and the cylinder moved away from the body of the gun. Five bullets and one empty place for a sixth one. I could smell gunpowder, and wondered if the gun had been used recently. I was nervous in handling it. I've never liked guns, and I was afraid it might go off even with the gentlest handling. Replacing the cylinder to its closed position, I put the gun back into the secret compartment.

I thought back to the other evening. The Oriental man had taken something from the desk. I was unsure what, exactly, as his back was to me and blocking full view. Had he also placed the gun in there, too? What else had been in the desk compartment?

The only items I could see in the desk were bills and letters that appeared to be from friends or family. So I closed up the desk panel and locked it, returning the key to its hiding place under the seat cushion of the desk chair.

If the gun had been there all along, I mused, why hadn't the Chinaman taken it, too, along with whatever else he had taken? Another thought: Could the gun have been placed there *after* our visit?

It was no longer a mystery of identifying the Oriental. He had been employed, I heard tell during the reception, by Reggie, to serve as houseboy in his new apartment. But since Reggie's death, there was no sign of him.

I needed to think, to sort it all out, but before I left to join my friends at Tony's for a drink and a talk, I had to see if there was something obvious I was missing that might lend a clue to why Reggie was murdered. This was the very room he was found in, after all. He was found dead at the refectory table, in front of a steak, baked potato, and string beans— half-eaten—and with a cherry tomato stuck in his throat.

I paced around the room, trying to take its inventory to store in my little brain for later consideration.

As I had never been in the room before the other night, I couldn't tell if anything was out of place or missing. I checked over the fireplace; there was nothing stuck up the flue. I lifted a potted plant and a couple of statues and found nothing. I opened a door, but found only a small bar set-up. I wanted to pour a drink, but knew I'd best not, as I was moments from discovery. People would be leaving the apartment, and I heard voices exchanging farewells.

I closed the bar and moved toward the Egyptian collection. The sarcophagus coffin stood upright against the wall; the image of an ancient queen with huge, compelling, black-rimmed eyes stared at me as if demanding answers. What secrets was she privy to? I doubted the coffin contained the dusty mummified remains of her majesty, but with nowhere else to look, I stepped closer to her, drawn by the hypnotic bidding of those painted eyes.

There was a scuffle at the library door, and I feared discovery of my snooping. So on an irrational impulse to seek a hiding place, I opened the lid of the ancient coffin just as the library door swung open.

In through the door walked Wilfred Harrison; out from the sarcophagus fell a very dead Lucille Montaine.

Sarcophagus — *I never guessed what I'd find inside.*

Lucille Montaine—
Posed for this risqué photograph back in '19 when she first came to New York and needed the money.

Times Square from 46th Street— Looking down toward the Times Tower during the daytime. The busy streets inspired my friend George Gershwin to compose Rhapsody in Blue. *Can you hear it?*

Chapter Three

"A bullet through her head," I said, in answer to Mr. Benchley's question.

The three of us were commiserating at a table at Tony Soma's.

Aleck looked soulful, full of remorse. "I am sorry to have said all those things about her, even though they were true, and she *was* dreadful, but when I wrote that somebody should put her out of her misery—"

I said, "I believe you said something along the lines of, 'clunked around the stage like a swaybacked cart mare on the way to the glue factory.' And you added, 'It would be kinder to put her out of her misery—'"

"Oh, Lord! I *did* say that, didn't I?" groaned Aleck.

Mr. Benchley added, "You did go on to say, Aleck, you'd've shot her yourself, but you knew your pen would do the trick, requiring little to no cleanup from the janitorial staff."

"They don't suspect *me*, do you think?"

"I'd not worry about being arrested, Aleck," I said. "Your motive—to ban Lucille from the Broadway stage—is not so compelling to the police."

Mr. Benchley wouldn't let Aleck off the hook so quickly, however; he believed Aleck should be more contrite, so he added, "Although, you are rather violent against the desecration of *The Stage*."

Aleck waved for the waiter to refill our drinks, and then sank back into his chair, a hand rubbing a troubled brow. Mr. Benchley turned his attention back to hear the rest of the account of my day. I relayed the events immediately following the discovery of Lucille Montaine's dead body: how Wilfred Harrison entered the library just as I had opened the standing sarcophagus coffin; how the very stiff and wide-eyed corpse of the late actress came crashing, face down, to the floor at my feet; how the scuffle of people, remaining mourners, and later, police and coroner, had piled into the apartment to question me and the others about the events leading up to the discovery of the body.

"I told the police the truth, that I had been admiring the Renoir that Reggie had left to me, and that on the way out, I was curious to peek inside the sarcophagus, which was—'only natural, don't you think, Detective, to want to see if there was a mummy inside?' There was no reason to complicate things by saying that I was snooping, or that I had gone through the desk and found a gun hidden in a secret compartment."

"But, the gun might be the murder weapon, Mrs. Parker," noted Mr. Benchley.

"How was I to explain why I was riffling through the desk in the first place? How was I to explain where I got the key to open the desk? How was I to tell them about the secret compartment? As far as anyone knew, I had never been in the apartment before this afternoon, so how would I explain how I knew my way around, unless I told them we had broken in the other evening?"

"I see your point," said Mr. Benchley. "All right, let's put together what we do know, and see where that gets us," he prefaced.

"Reginald was found dead in his apartment Thursday morning," said Aleck. "Nobody had seen Lucille since Thursday, too. She missed her Thursday-night performance, and that raised a red flag that something was wrong," I said.

Mr. Benchley asked, "But, what was she doing in Reginald's apartment that got her killed and put in the coffin? Could she have had anything to do with Reggie's murder? Or witnessed it or seen the killer?"

"My God!" yelled Aleck. "Do you think she was in the box when we broke in Thursday night?"

"If so, did the Oriental or Marion have any idea that a dead Lucille was in there? Had one of them known, he or she could be the murderer," said Mr. Benchley.

I shook my head, "If she *was* in the coffin while we were there hiding behind the window curtains, neither acted like they knew about it. Remember, I could see them through the break in the draperies," I said. "Each had only one intention, and that was to find something in the room that they wanted to take away. I didn't get the impression that they had any idea about Lucille. And she might not have been in the sarcophagus at that time; she might have been killed elsewhere, or after we left the apartment. But, let's go back to the first problem, the cause of Reggie's death."

"Yes, Dottie," said Aleck. "I think if we know why, and by whom, Reginald was murdered, we might be led to Lucille's killer."

"As far as I know, after spending the past few hours with the family and the police, nobody has mentioned the fact that he was allergic to tomatoes!"

"Why not, do you think?" asked Mr. Benchley, and then proceeded to answer his own question: "Because any one of those people who knew of Reginald's allergy would immediately become suspect."

"But, who else knew?" asked Aleck. "Dottie and I, who sat with Myrtle at an opening-night party two years ago when the dog-meets-skunk story was told; his sons; probably Gerald Saches; his cook and house staff. Damn! Probably everybody."

"But not everybody had a strong motive," said Mr. Benchley.

It was six o'clock in the evening and Tony's place was packed with businessmen stopping in for cocktails before catching trains to the suburbs, friends gathering for drinks before going off to one of the many restaurants around town, and a few hard-drinking regulars seeking solace in their cups. Our discussion was interrupted several times by friends who stopped at our table to say "Hello." I knew that in order to sort things out we would have to find a quiet place to do so.

I thought about the odd behavior of all those who knew of Reginald's allergy, but had failed, as far I as could see, to bring it to the attention of the police. Perhaps my thinking was too linear. Maybe I was looking at the situation from the wrong point of view. Maybe I was seeing what I wanted to see, what *seemed* obvious. What if I was just grabbing at the easiest solution?

Groucho Marx came to mind. Our friend, whose one-liners were often built upon ambiguous and misleading sentence structures—"I once saw an elephant in my pajamas"—made me realize that perhaps we were looking at things the wrong way.

"Maybe he didn't die from the allergy," I said. "What if the tomato was placed in his throat to make it *look* like he choked? A way to eliminate from consideration the way he really died? What if the murderer didn't even know about his allergy?"

"If that were the case, then the suspects are not limited to the few who did know. Was there an autopsy?" asked Mr. Benchley.

"Aleck?"

"I'll call Cousin Joe at the Twentieth. He can get us a copy of the coroner's report with no questions asked."

There was little time left to talk further on the subject as Aleck had an opening-night show to review. From the bar he put in a call to Sergeant Joe Woollcott at the Twentieth, who promised to get him the report by the following morning. Later this evening, Aleck would come to my rooms, after he handed in his review of tonight's show. In the meantime, Mr. Benchley and I would be making a short trip up to the murdered actress's apartment on West 51st Street.

———◆———

Mr. Benchley and I walked several blocks north and then turned west toward the brownstone apartment of Lucille Montaine. We dodged automobiles as we crossed under the Sixth Avenue El, over the trolley tracks on Seventh Avenue toward Broadway, and into the traffic-congested streets of the Theatre District.

Trains rumbled like snare drums overhead, shaking the ground with deep bass tones; trolley car bells clanged, amusingly sprite-like; motorcar horns blasted brazen brass, or hee-hawed like a chorus of donkeys on the run; a cabbie and a motorist shouted obscenities at each other, and police whistles, blocks away, flitted lightly through the air. Scraps of syncopated songs spilled out from honky-tonk gin joints and tacky dance halls. Capricious tunes rang up from the streets like jazz, an improvisational melody reverberating along the strings of towering structures. The city was bright, vibrant with life and the excitement of rich possibility, its people racing in pursuit of inspiration or whimsy. Even the cold, determined wind from off the Hudson would slap your face, stiffen your back, or nip at your heels; revive the spirit, or knock you for a loop; quicken your pace, quicken your pulse, and give renewed purpose to the pursuit of success, and meaning to the phrase, "If you can make it in New York, you can make it anywhere." My friend George Gershwin feels the rhythm of this city, hears its ever-changing tune, rejoices in its singularity, and has so well captured the heart and spirit of New York in his new *Rhapsody in Blue*.

The discovery of Lucille's body had been the most stunning event I told my friends about when I had arrived at Tony Soma's. But there was quite a bit more. As we braced ourselves against the sharp wind, I told Mr. Benchley the gossip and the few facts I'd gleaned from my afternoon at the reception and reading of the will: Reggie had never filed for divorce to be with his mistress, Marion. Myrtle hadn't wanted the divorce, either, just a separation, so Reginald and Myrtle were still married at the time of his death. Also, Mistress Marion had not been seen anywhere near the funeral home, or at the service, or at his interment.

According to the terms of the will, aside from bequests to friends and employees, gifts for medical research, charities for the poor, a foundation in his name to fund artistic development in the Theatre, and his collection of Egyptian artifacts bequeathed to the Metropolitan Museum of Art, all was left to his wife. He left modest amounts of money in trust for his sons, but with stipulations: not to be received until reaching the age of 26 and the completion of their university educations. As for my observation of the young men, they appeared sullen and impatient with the traditions of the past couple days, rather than mournful; they had obviously been at odds with their father, for what reason I would have to investigate, and they did not bother to hide their resentment.

When we arrived at Lucille's apartment building, a four-story brownstone on 51st Street just west of Eighth Avenue, we were unsure what we might be walking into, so we stopped at the stoop leading up to the front entry door. If the police had not been to her apartment yet, they surely would be soon. There was no patrol car parked on the street. There was nothing for it but to buck up and press on, so we braced ourselves and climbed the steps.

The front door was unlocked. We found Lucille's name and apartment number on one of five letterboxes. The house was quiet as we climbed the stairway up one flight. The sound of a tune playing on a Victrola from rooms on the floor above was the only sign of life. Her door led to rooms at the front of the building. Its lock was easily jimmied by Mr. Benchley, a.k.a. Bobby the Burglar.

Light filtered in from street lamps and lit a path

to the windows, where I lowered the shades and pulled the draperies closed before Mr. Benchley hit the light switch on the wall. Light fell in pools from table lamps around the room and onto a red-plush sofa and a matching easy chair. A thick, cream-colored acanthus-leaf-sculpted carpet anchored the living room suite set before bay windows. Lots of photos, all containing images of the dead woman posed with Broadway's stars, stared back at us from sparkling silver frames grouped on various mirror-topped tables and on the fireplace mantle. A sleek mirrored bar separated a small kitchen just off the entry foyer and a door leading to a bedroom and bathroom.

"What now, Mrs. Parker?"

"I'm not sure, Mr. Benchley."

"Well, we didn't come here out of simple curiosity."

"I suppose we came to search for . . . what *are* we searching for, anyway?"

"Something that might give a clue as to why she was murdered and who may have done the gruesome deed."

"Right! And while we're at it, anything that might tell us more about who Lucille Montaine really was."

"What do you mean? Her real name? You think Lucille Montaine was a stage name?"

"Well, yes, that, too, but what I mean is, if we know more about the victim, who she really was, who were her friends, what were her habits, her troubles, maybe we will know why she was murdered."

"Very good," said Mr. Benchley, looking over the room. "Well, we know that the last time she was in the apartment it was during the daytime because when we entered, the window shades were up."

"Very good deduction, indeed, Mr. Benchley. So that means she'd been missing since Thursday, but before five o'clock in the evening. Why don't you look around the living room and gather up anything interesting. I'll search the bedroom."

I pulled the shades and curtains before turning on the bedroom lamps, and then went through her bureau drawers, the vanity, and bedside table. Aside from the usual array of lingerie—camisoles, slips and panties, hosiery—and jewelry boxes, perfume bottles, and face creams, there was little of anything that might tell me more about her than that she shopped at Bendel's and Bergdorf's. The armoire and closet boasted numerous hat boxes and dozens of pairs of shoes and purses, as well as many shimmering gowns, a silver fox fur–trimmed coat, a couple of evening capes, four or five suits, silk blouses, and negligees.

I quickly went through pockets and purses and gathered up note slips, sales receipts, business cards, and several theatre tickets and programs, to more closely scrutinize later. I was about to pull the chain of the closet light when I noticed that the lid of a wardrobe box was slightly a-kilter. I lifted the lid, and behold! A treasure trove of letters, a scrapbook, photos, and news clippings! Quickly, I checked the other boxes lying beside it and found in one of them a man's shirt and suit jacket tossed and wrinkled, the clothing labels from a more pricey men's tailor in midtown, and in another, a costume of black trousers, turtleneck sweater, and knitted cap. Tossed in a corner of the closet was a pair of very soiled tie-up flat-heeled shoes. Encrusted mud caught in the step where sole meets heel made me wonder where in the city one could find such heavy mud, except maybe in Central Park. I made a decision to leave the clothes and shoes but take with me the box of papers.

After shutting the bedroom lights and raising the shades, I went in to join Mr. Benchley, who had collected several items from the living room, which we added to the box of mementos.

Just as we took a final turn around the room, the telephone bell rang, causing both of us to freeze. We looked back and forth from the phone to each other with dreaded expressions, as if we were certain that whoever was on the other end of the line *knew* we were in the apartment. We were like kids caught with our hands in the cookie jar, like teenagers caught necking on the living-room sofa, like—oh, what were we to do? Hide behind the draperies from some omnipotent entity seeping through a telephone receiver? *I'm getting too old for intrigue*, I thought.

But the bell seemed to ring more loudly and more insistently, as if demanding to be answered with every consecutive jangle. I reacted on instinct. I picked up the receiver.

"Hello?" I said in a weak monotone, expecting

the deep, resonant voice of The Lord to bellow out, before reaching out through the receiver to box my ear.

A woman immediately chattered on about a problem with the laundry, and it took me a minute to decipher that the caller was Lucille's house maid, and she was so sorry, but she could not get the stain out of the negligee. "What should she do?"

When I had an opening to speak at last, I informed the woman that she had reached the wrong number, and I hung up.

It was time to leave before we were discovered, and we set about shutting lights and raising shades. But as we were peeking out the door into the hallway to see if the coast was clear, the telephone bell began its sharp jangling again. We both jumped in surprise, and irrational fear sent my heart flying up to my throat. When I looked over at my friend, Mr. Benchley's usually cool demeanor was betrayed by droplets of moisture on his neat moustache; his normally expressive face looked not unlike that of the proverbial deer-caught-in-the-headlights.

Neither of us wanted to move, nor look at the source of the ringing, but when I finally turned to face the thing that beckoned unrelentingly, I had the impression that the apparatus was actually shaking furiously, jiggling on the table; if the candlestick had had feet, it would have been stamping its demand. I *knew* it would not be the house maid calling again. Somehow, ridiculous as it sounds, the ring was different, meaner, more menacing. Perhaps it was that we were rooted stock-still in shadowy darkness, on the verge of discovery by the police or a murderer, and that was why the phone rang out with a shrill, unworldly and sinister bent. I was as afraid *not* to answer the frenetic appeal as to answer it. I have always believed that, at times, to learn the truth is to shine light on the unknown, and in so doing, menacing shadows are chased away. It is far less scary than blundering around a problem, ignorantly and idiotically, in the dark.

Ignoring Mr. Benchley's head shaking, I picked up the receiver, but cupped the mouthpiece and said nothing.

I could hear *his* breathing. Yes, there was a *man* on the other end. I waited for him to speak, but he didn't. Finally, I whispered, "Hello?"

There was a pause, a long pause, enough time for me to know that wheels where turning in the caller's brain, spinning in search of explanations. A click, and the line went dead.

"Let's get the hell out of here!" I said, just as we heard the screeching of tires on the street.

We closed the door after engaging the lock and hurried down the staircase, reaching the bottom landing and the foyer just as a pair of police officers arrived at the outer door. I was worried that they would recognize me, not necessarily for my celebrity, but as the woman who had released Lucille Montaine from her exotic casket.

The interior layouts of most brownstones in

Manhattan are identical. As this house had been only modestly modified to convert from private residence to apartment living, I hoped that the stairway leading down to the basement apartment wasn't blocked off. I had hoped right, it wasn't, so Mr. Benchley and I ducked out of sight around the stairwell and down the stairs, aware that the stairway would end at a locked door to the basement apartment, but at least out of sight of the police officers coming through the main entry door. We waited as the footfalls on the creaking stairs overhead diminished, and then we came up to peek around into the hall to see if the coast was clear for our escape.

A few minutes later we were safely in a cab heading downtown to my rooms at the Algonquin, laughing and joking inanely in an effort to release the tension of the past hour. It would be quite a while before Aleck joined us, but that gave us time to look through all the papers and pictures we'd carried out of Lucille's apartment. As none of us knew Lucille Montaine very well, I was hoping these items would give up any secrets in the dead woman's past.

Woodrow Wilson greeted me enthusiastically when we walked through the door, and then slunk away across the room to lie beneath a chair when he remembered his shameful behavior while I was out; I discovered the puddle on the floor; it wasn't the first time. . . .

I grabbed a towel, cleaned up the mess, and then took my neglected pup out for a spin along the street, leaving Mr. Benchley to begin organizing our stash. Before I came back up on the lift, I ordered room service at the desk. A plate of sandwiches to tide us over until Aleck arrived, and a snack for Woodrow Wilson, compliments of Henri, the chef of the Algonquin dining room, who saved special morsels for his most beloved and appreciative pooch. By the time I returned to the apartment, Mr. Benchley had not only spread all the papers around the room, but also fixed us a shaker of Tom Collinses.

"But, Fred," I said, looking around the room at the scores of items strewn on the floor. "What fresh hell is this? How the hell do we make sense of this madness?"

"Ah, my dear girl, but there is method to this madness."

"More like madness to the method, if you ask me!"

"Well, I'm not asking; I'm telling," he said, handing me my drink. "Now take a sip and tell me that isn't the best Tom Collins you've ever tasted."

"I cannot say such a thing. It *is* the best Tom Collins I've ever tasted."

"Good," he beamed, then took my hand to lead me through a path of uncluttered carpet. "Now, if we stand right here we can turn in a three-hundred-and-sixty-degree—"

"Please! I'm not a mathematician!"

"—and we have it all spread out at our feet."

"You remind me of the Kaiser standing on a map of Europe."

"It's more like a labyrinth, really," he said, considering the layout with a frown. "Make fun, if you want, Madame, but there is science here!"

"Math, and now science!"

"There you see?" he said pointing to the floor. "First circle: letters in chronological order; second tier: photos—Lucille was organized and marked the dates and events, and identified the people in the pictures; and then, there," he pointed, vaguely, "are receipts: ticket stubs, programs, store charges, notes. *Voila*: Last circle—news clippings, mementos, and a scrapbook!"

"Fred, you are brilliant! But where is the Ninth Circle of Hell?"

"Let's dive in."

An hour later, after a short break (we'd finished off the last crumbs from our turkey sandwiches, and licked out the last dregs from a second shaker of drinks), we went back to the task of sorting through Lucille Montaine's life.

Soon we'd learned that she had been born Ethel Mae Herring, was raised in Des Moines, Iowa, one of two children to middle-class parents, her father, a pharmacist, her mother, a homemaker, who also gave piano lessons, and that Ethel Mae had been the star of her high school's senior production of *A Midsummer Night's Dream*, which we might have learned had we read the *Playbill* biography from one of her Broadway shows. There was a cast photo in her yearbook, where she was flanked by wood nymphs and a Puck who wore his mischievous grin for the camera.

Through several letters from her mother, we discovered that she had come to New York to make a career in the Theatre. As if that was news! And from several love letters we learned that Lucille had had a very serious romance, which she had abandoned for the Great White Way.

From a much-handled scrapbook of clippings and theatre photos, many of which had come unglued, leaving behind yellowish, rectangular ghosts on its pages, we learned that she had appeared in several chorus lines with touring companies across the country. For two years she'd traveled the circuit from Portland, Maine, to Portland, Oregon, even returning to her hometown's Palace Theatre in a Lee Shubert extravaganza. Her biggest out-of-town role was as the Month of April, for which she wore a gown of cherry blossoms and carried a silver umbrella, while being rained upon with silver confetti. She had cut out the reviews from each newspaper of the cities on the circuit, which noted her delightful costume and graceful form. Soon, she'd advanced to a walk-on in the 1922 production of *Fashions for Men*, and later that same year, a walk-on in the production of Eugene O'Neill's *Anna Christie*, which starred Pauline Lord. She'd yet to cut out the notices from her first starring role in RIP's show that had opened only a week earlier to mostly dreadful reviews. But then, she probably would not have pasted them in the book, except for the benign, if syrupy, notice by critic Ralph Chittenham.

Also among the usual debris of useless, little

used, or forgotten items in the wardrobe box were such things as an old powder compact, hairclips, hat feathers, a tired-looking box of blue note cards, a broken comb, a rolled-up high school banner, a bottle of glue, manicure scissors, and a wrinkled red satin ribbon.

The items that Mr. Benchley had taken from the living room included a notepad from beside the telephone, several pearls found under the sofa seat cushion, a torn-off high heel tossed behind a chair, and a box of matches from the 21 Club.

Mr. Benchley rubbed the angled point of a pencil across the blank surface of the notepad paper to reveal the ghost of messages past: "Biltmore 1130," it read. Was it A.M. or P.M.? We didn't know. A meeting? Under the Biltmore's famous clock in the lobby, the designated meeting place for thousands each day?

Obviously, a strand of pearls had been broken, whether by Lucille or a visitor was anyone's guess, and several pearls had rolled back into the crease of the sofa cushion. That lent little information, as I have a box chuck full of bits and pieces of broken jewelry in my closet. No sinister meaning in that, anyway.

But the discovery of a broken heel—likely from a dress shoe, as it was covered in satin—coupled with the loose pearls, gave rise to visions of a struggle in the living room. (Although, you never know what you'll find under my sofa.)

As for the matches, Mr. Benchley pocketed them, having used his last one for lighting his cigarette.

After three hours of rearranging items and taking an inventory for quick reference in the future, we returned everything to the wardrobe box, having found nothing that could explain her murder or be a connection to anyone who might have had reason to kill her.

Aleck arrived at midnight, having filed his review of Irving Berlin's new *Music Box Revue of 1924*. Entering, with a flourish of his hand, he removed his red-satin-lined black opera cape and laid it across a chair, resting his top hat, opera scarf, and gloves in a neat stack.

"I thought you'd be ready for a night on the town," he scolded. "First to the opening-night party at the Waldorf for the *Revue*; I thought it would be fun to say 'Hello.' Fanny Brice was hilarious, the little yenta; Grace Moore, Bobby, was magnificent, as usual, but I did miss you in this production, kiddo!"

"Did you really, Aleck?"

"Go home, Bob, and get some duds on. We'll go on to dinner—What have we here? Reluctance?"

"Let me slip into something for the occasion," I said, retreating to the bedroom.

In the bathroom, I rinsed off the day's grime, and then pulled from my closet a simple black satin sheath dress, changed into nonsensical shoes, powdered and rouged my face, put on lipstick, darkened my eyes with mascara, pushed my untamed locks under a sleek, purple satin evening hat, decorated with gold fringe that frames the face, wrapped a gold-threaded shawl around my shoulders, grabbed an evening purse, and then finished with a cloud of Coty's Chypre, my favorite cologne. All in all, a record-breaking six minutes, start to finish.

"Bob left to run across the street to dress. He'll meet us downstairs in ten minutes," said Aleck, relaxing on the sofa, having poured himself a whiskey. "So tell me about your evening."

I filled him in on all we'd been up to since we parted after drinks at Tony Soma's. He frowned when I told him about our breaking into Lucille's apartment, gasped when I mentioned the sinister telephone call, and clenched fist to mouth when I talked about the arrival of the cops. Although his reactions were words enough, he reserved comment until I finished telling him about our lack of discoveries.

"I don't like it," was all he had to say, and knowing the normal loquaciousness of my friend, I knew he was serious.

"Neither do I, Aleck."

"No, that's not what I mean. I don't like that you are taking such chances. You and Bob could have been arrested!"

"Then we'd've been mentioned in FPA's column tomorrow after you bailed us out," I said, making light of the situation, while checking my evening bag for essentials—lipstick, pressed-powder compact, eyeglasses, handkerchief, cash. I filled Woodrow Wilson's water bowl and then waited as Aleck donned his cape.

At the door he touched my shoulder and said, "I worry about you, dear Dottie. There is a murderer out there. I fear what might happen should you get in his way."

I was touched, really, by his genuine concern. We are good friends, but it is rare that a display of affection from Aleck arrives unaccompanied by insult. I kissed his cheek, and so I wouldn't cry, as I am easily melted to tears by sentimental gestures — the appeal of doggie eyes, road-weary hack horses, and kind words — I changed the subject by asking what he enjoyed most about the show he'd seen earlier.

———————

The Waldorf is a grand hotel, boasting several ballrooms, marvelous dining, and a first-class nightclub and orchestra, and is the midtown home of many famous visitors and residents. I adore walking into its spectacular lobby.

The opening-night party was in full swing when we arrived, and a glass of champagne was placed in my hand before I had barely crossed the threshold of the ballroom.

We three remained near the entrance as we perused the crowd. It was what usually is done. Not only can we be seen to best advantage, we can take in the entire room and determine whom to avoid and whom to approach. Mr. Benchley and I let Aleck take the lead tonight, and once he spotted her, he walked straight over to Fanny Brice.

Unfortunately, Ralph Chittenham was extolling the various virtues of Grace Moore's performance and her glorious operatic voice just a few feet from where we stood. His loud baritone carried the distance.

". . . While I was in Boston last Thursday, I caught a marvelous production of a little play entitled *Grounds for Divorce*, with Ina Claire and Philip Merivale. Ina and Phil gave delightful performances."

"I've heard wonderful things about the play. Ina and I go way back, and I wish I could see the play when it comes to town, but that's not likely with our performing on the same nights and matinee days," said Grace.

"It's a pity. But, then, she won't get to see your terrific numbers in the *Revue*, either."

Ralph spotted us. "Hello, you two!" he called out.

I nodded and smiled at the critic, greeted Grace with a hug and complimented her gown, told her I would be around soon to catch her show, even though I wasn't assigned to reviewing it for *Ainslee* or *The Smart Set*.

Mr. Benchley greeted Grace, with whom he had starred in last season's revue, with an embrace and kiss. Ever cordial and charming, he asked after her health, gently gossiped about mutual friends, and then fell into conversation about the vast number of laryngitis cases plaguing actors this past fall. Ralph Chittenham and Mr. Benchley enjoyed a friendly relationship. But then, Mr. Benchley was a much more tolerant person than I.

After Grace moved on to greet new arrivals, I lingered a while, observing the lovely assemblage of Theatre folk, as the two men swapped pleasantries and harmless gossip, before excusing myself to go "powder my nose." I had no intention of powdering anything, actually; I just wanted to get some distance from Chittenham before he tried to engage me, too, in conversation. I took the opportunity to congratulate my friend Irving Berlin, and to share in a toast to the long run of his new hit show.

Light reflecting from impressive chandeliers flashed on sequins, drawing my eye, in particular, to a stunning gown worn by a familiar blonde. The Mary Astor look-a-like walked through the columned arch leading to the ladies' lounge. It was not the surprise of seeing Marion at the party that prompted me to follow her; it was the man who made fast tracks after her that drew my curiosity.

I squeezed around a clot of celebrants to the archway, where I found partial cover beside a palm. I hoped that no one would approach me while I peeked through the fronds. The ridiculousness of my concealment brought to mind scenes from Oscar Wilde plays, and the realization that everything I had done today held a fancy of intrigue.

There stood RIP's mistress, Marion Fields, in huddled debate with Wilfred Harrison. I couldn't do anything other than listen to their conversation, as Marion's eyes were flitting about in search of eavesdroppers. She spotted me and our eyes locked. She touched Wilfred's arm, and nodded in my direction.

There was only one thing for me to do, so rather than sheepishly retreat, I decided to draw full attention to myself, pretending to use the cover of the palm to re-fasten a wayward stocking. Rising up, I walked toward them as if on my way to the ladies' lounge.

As I had never officially met Mistress Marion, all I could do was smile and nod in passing. I did know Wilfred, and even though he made sure his back was to me, I stopped short a few steps after passing, turned on my heel, and said, "Wilfred Harrison? Is that you?"

The handsome face that turned toward me blanched before a rosy flush colored his features.

"Oh, Wilfred," I drawled, making a show of how delighted I was to see him again. "Fancy meeting you here, of all places! I suppose you are slumming it this evening?"

I touched his arm, batted my lashes in blatant flirtation, and although I knew that I sounded like an ass, I wanted to see Marion's reaction.

"Hello, Dorothy, nice to see you again," he said politely, but noncommittally. It was obvious he was anything but glad, and I wanted to know why.

As he did not introduce me to Marion, I became suspicious of his bad manners. I wouldn't let it lie.

I stuck out my hand and said, "Hello, I'm Dottie Parker, marvelous party tonight."

She met my handshake, "Marion Fields, Mrs. Parker."

"Call me Dottie." I looked up at the six-foot-tall Wilfred, waiting for him to offer something to the conversation, but the tongue-tied dullard only produced a tepid, "Yes, that's grand."

I wasn't going to let either of them off so easily. "Lots of very interesting people here tonight, Marion; Theatre folk are lots more fun than we writer types, you know. I suppose Wilfred has introduced you to some of them?"

Wilfred dove in awkwardly. "Actually, I have only just now met Miss Fields. She dropped her purse in passing and I was helping her retrieve a lost lipstick that rolled under the table there."

"Oh, well that explains it." Now, to really put them on the spot, I said, "Forgive me, but it looked like you were avoiding me."

He turned green.

"My silly paranoia, really, pay me no mind."

Then, before he could say a word, I said, "You look awfully familiar, you know. Do you waitress at Schrafft's?"

"Marion is an actress, and she has friends in the show. She was in the chorus of last's year's *Music Box Revue*."

"My, you can learn a lot about a person while retrieving a lipstick," I said, and added in my pathetic little singing voice before either could reply, "'*Yes, we have no bananas; we have no bananas today!*' Nifty little tune. Stays with you, you know—humming it around town all day, can't seem to sleep because it's rolling around your head at three in the morning . . ." I was

referring to Irving Berlin's hit song from the 1923
Music Box Revue in which Marion was in the chorus.
"But, it's not from the show that I know you, is it?
But from where?"

"I've been around—"

"I'll bet you have," I said, burying my words into
the bubbles of my champagne.

"I was saying that I've been around many of the
same places you frequent, Mrs. Parker."

"Call me 'Dottie,' dear."

"I used to work for Reginald Pierce. I was his
assistant."

Vanity revealed!

"Really, now! Why, I was just—" (I hoped to
appear appropriately flustered) "Why, I didn't see
you at the wake or funeral or the reading of the will,
so you must have been so devastated by his murder
that you—"

"Murder!" she yelped. She looked genuinely
shocked, or she was one damn hell of a good actress,
for I glimpsed a feral flash of fear rush over her features. "I thought he choked on a cherry tomato?"

I knew in that instant that she could not possibly have had anything to do with Reggie's death.
But, why were she and Wilfred pretending they hadn't
met until a few minutes ago? If she had been RIP's
assistant, even if her duties were to turn down his bed
covers and warm his sheets, she surely would have
known Reggie's attorney. These two were guilty of
something, that was for sure. But, they were not going

to share their secret with me no matter how much further I pushed on with boorish taunts.

"Well, then, as this gentleman hasn't had the chance to tell you yet—as you two have just become acquainted—Mr. Harrison, here, is the executor for Reginald's estate. Small world, ain't it? Well, must be off—so nice to have made your acquaintance, Marion." And with that, I continued on to the ladies' lounge.

I caught up with a very jocular Aleck, sitting at another "round table" with a group of his fans including Fanny, Grace, Irving, and FPA. I stood beside his chair, after having waved the gentlemen to remain seated.

Aleck had before him the three key ingredients of his newest heavenly confection. He poured a pint of cream into a shaker of ice, added to it eight ounces of an excellent Napoleon cognac, and then an equal portion of crème de cacao to the mix. Gently, he stirred, fixed the strainer, and poured the elixir through and into glasses for everyone at the table to taste. There was quite a bit of moaning and humming, a lip smack and a comment from FPA that he really wasn't into mixed drinks; liked his rye straight up. But, Aleck's drink, "let's call it the 'Brandy Alexander,'" was certainly a cut above his nightly hot cocoa.

"Well, all you crazy kids," said Aleck, after finishing off his drink and pushing back his chair, "I came to this dance with Mrs. Parker, so I must see her home."

We found Mr. Benchley, who was more than

eager to leave, and we wove our way to the hatcheck, through the lobby, and out into the night. A light drizzle had dampened the streets to a glossy sheen; city lights rippled over the mirror-slick surfaces. We waited under the canopy as the doorman hailed us a cab.

Once settled in, and as Aleck was instructing the driver of our destination, I saw Ralph Chittenham walk out of the hotel and into his limousine. The chauffeur, in full livery, closed the door after him and was walking around to his driver's side door when the streetlight washed over his face.

"That's him!"

"What are you babbling about, idiot child?" said Aleck with feigned impatience.

"The Chinaman!" I spat out. Both men looked in the direction of my pointed finger. All they saw was a car door closing.

"The little Oriental I saw at RIP's apartment that night fishing around in the desk, Reggie's house-boy. He's chauffeuring Ralph Chittenham."

"He made fast work of getting a new job, didn't he?" said Mr. Benchley.

"But, people are looking for him."

"What people?" asked Aleck.

"The police wanted to question him. He may have been the last person to see Reggie alive."

"Then someone should let the police know where to find him,' said Aleck.

"Not someone. Not yet, at least. I want to talk to him first."

"Hold onto your deerstalker, Sherlock," yelled Aleck, taking my hand. He turned to Mr. Benchley. "Bob, this is getting serious and potentially dangerous."

"Yes, Aleck, but I don't think that we're in any real danger. First of all, we've never been taken seriously by anyone before; we're known as frivolous wits; our banter is louder than our bite, and secondly," he turned his attention to the street, as if searching the pavement for words as the cab whizzed along the avenue, ". . . well, there is no secondly that I can think of at the moment."

"Well said," said I.

Broadway & 42nd Street— Looking west toward the Hudson River. The street is lined with theatres.

Coat Advertisement— Gorgeous but pricey furs at Stewart & Company.

John Barrymore— That's our friend, Johnny, frightening his audience and delighting the critics as Richard III.

Chapter Four

Ten minutes later, we three sat down to a late meal at a little Hungarian restaurant on 50th Street, whose owner was not averse to serving supper at two in the morning. It was our first chance to discuss the events of the evening.

I have never known anyone who enjoys food more than Alexander Woollcott. Each meal is like a ritual, and to watch Aleck dine is not unlike watching a priest performing transubstantiation during Holy Mass: Cloths are unfolded and used to wipe the silverware and then the wine and water glasses, before being refolded and placed to the left of the plate. When the waiter arrives with the rolls, a new napkin is brought before the gourmand, and with a flick of the wrist, like the snapping of a courtesan's fan, it is placed on his lap. Water is poured, the appetizer and drinks (the first of many beverages) are ordered. The captain and waiter move about like altar boys, and know precisely when to genuflect and retreat.

Aleck reaches for his first roll. If it is cold to the

touch, he bids the waiter to warm them. If they are warm, he nods to the man, as a priest to his deacon, and then he gently tears it into several pieces, as he might break the wafer host. He blesses a morsel with butter, always sweet, never salted. With solemnity, his eyelids fluttering shut behind the thick glasses, the first morsel is placed upon his tongue, in silent thanksgiving. All in all, breaking bread with Aleck is a religious experience.

It is not unusual to see set before him several main courses, and at meal's end nary a crumb left on four or five dessert plates. Throughout, there is the constant flow of mixed drinks, bottles of wine, and cup after cup of coffee. Aleck did not achieve his great weight of nearly three hundred pounds by skimping on the Hollandaise or refusing the third piece of cheesecake.

When he isn't enjoying the excellent fare of the dining room at the Algonquin, he prefers the dining room at the Kaufman apartment. Bea Kaufman, George's wife, is the most proficient of cooks, and for Aleck, an invitation to dinner is always a standing one. Bea never cuts corners on flavor and texture, so the cream and butter and sauces flow heavily, and so do the beverages, for the household is supplied by a most reputable bootlegger. As she and Aleck have padded up, George, miraculously, remains reed thin.

This night, or should I say, this morning, Aleck's final meal of the day was a light one—just goulash, spätzle, beets, half a loaf of black bread, and a Linzer torte for dessert.

"We haven't gotten the coroner's report, Dottie, so we can't be certain," he said as he dunked a well-buttered piece of bread into the Hungarian stew.

"Oh, he was murdered, all right."

"It does seem likely, Aleck," said Mr. Benchley. "There are so many people with motive; it would be unlikely if Reginald's death was *not* a murder, *statistically* speaking, that is."

"What the hell does that mean?" said Aleck. He stopped chewing, swallowed, and squinted through his frames at Mr. Benchley. His moustache twitched. "Do you think that what you just said makes sense?"

"Statistically, yes," twitched back Mr. Benchley's neat fringe.

"You're bonko, boyo Bob!" said Aleck, his eyes growing huge behind the eyeglasses.

"Well, it is two in the morning, Aleck, and—oh hell! I stand by my numbers!"

"Don't listen to him, Fred," I said. "You've got a very good point there, whatever it is, and no matter the hour!"

Aleck pointed his fork and wagged it like a finger at me and then at Fred. "You realize, don't you, you two congenital idiots, that you've taken evidence from what may have been the scene of a crime?"

"I don't know what you're getting at."

"Lucille's apartment! Pearls, papers, all the stuff—"

"We'll put everything back," I said, knowing Aleck was right, but still feeling on the defensive.

"That's not the point, you naughty girl. So which one of you two dolts is the troublemaker, and which of you is along for the ride?"

Mr. Benchley and I simultaneously pointed at each other.

"*Tsk, tsk!* What am I to do with you children!" said Aleck, shaking his head, his jowls following the lead.

"You know, Aleck," said Mr. Benchley, the model of sudden sobriety, "You'd make someone a very good wife."

Aleck guffawed, nearly sending a mouthful of potato to his lap. He did have a sense of humor, even if at times, though rarely, he was the brunt of the joke. He hated being around dull people, and respected a fast and clever barb. Many friends have affectionately tried to describe Alexander Woollcott, the man most responsible for setting the witty tone of astringent and outrageous humor for our generation. In some respects he is an aberration. He possesses equal parts of the feminine and the masculine aspects of human nature, and often, depending on his mood, vacillates between the two. It is because of his blatant effeminacy, his flowery, exuberant praise for the theatrical achievements of an actor or playwright, or his deliberate and bloodthirsty disembowelment of one he wishes banned from the stage, that he has been dubbed "vitriol and old lace."

On the subject of his sexual relations with women, no one is quite sure, although his claim to having contracted the mumps when he was twenty is a handy excuse for his celibacy, and, as he assumes we know what that implies, nothing more needs be said of the matter.

Groucho Marx once asked Aleck about his time in the army during the war.

"Tell us, Aleck," he asked, "when you were in France, did you get laid?"

Aleck considered the question, and then replied, "Infinitesimally."

A mean-spirited fellow, who shall remain nameless, blurted out that Aleck was "a fag who just never got caught." Whether asexual or homosexual, it would not lessen my great esteem for the man. Anyway, the truth be told, half the people in the Theatre are homosexual; the other half are just plain psychotic— with the Marx Brothers and John Barrymore on the psychotic side. But, I think Aleck is body conscious, and too shy (believe it or not, for all his bravado!) to indulge in physical intimacy. And I can see beyond his vitriol that he possesses a deep fear of rejection, in spite of the face of confidence he shows the world.

I've never known anyone like Aleck. He is at once both male companion and gossipy girlfriend to me. George Kaufman summed him up most succinctly when he described Aleck as "improbable." And that is exactly what he is: singular.

We discussed "The Case." I think it was that evening that we first referred to the murder of Reginald Pierce as "The Case." In spite of Aleck's very logical concerns about safety, and the obstruction of justice through our meddling, we were drawn to the task of solving the murder of the producer. And we were certain, in our guts, at least, that Lucille's murder was connected.

"Do you think the understudy murdered Lucille?" I asked.

"What, because she was hungry for a part in a play?" said Mr. Benchley.

"I've known actors who'd kill for a fava bean," said Aleck.

"The problem is this: If both murders are connected, why would the understudy have killed the producer of the show? Where would that get her? Why not just knock-off the star?"

From my evening purse I took out the short list of suspects and the objects taken from Lucille's apartment. "All right, let's consider each suspect. Who on this list stands to gain the most from RIP's death?"

The boys glanced at the list.

"The wife, for his money."

"Gerald Saches, because with Reggie out of the way, he can move in on Myrtle."

"Or, the mistress, Marion Fields. She gets revenge on Reggie for not divorcing his wife. But, she inherits nothing, so it is a rather vacuous reason to kill."

"You don't think revenge is enough? Ever see *Hamlet*?"

"If she did do it, she needed help. Reginald was

a big man, and she is a tiny bit of a thing. We'll find out in the morning just how he was murdered."

"What was she doing with Wilfred Harrison, huddled in clandestine conversation?" I asked, rhetorically.

"Are you so certain it was anything more than an innocent encounter?" said Mr. Benchley.

"I'm sure it wasn't innocent. And then there is the mysterious Oriental driving 'Ralph Shittenham.'" (I knew what I'd said.)

"What we need to do is find the connection to RIP among all the suspects. One of them had to have had some motive, albeit some secret motive, for wanting both Reginald and Lucille dead," said Mr. Benchley. A look of puzzlement crossed his features, and then he said, "Unless Lucille was killed by someone else, for reasons unconnected to Reggie, and the murderer wanted it to *look* as if the same person killed them both."

"We won't know unless we delve into the lives of each victim and each suspect to find a link or a motive so compelling it eliminates everybody else."

Aleck looked at me and then over his glasses at Mr. Benchley. "Just make sure he or she doesn't eliminate you."

"You know, Aleck," said Mr. Benchley, "I've reconsidered: You're not a wife; you're a real mother."

If Alexander Woollcott and Robert Benchley
are a bit . . . unusual, the members of the Algonquin
Round Table might be described as an odd menag-
erie of contrasting talents and personalities: writers,
journalists, theatre people, but artists, all—Jascha
Heifetz and Irving Berlin; Harpo Marx and Robert
Sherwood. Our commonality is our luncheon club,
our notorious wit, and the great joy we share in each
other's company every day. I believe our enthusiasm
to be together comes from our neurotic, yet endearing,
need to belong to a family. Many of our members have
come to New York from other places to build careers,
and there is the natural desire to seek the emotional
acceptance families provide. So it is not unusual for
us to meet at the Gonk for our one o'clock luncheon
as often as six days a week, and later, at five-ish for
cocktails in my rooms or at Tony Soma's, or at Neysa's
studio, and then, if there isn't a play to review or a
deadline, on to supper.

Then there is the Thanatopsis Literary and
Inside Straight Club, a poker game that has been meeting for years every Saturday night. It is not unusual
for the games to continue on into Sunday evening,
or even into Monday morning! The marathon card
games have recently been moved from a room at the
Algonquin to the home of Jane Grant and Harold Ross,
a residence that they purchased with Aleck on West
46th Street. I rarely attend, unless it is to commiserate
with Jane.

When one of us is separated from the group

for more than a few days, he or she suffers withdrawal symptoms. Like members of any family, we don't always get along; we have our "moments," but the bond of our friendships is stronger than any gripe that might threaten to tear us asunder.

Back a few years, in June of 1919, Robert Sherwood and Robert Benchley, alongside whom I worked at *Vanity Fair*, were invited to a luncheon to welcome back from the War Alexander Woollcott, the new drama critic at the *New York Times*. A select group of newspaper journalists and editors were invited to the free lunch. As the two "Bobs"—we got to calling Sherwood, "Sherry," to end confusion in the office—and I usually spent our lunch hours together, they insisted I tag along with them to the welcome luncheon.

The meal was set in the Rose Room of the new residential Algonquin Hotel on 44th Street between Fifth and Sixth Avenues. I was the only woman at the table, and although I would never allow anyone to believe I was intimidated by the mental brawn of a room full of men, I sat quietly, observing the competitive verbal gymnastics of the masculine participants. I remember remaining very still as I took in the playful cadence of their comments, their pungent but humorous insults, a sort of rebirth for our modern times of the old men's club parlance. Nothing was sacred, and they did not edit for the benefit of my feminine ears. These men, a motley assortment of unsavory-looking characters, whom I never would have sought out for friendship under ordinary circumstances, accepted little me without prejudice, and I in turn became devoted to them. When just the right moment arrived for me to add my voice, I made a little comment (I haven't the foggiest idea what I actually said!), and owing to the riotous reception, I was instantly admitted into their exclusive club.

Aleck's cutting wit set the tone of the luncheon, and everyone present was very young and ambitious and yearning for acceptance from his peers and the world at large, in a city that each was desperate to conquer. Spirits were high, the high-jinks ongoing, and in spite of the icy glares from surrounding diners, the manager, Frank Case, tolerated our noisy exuberance. He saw that we were babes in the concrete woods of Manhattan. He must have seen the flash of brilliance evident in the prodigies, felt the rising pulse of creativity energizing the room, because instead of throwing us out, he banked on our success and built from it a living legend—born in the Rose Room of the Algonquin Hotel. They say eating a good breakfast keeps you healthy, but I never knew that eating lunch would make us famous!

Aleck made comment that the luncheon was so much fun all the "fellas" should do it on a regular basis. And being one of the "fellas," I was invited to join the boys the following week.

Soon it became a daily function of the restaurant to see us arrive at one o'clock, and for Frank Case to seat us near the entrance of the dining room, right off the lobby, for all passersby to see. Frank figured that other people would be encouraged to lunch there, too, just to hear the names of famous people being tossed about the room from our table. He assigned to us our own waiter, Luigi, and because most of us were so poor back then, our table was graced with baskets of popovers and celery stalks, compliments of the house. Scrambled eggs being the cheapest plate on the menu, I'd often have a half-order. We must have been quite a sight: Aleck dressed to the nines, his dinner bill alone more than the total of the ten or twelve others who happened to show up each day.

There was Harold Ross, a fellow reporter Aleck met overseas during the War, whose wife, Jane Grant, a social columnist for the *New York Times*, cited him as "the homeliest creature she ever met"—a description compounded by Edna Ferber, who, upon first meeting Ross at a dinner party, believed him to be "a vagrant brought in by her dinner host as a joke," saying the man looked like "a plucked woodchuck." He did, actually, because of his bristle-brush head of hair, his feral, beady stare, and bucked front teeth. If Ross's and Jane's magazine, *The New Yorker,* takes off, they might fare well.

FPA, one of the highest paid and most widely read columnists for the *New York Tribune*, has a rumpled face, long neck, small head, and a bulbous nose, and is often mistaken for a particular moose head hanging over the hearth of an Adirondack sanatorium.

Groucho Marx never wears his ridiculous fake

mustache offstage, but he does enjoy raiding the costume master's domain for unusual evening wear. His velvety baritone rolls out a nasal Manhattan sing-song of pure silliness. As for Harpo (Adolph), there is nothing quiet about him.

With us, too, is Heywood Broun, sport columnist, social and political commentator, and jazz maniac, who writes for the *World*. He is big, bulky, brilliant, and endearing. His suits are as rumpled as FPA's face.

I dress in a very ladylike fashion, have impeccable manners, and speak in dulcet, finishing-school tones, but have a propensity for off-colored humor and dropping numerous four-letter words into everyday conversation.

Robert Benchley, Harvard man, past editor of the *Harvard Lampoon,* and star of the *Hasty Pudding* shows, is the kindest of souls, truly interested in people and universally loved by all who meet him. He is the model of class, integrity, and masculine beauty. He can listen to the most mundane story told by a bore at a dinner party, and leave the storyteller with the newfound belief that he is the cleverest fellow in the world, next to Bob Benchley. I often feel that we, our friends and I, have corrupted him. When we first met, Mr. Benchley neither smoked nor drank; he was a real little White Ribboner! But, I, too, had been no different from Mr. Benchley, until I found how much more bearable life could be with a little bathtub gin smoothing over my orange juice. I suppose the reasons why we drink are different for each of us. I drink because it makes me less miserable. Mr. Benchley drinks because it makes him even happier!

George S. Kaufman is rangy, pompadoured, and, at the time of our first meeting, Aleck's assistant at the *New York Times*. He is at once both a handsome and grotesque figure, sexy and flamboyantly attired, with a smile that dazzles. Impeccable in all things, during the five years of our friendship George has co-authored that many hit plays, amassed a small fortune, acquired an extravagant apartment, and yet guards his seventy-five-dollar-a-week job at the *Times* as if his success and fame might evaporate at any moment. The best card player of the Thanatopsis Literary and Inside Straight Club, usually winning the hand he's dealt, he is the happiest of any of the married men at our table, freely admitting to not having bedded his wife Bea for five years, and convinced that their relationship has improved because of it!

Then there's Marc Connolly, reporter-turned-playwright, who is as short, fair, and bald as his collaborator, George Kaufman, is tall, dark, and hairy. They are as different as night and day, and yet, together they are the sun and the moon over Broadway. Marc is the antithesis of George. If one tried to measure success in relation to effort, one would never guess that this young man is one of the laziest people in town. How Marc manages to produce such fine work with such little effort is a talent in itself. After his first hit show, Marc promptly quit his reporter's job with the *Morning*

Telegraph, wanting to travel leisurely through Europe with his mother, with whom he lived, and remains living with at the time of this writing. George, who lives for his work, is frustrated at his collaborator's disinterest in finishing the last act of their play. Upon hearing that a novel by Charles Dickens was to be post-humously published, he noted that "Charles Dickens, dead, writes more than Marc Connelly, alive!"

As for Bunny (Edmond) Wilson: When we first met, he was a pale, round-faced, balding, russet-headed boy of twenty-four; a Princeton man returned from the War, he was eager to make his mark as a writer. I discovered one of his story submissions when I was wading through the slush pile at *Vanity Fair*. He was as timid as a virgin; in fact he *was* a virgin, and probably still is, although ever-ready, for in his pocket he's been carrying the same condom he carried on the day we first met, five years ago. (Don't ask me how I know this.)

Bunny carries a torch for Vincent—Edna Millay, that is, who is, in my opinion, a second-rate poet who doesn't deserve the devotion my Bunny bestows upon her. Why do nice men waste their love on such mean women? I'm very protective of Bunny, and the fact that he dislikes Condé Nast as much as any sensible person should only endears him to my heart! He will move on to greater things, I am sure. A more honest man, there isn't.

At the beginning we had been dubbed "the greatest collection of unsalable wit in the country."

But, after a little time, thanks to FPA, who dined with us every day and was a regular companion going to first nights with Aleck, and in whose column, *The Conning Tower*, were chronicled all the people he'd met throughout his day, we became known to all New Yorkers as the models of wit and sophistication.

Now, five years after our first luncheon, there are few clever remarks that haven't been attributed to any one of us, but I have to admit many of *my* witticisms go unpublished because they are, well, quite frankly, unpublishable.

But, I digress. There are many more stories I will tell about at a later time, like Robert Sherwood and the midgets, Heywood Broun and the dime, and Scott Fitzgerald and Zelda and the magnum of champagne.

This afternoon, after suffering the effects of too little sleep and too much champagne, Woodrow Wilson and I were met in the Algonquin lobby by a very excited Alexander Woollcott.

After guiding me to a quiet corner, he pulled out of his coat a sheaf of papers. He shuffled through pages and then pointed at one particular line.

"Asphyxiation?"

"The cherry tomato was to make it look like he choked to death," said Aleck.

"That narrows the field of suspects. Whoever killed Reginald had to have known about the tomato allergy."

"Yes, I doubt the placing of a tomato in his airway was a coincidence," he agreed.

"I don't believe in coincidences. That's the only possible proof I might entertain that there may be some sort of meaning to our crazy existence on earth: not accepting the concept of coincidences."

"You're waxing metaphysical, Dottie; it doesn't suit you."

I searched through the coroner's report for any possible clue toward identifying the murderer. "No marks on his body, so he wasn't pushed around or beaten before he was killed. I don't see anything that indicates how he was suffocated."

"The coroner found a feather in his hair. Goose feather."

"A pillow."

"Likely. And the clothes he was found in? He didn't dress himself."

"The autopsy could figure that out? Amazing."

"Not amazing; common sense. The way his shirt was tucked, and his tie was done up by someone *facing* him to do the task. Same with the way his shoes were tied; they found fingerprints on his shoes that were not his. He was killed a few hours after midnight; he was found at 7:30."

"Having a breakfast of steak, potatoes, and— don't you think that kind of a meal at that hour—" I forgot for a moment with whom I was speaking. Aleck would eat a five-course meal at three in the morning. But Reginald Pierce probably wouldn't; he was reed thin, and long suffered gastric distresses. He was the poached-egg-on-dry-toast sort of guy. I said, "Perhaps someone wanted it to look like he was having a late supper, to make it appear as if he died earlier in the evening. Who found him?"

"The maid."

"Live in?"

"No. Comes in at seven in the morning. That last page is the statement she gave the police. Joe thought we'd like to see it. Maid came in at seven, got coffee started, washed a few plates in the sink, her usual routine. She found Reggie a half-hour later."

"We've got to talk to this woman," I said. "There's nothing in this report that tells us much about how she found the place when she arrived. I mean, had the bed been slept in? The icebox was nearly empty of food when we raided it the other night; had the maid thrown out anything? Was dinner delivered from a restaurant? Did the police go through his garbage? When did they suspect foul play, after the coroner's report?"

"My head is reeling, dear," said Aleck. "I have no answers for you."

Aleck looked up and over my shoulder. Mr. Benchley joined us, and I handed him the report.

"Looks like we have our work cut out for us, Mrs. Parker, dear."

I handed the reports back to Aleck, who tucked them into his coat, and then the three of us walked toward the dining room to join the others for lunch. Just before we passed the threshold, I halted abruptly, touching Aleck's arm.

"Tell me, Aleck. Have the police released to the press the real cause of death as yet?"

"No. I've sworn to Joe that I'd keep it quiet, in order not to alert the murderer."

"All right. Then we won't talk about what we know during dinner. There's a room full of reporters in there!" I turned to Mr. Benchley. "What's your afternoon look like?"

"What do you have in mind?"

One of the most difficult things for a newspaperman to do is to sit on one of the biggest stories of the year, while pretending his bottom rests on nothing lumpier than the cushion of a chair. Knowing all the while that the room would clear in seconds should the truth be revealed to the greatest gathering of newspapermen in the city, I watched nervously as Aleck's eyes literally burned with frustration from the urge to impart the explosive news. His cheeks were flushed, and he actually left food on his dinner plate. Watching him tap his fork on his bread plate to the rhythm of "Ain't We Got Fun?" (that trite and altogether detestable ditty that has swept across the country like an unstoppable wave of influenza) led Harold Ross to ask if Aleck was feeling ill; there was that "thing" going around and people were getting sick. Ross is a paranoid hypochondriac; he sees germs in everything, and if people weren't out to get him, germs certainly were. Aleck called Ross a "fawn's behind" and told him to pass the salt.

Mr. Benchley easily managed to set the hot

newsflash aside while he lunched and talked about his friend Grace Moore and the opening of the new *Music Box Revue* in which she stars.

As for me, I supplied FPA with no clever remarks for his column, and I became so antsy that Ross turned toward me to ask if I was not feeling well.

"Oh, for cryin'outloud, Ross, nobody's sick except you!" Aleck screeched. As Ross was often the brunt of Aleck's jokes, there seemed to be nothing unusual about Aleck's outburst. It may have been the first time in our history that I was glad to leave my friends behind in the dining room.

I took Woodrow Wilson out for a stroll, and Mr. Benchley met me by the elevator upon our return. Up in my rooms, we went over my notes, checking off or scratching out items. We started a new page to guide us toward a solution of the case.

"We have a shit-load of things to do, Fred," I said, handing him the notebook and pencil. "I suppose we have to return the items we took from Lucille's apartment?"

"Are you asking me?"

"I guess we have to return them."

"You don't sound convinced."

"I'm not, really," I said, removing the lid of the wardrobe box and taking out the scrapbook. "I feel like there's something here, some clue we're just not seeing yet."

"Well, a day or two won't make any difference now. We've already obstructed justice and sullied evidence."

"We agree, then; a few more days."

"I didn't say that, but what's done is done."

"Yes, what's done is done," I said, taking the box back to my bedroom. "We have to go back to Reggie's flat to get the gun."

"Let's not steal anything else, especially not what may very well be the murder weapon that was used to kill Lucille."

"Wiping off my fingerprints might be a good idea, though."

"I see your point, my dear."

"I was thinking that we can get into the flat with the excuse of wanting to speak with Reggie's maid. Her name is Mrs. Kramer. While you talk to her in the kitchen, and ask her about the morning she found Reggie, I'll sneak into the library and get the gun."

"Let's be clear, Mrs. Parker—"

"Yes, yes, all right. I'll just wipe off my finger-prints, you old fuddy-duddy."

I sat down beside Mr. Benchley on the sofa. "There were lots of unanswered questions in the police report."

We made a list of questions to ask Mrs. Kramer, and then turned our attention to the next part of our investigation: the Chinese houseboy.

"A visit to Ralph Chittenham is in order," stated Mr. Benchley. "He's got some explaining to do. I think we should stop in and see the old sport, first."

"And what about Wilfred Harrison?"

"What about him?" asked Mr. Benchley, a slightly perplexed look raising his brow.

"He figures in this somewhere."

"How so?"

"His tête-à-tête with RIP's Mistress Marion last night."

"You're just miffed that he hasn't fallen for your charms, Mrs. Parker."

"*Awww, phooey!*"

A few minutes later, after refreshing Woodrow Wilson's water bowl, we were off on our afternoon of investigation.

My Edith Sitwell pose when I aspired, a few years back

Robert Benchley —
Boulevardier, bon vivant, best friend.

Alexander Woollcott —
Better known than Calvin Coolidge.

Chapter Five

I never really gave much thought to why I didn't like Ralph Chittenham. Like me and my friends, he is a drama critic for a major New York newspaper. It's not just a matter of taste that separates us; we often agree on the worthiness of productions. But, when I feel that crap has been foisted on an unsuspecting public, or that there is dishonesty in the writing or the acting of a play, or that the production qualities fall short, I do not resort to euphemisms or pleasantries. I resort to my mightier-than-the-sword pen and my rapier-sharp wit to cut away at the offending malignancy. The truth is I love the Theatre. I can't wait to go to the Theatre. Every time an orchestra tunes up and the houselights lower, and the lush velvet curtain lifts to reveal a world created from the imagination, I feel a great rush of excitement. More often than not, I am disappointed, but I always return, forgetting the past disappointments, looking forward to the next play, and the *possibility* of a transcending experience that is to be had only in the Theatre.

I suppose I think Ralph Chittenham is smarmy. In trying not to offend, he becomes suspect, for one wonders why so powerful a critic feels he must pussy-foot along the catwalk between truth and mendacity. Where I choose to toss the stick of dynamite to the stage below, he chooses to dribble confetti over the mess.

Now that I think about it, his milquetoast approach to an art form that I am passionate about makes me angry, and for that reason alone, I do not respect him.

Is he a bad man? No. I have no reason to believe him bad. He is liked by most people, I suppose, as he's never offended anyone by his critiques. I should think him a sympathetic soul. His wife died several years ago. I've never heard him actually indulge in mean gossip, and, well, I hate to say it, he spends his money on charitable good works and I spend mine at Bonwit's.

I should be ashamed of myself.

"You know, Fred," I said, after we paid the taxi driver and walked toward the courtyard entrance of the Dakota, the luxurious sprawling apartment building on the corner of Central Park West and 72nd Street, "I may have been unfair."

"Oh? How so?"

"About Chitty; I haven't always spoken kindly of him."

"You haven't always spoken kindly of anyone."

"Low blow, Mr. Benchley. I've always spoken kindly of you."

"My dear, why wouldn't you always speak well of me? I am the ideal gentleman, a good and faithful friend, morally beyond reproach—"

"I have been known to turn, Mr. Benchley."

"I stand warned, then. But, my dear, talk about being unfair to Ralph Chittenham? Why, it'd be unfair to single him out for compassionate treatment."

"You do think me pathologically bitchy?"

"To change the subject before I get hurt, how many people do we know who live in this building?"

I rattled off a list of friends, acquaintances, and people of note, ending with Myrtle Price Pierce and Ralph Chittenham.

"Interesting coincidence, Mrs. Parker."

We were announced to the concierge by the uniformed gatekeeper at the front gate kiosk, and then taken up on the lift to the fourth-floor apartment of Ralph Chittenham. I was quiet as the operator, an elderly woman draped in old-fashioned black bombazine fabric, in disuse since the last century, took us up to his floor. I was lost in thought, reflecting on my occasional cutting remarks. All right, more than occasional.

Was I a spitting fire-dragon lady? Wasn't I just being honest in expressing what I'd observed in other people? I was paid for my opinions. People, my readership, eagerly looked forward to my reviews. They liked my stories, too, because I exposed the interior living truth of my characters. I cut to the bone and showed the less salubrious motivations that spring from the human heart and the underlying ambivalence behind the smiles we wear like cloaks to cover our nakedness.

It occurred to me that the people who were eager to know what I had to say about this, that, or the other were voyeurs, reveling in watching the bloodletting. Romans enjoying an afternoon of blood sport at the Coliseum. I resolved to be nicer. Scratch that: "nice" is too insipid. "Embracing," that's what I'd be. I'd be embracing. I'd start with Ralph.

And when he came into the drawing room to greet us, after we had been admitted by the very Chinaman we had come to inquire about, I decided that I would try to embrace Ralph spiritually, as I could not bring myself to do so physically. It must have been the bad mustache.

His wide-eyed surprise at our unannounced visit melted into an expression of delight. "Bob, Dorothy, this is great that you've stopped by! Maxwell, take Mrs. Parker's coat."

The perfect host, he motioned us to chairs, and then made for the bar. "What can I pour you? My bootlegger, Joe Morley, just brought me an eighteen-year-old single malt this morning—or would you prefer coffee or tea?"

"We've had lunch, Chitty, dear. Straight up would be lovely."

"Ditto, like Dottie," nodded Mr. Benchley.

"Nice digs you've got here, Chitty. How many rooms?"

"Ten, plus servants' quarters."

"Nice view of the park, too," I said, ambling over to the beautifully draped windows to take in the lush landscape of yellow and orange treetops laced with the crisscrossing geometry of roads, paths, and bridges.

"That's why I wanted this place, Dorothy," he replied, crossing to me and handing me the drink. "I grew up in the country, you know, and I sometimes miss the trees and the birds. I have a little of it here, right out my window."

"I grew up in this neighborhood. I know every inch of Central Park."

Mr. Benchley piped in, "I grew up in Worcester, Mass; we had parks there, if I recall. I bought a house for Gertrude and the children in Scarsdale, which is one big park."

My withering look conveyed my annoyance: Mr. Benchley twitched his impeccably groomed moustache and sat back in his chair. Ralph handed him his scotch, and my friend was restored to sanity.

"I had a friend in school who lived on the floor below," I said, "and isn't the Pierce's apartment . . . ?"

"Next to mine," said Ralph.

"Is it really?" asked Mr. Benchley.

"It's accessed by the west elevator," said Ralph. "Another?"

"Yes, please; fine, very fine scotch," said Mr. Benchley.

Had he forgotten why we'd come to see Ralph? What was he doing? We had places to go, people to see, and drinking away the afternoon was not part of the plan.

"Do you mean that even though you're on the same floor you can't shuttle through to each others' apartment by a common hallway? You have to go down the elevator and up again?"

It was as if he didn't hear my question, for he shouted for his servant to bring out a tray of cheese.

"The young fellow who answered your door— he was Reginald's houseboy, I believe," commented my dear Fred, who, I am so relieved, and a little bit ashamed, to admit, was not half the idiot I had been imagining him to be.

"Maxwell. Yes, he once worked for the Pierces."

"The police have been looking for him. They want to talk to him about Reggie."

"Why?"

"Mrs. Parker, have you any idea why?"

"I believe, Mr. Benchley, that . . . Maxwell, is it? Maxwell may have been the last person to have seen Reggie alive."

"Why should that concern the police?"

"Tie up loose ends?" I said.

"Maxwell!" called out Ralph, and in a moment the servant appeared, cheese board held in white gloved hands, his head bowed in subservience as he awaited instructions. "The police want to talk to you."

He looked up and smiled. "Do they, really, Sir?

Why ever would they wish to speak with me?" He turned to face Mr. Benchley and said, "I'll try to answer your questions as best I can."

Ralph laughed. "No, Maxwell, this is Bob Benchley. Mr. Benchley is not a policeman." He chuckled, and then, after considering, said, "In a way he is a policeman, though; he is a theatre critic, a policeman of the artistic sort, isn't that what we all do, now?" He chuckled, and Mr. Benchley smiled and nodded agreement. "No, Maxwell, you'll have to go to the police station."

"Very well, Sir."

The cultured voice coming from the slight figure was unexpected, and completely belied his demeanor: upper class, British public school, Oxford or Cambridge?

"Tie up loose ends, I'm told," said Ralph. "Whatever that means. But, you see, you may have been the last person to see Mr. Pierce before he died."

"Very well, Sir, I shall go to the station and speak with someone in charge," the servant replied. "Is there anything else, Sir?"

"No, Maxwell, take the rest of the afternoon off, so that you can do that."

Was I surprised! For the third time today, I felt ashamed of myself, and as it was only a little after three o'clock, it did not bode well for the remainder of the day. I was guilty of believing that because this young Asian possessed the deportment and refinement of a gentleman, he was superior to the poor, lowly Chinese coolie I had first thought him to be!

I have to admit, I am as race conscious as most people. Being Jewish—actually, I am half-Jewish (and to some people, half-Jew is better than all-Jew)—I am no less reactive, or more race tolerant, than the next white Anglo-Saxon Protestant. So I was instantly slapped aware of my unfortunate assumption that a Chinaman in servant's attire did not necessarily have to be named 'Sing Lee,' work in a Chinese laundry, drop articles when speaking English, or substitute the letter L for the letter R.

I should know better, is what I mean. I was born a Rothschild—but I must let it be known that I was not born into the famous blue-blooded Rothschilds; there was no great inherited fortune, only one, long gone, made by my hardworking father manufacturing coats in his sweatshop. I was educated by the Catholic nuns of the Blessed Sacrament Academy, where they never ceased talking about Jesus. As a descendant of what I euphemistically like to call "the folk of mud and flame," I burned when my stepmother would ask me, "Did you love Jesus, today?" I felt her Christian displeasure and her smug sense of superiority. I vowed never to view any human being as less than worthy of respect because of race or religion.

Always made to feel outside the circle of God's light (more like a lost soul destined to travel Dante's circles of hell), I am loath to admit that I was happy to lose my Jewish moniker when I married Eddie Parker.

My Jewishness was viewed by his parents as a pox set upon his family, and no matter how I tried, there was little I could do to diminish their prejudice. But, my own inherent *fear* has led me to the decision that if Eddie and I divorce, I will retain the Parker name. Unless you are a member of a lowly minority living among a righteous majority, you cannot understand the trepidation one feels while walking through one's day, through one's life, being judged by a name.

The world that came to know and accept Dorothy Parker might not have been so willing to swallow my acerbic wit, or see me as the paradigm of style and deportment for my generation, had I retained the name of Rothschild. I would have been seen as inconsequential, and dismissed as "that cheeky little Jewess, Dorothy Rothschild." Had I kept my maiden name, I doubt I'd've been so eagerly accepted. My *fear* is that my true name, my maiden name, would mean my end. *A rose by any other name no longer smells so sweet: It stinks!*

It is my *fear*. I try not to show it. (No one will ever read these thoughts I put down here. They might not like me if they did.)

As the servant started for the door, I asked, "Maxwell, may I ask, how long had you worked for Mr. Pierce?"

He turned and glanced at Ralph while nervously shifting his feet. "Not so very long, Mrs. Parker." I noticed that his white gloves were soiled black at the fingertips.

"Since Mr. Pierce moved to his flat above his theatre, wasn't it?" offered Ralph.

Again, looks exchanged between the men. "Four months, I believe; since the spring, yes."

"The timing couldn't have been better," said Ralph.

"How so?" asked Mr. Benchley.

"Oh, I didn't mean that the way it sounded, Bob. What I meant was that last month my housekeeper gave notice because she was moving in with her daughter in New Jersey, and, well, after Reggie passed away, well, you understand, don't you?"

"How so?"

Dear God! Mr. Benchley had no right to make fun of Maxwell! Or was it only an innocent Freudian slip that he kept using the same phrase that was decidedly used for mocking the Chinese? Maybe it was like saying, "I'm dying for a cigarette," at the funeral of a consumptive. I wanted to shut him up before he made a bigger fool of himself.

"Mr. Benchley," I said quite firmly, startling him to attention. "It wasn't grave-robbing, that's what Shitty was trying to say."

"Language, Mrs. Parker!" said Mr. Benchley.

"*Shitty?*" asked Ralph, his jaw fallen.

"Chitty!"

"Just sharpen that 'C,' Dottie, dear," said Ralph with a good-natured chuckle.

"Of course." I was befuddled, and making a bigger ass of myself than Mr. Benchley.

"It wasn't grave-robbing. Maxwell was—available."

"Of course," I agreed. I was worse than Fred sitting there, a silly grin on his face. I had not only put my foot in my mouth, but tried to swallow it, too. This was not going well.

"It's time to leave, Mr. Benchley."

"Going somewhere without me?"

"No, Mr. Benchley: We have to leave."

"Who do?"

"We do."

"We do what?"

"Oh, for cryin'outloud!"

"Do we?" He made no attempt to rise from his chair, only smiled his silly smile.

"Of course we do," I reiterated firmly, offering my hand to help him out of the chair.

"How so?"

I was red with embarrassment. I turned to Ralph, "So kind of you to see us. And thanks for the first-class refreshment."

I said nothing on the lift down to the lobby, and remained quiet as we walked out through the courtyard and into a taxi that conveniently dispatched a passenger as we stepped onto the sidewalk.

"Your comments smacked of racism, Mr. Benchley!"

He burst out laughing. "I swear to God, my dear Mrs. Parker, I had no idea what I was saying. 'How so?' is interchangeable with 'You don't say?' or 'Please explain' and stuff like that. I suppose the phrase has just rooted in my brain."

"Something's taken root, that's obvious, and yes, I have noticed that you've used the phrase quite a bit since seeing that dreadful play, *Shanghai Suzie*, but it was an unfortunate coincidence that we were in the presence of a Chinaman when the seed sprouted from your mouth! As bad as Al Jolson wearing blackface in Harlem!"

I looked at Mr. Benchley, who cast a look back at me of less than sorrowful innocence. I burst out laughing. "Between the two of us—"

"Shitty?" interrupted Mr. Benchley. "You called him 'Shitty'!"

"I called him 'Chitty'!"

"I was there, remember?"

"We have to improve our interrogation technique."

"How so?"

"We got very little information from our visit, and if you 'how so' me again I'll—"

"I don't want to know how you'll punish me, so I'll behave. Actually, I think we found out quite a bit from our little visit, most importantly, the name of a very good bootlegger of some quality imported hooch. Yes, we've learned a lot."

"Have we? How so?—*damn!* You've got me doing it, now!"

"Did it not occur to you that your 'Chitty' didn't seem at all surprised that we, of all people, should know that the police were interested in speaking with Maxwell, and didn't question why we, of all people, would take time from our busy day to stop at his home, rather than telephone with the request?"

"You are right, Mr. Benchley."

"And, Mrs. Parker, did you not observe how Maxwell kept looking over at 'Chitty' when you asked him how long he'd been employed by Reggie?"

"I did!"

"As if they were in cahoots."

"I rather like that word 'cahoots.'"

"Well, they were in it."

"I agree. There is something they are in cahoots about, and they wanted to get their stories straight."

"Yes, that's right. And why is an educated young man working as a houseboy in the first place? What I mean is, he isn't really anyone's houseboy, is he?"

"How so?" I was saying it now, too! "*Shit!*"

"Language, Mrs. Parker!"

"*Aaarrrgh!*"

"I'll bet he is just *posing* as a servant."

"Very astute of you, Mr. Benchley. I presume you've arrived at the conclusion that he is too well-spoken and educated to be a houseboy?"

"Well, with a name like Maxwell, it's a giveaway he's nobody's coolie, Mrs. Parker."

"Mr. Benchley!"

"Yes, Mrs. Parker?"

I decided to ignore his unfortunate verbal phrasing.

"I see you've never dined with Lord and Lady Worthingham, or been a guest at the Hyde Park home of Sir Jeremy Canterbury and his seventeen Springer spaniels. Therefore, you have never met the educated and refined butlers of such households."

"That Sir Jeremy Whattchamucallim, with the seventeen spaniels? Wasn't that a music hall act come to vaudeville? No, I suppose not. That's Al Gordon and his Comedy Canines. I think he has twelve dogs . . ."

At times like these, it's best to ignore my friend and plow ahead. "But, I am inclined to agree with you in spite of your faulty analysis. Maxwell *ain't* no houseboy."

"Language, Madame! And what do you mean, 'my faulty analysis'? Faulty! How so?"

"It isn't that he speaks and carries himself like a prince that gives him away. Did you not notice his hands?"

"Should I have?"

"Shoe polish."

"Shoe polish?"

"Shoe polish. Shoe polish stains on his fingers."

"He was wearing white gloves."

"Of course he was."

"Stop being obtuse, Madame, and share just how you could tell he had shoe polish stains on his fingers when you couldn't see his hands for his white gloves?"

"He wasn't wearing them when he answered the door to us."

"Ahhh! And it was then that you noticed the stains on his hands!"

"Actually, I saw no such thing; he had his hands behind his back, like he was hiding something."

"Then what are you getting at?"

"Why would he put on gloves when he was called into the drawing room?"

"Shoe polish?"

"Shoe polish. I *smelled* shoe polish."

Mr. Benchley gave me a vacant stare that spoke volumes.

"Ah . . . you *smelled* shoe polish. All right."

I said, "I'm *guessing* it was polish stains he was covering up, or some kind of marks on his hands he didn't want us to see."

"Butlers wear gloves; he was carrying a cheese tray."

"You've seen too many drawing-room comedies, Mr. Benchley. Butlers only wear gloves while serving supper."

"I stand corrected."

"And the glasses."

"Glasses?"

"Eyeglasses, yes."

"Houseboys and butlers, although educated, don't wear glasses?"

"Not atop their heads. Those were reading glasses."

"Can we move on to the point of this conversation, Mrs. Parker?"

"Oh, look! We've arrived at Reginald's flat," I said as the cab pulled up to the Reginald Pierce Theatre. "We'll have to discuss this later."

"Oh, I hope not!"

———◆———

Mrs. Kramer's services were no longer needed at Reggie's apartment, she told us, when we met her coming down from the elevator. I couldn't believe our good timing in catching her before she'd gone.

"I come in every morning to the apartment," said the middle-aged woman with a heavy Brooklyn accent, "and I leave at noon. I seen nothin' unusual, 'til last Thursday, when I find Mr. Pierce dead in the library."

"Did he have any other visitors besides Miss Fields?"

"Oh, sure, hundreds of people visited him."

That narrowed it down.

"Did you cook and shop for him, too?" asked Mr. Benchley.

"No, only the cleaning. The Chink, Max, he did the cooking."

"The dinner he was eating when he choked. Did Max cook that?"

"I'm not sure, but it looked like it was the food left from the play that's goin' on down in the theatre."

"Food from the play?"

"Yeah. Every night. The part where they have dinner, but never get to eat the food? You see the play? It's mighty funny."

I begged to differ, but kept it to myself. "Yes, I remember now. The dining room scene; using real food because the steak has to be cut up."

"Did he often eat the stage meal?" asked Mr. Benchley.

"I never seen it. I just get dirty plates in the sink to wash each morning."

"Did you tell the police that Mr. Pierce's last supper was from the show?"

"Nobody asked me."

"Have you seen anything else unusual while you've worked for Mr. Pierce?"

She giggled ashamedly, "Are you kiddin'? The place was crazy. All them actors around all the time, whatcha'spect?"

I thought of the Marx Brothers and their antics, Tallulah and her gymnastics, Jack Barrymore and his adventures.

"Yes, I know what you mean."

We thanked her, and waited for her to disappear down the sidewalk before Bobby the Burglar easily slipped into RIP's flat.

The plan was to get in and out of the apartment as quickly as possible, so we wasted no time going into the library to retrieve the desk key and open the desk's secret compartment.

"*Shit!*" I hissed.

"Language!"

"The gun is gone!"

The gun I had handled, that bore my finger-prints, was gone!

"Oh, shit," said Mr. Benchley.

"My point exactly," I hissed. Panic rippled through my belly and weakened my knees; I felt light-headed and overheated and there was a buzzing in my ears.

Where was the gun? *Who* had the gun? I couldn't decide what was worse: a gun with my fingerprints on it found by the police or taken by a murderer!

Mr. Benchley suddenly took hold of my arm with a firm grip and told me to remain still. It took a moment for me to understand why he placed his hand over my mouth: Someone had come into the apartment after us!

As I was useless, paralyzed from dread, Mr. Benchley leaped into action, locking the desk, returning the key to its place under the seat cushion, and pulling me along with him behind the blue velvet drapery.

It was late afternoon, and I felt oddly exposed in the window with the sunlight glaring at our backs as we faced the screen of curtain. Muffled voices lingered for a time outside the library door, and then rang out clearly as they entered the room. We couldn't risk peeking through the joined panels as the sunshine would serve as a spotlight on us. Worse, I feared that even through the lined panels our silhouettes might give us away. My skin crawled with fear; Mr. Benchley was as keyed-up as I, for he did not release or loosen his grip on my arm.

"The police have gone over the sarcophagus thoroughly, Dr. Fayed, and it may be released to the museum, along with the other artifacts."

The voice was vaguely familiar, and as I felt Mr. Benchley's grip tighten, I knew that he, too, identified the speaker.

"Here is the list of the collection's inventory—"

"Shall we get started, then? Ah, Wilfred, I see they sent you. Glad you could join us."

"Sorry I'm late, Mr. Saches, I was held up in court—"

"Perfectly all right," replied Gerald Saches, tossing off the excuse. "Dr. Fayed, let me introduce you to Wilfred Harrison, of Whipple, Conrad, and Townsend, the law firm representing the estate of Mr. Pierce. Wilfred, Dr. Fayed is the director of Egyptian Antiquities at the Metropolitan Museum of Art come to do a preliminary evaluation."

"How'djado's" were exchanged, and I now knew to whom all the voices belonged.

"Shall we get some light in here?" asked Wilfred, renewing my panic. I could feel the tingle of adrenalin in the soles of my well-shod feet. Mr. Benchley released my arm and moved quickly away toward the side of the window. I realized what he was doing, but feared moving to the opposite end might jostle the fabric of the drapes. I waited for the curtains to part before I moved along with them. I heard the scratchy sound of the cord riding along the pulley before I took a step.

"I wouldn't open the drapes, Mr. Harrison." A man's voice sounded, English, but in accented Arabic, deep and commanding. It was Dr. Fayed speaking. "Sunlight is very destructive to treasures that have been buried for millennia. The lamps will do very well for our purposes right now."

The reprieve was fortunate; I doubted we would have escaped discovery had the drapes been opened even a couple of feet.

There proceeded to be periods of silence, alternating with brief queries for documents, related commentary, and the rustling of objects being moved about.

It seemed like forever that we stood there, our backs to the warm sunshine. I wished I had a book to read, and thought about dumping out my purse to straighten its contents, smoothing out my crumpled paper money with George Washington and Abe Lincoln right side up for a change and facing the same direction, but the click of the purse latch might give us away. I looked over at Mr. Benchley, who appeared to be snoozing as he sat on the wide casement ledge, his hat shielding his face, his back against the side of the window frame. If he snored, we were done for. I glanced at my watch. We'd been in hiding for more than an hour!

The longer one has to remain still, the more one is plagued by the itch that needs scratching, the cramp that needs stretching, the sneeze that needs— well, sneezing. I didn't know how much longer I'd last, and I was considering how best to remove my shoes when there was indication that the men might be about to leave.

"It's on the list, but I can't say where it is," spoke Gerald Saches. "Are you certain it was not taken as evidence by the police, Wilfred?"

"The room was searched, but nothing was removed from the room when they made their investigation. Items were dusted for prints, the sarcophagus coffin, mainly, but the display cases were locked, nothing appeared to be missing, so none of the antiquities were touched. And as none of the pieces were bequeathed from the collection to individuals, no one else has handled any of them. But, there was that Parker woman who was left alone in here after the reading, she found the actress's body. Perhaps—"

"Nah," said Gerald, much to my relief. "Dottie may have a fresh mouth, but she's not a thief."

I wanted to come out and slap him. Even if he was telling the truth.

"Then I suggest we continue our inventory tomorrow, from the point we left off today. It must be located, Mr. Saches," said Dr. Fayed. "If it is the gold, and not the bronze, it is the most valuable object of the entire collection. We cannot take possession of the collection without it, of course."

Gerald asked why they couldn't.

Wilfred explained. "As it is part of the collection and specifically named, the collection becomes incomplete without it, whether or not its authenticity is proven. Papers need to be drawn up, stating the specific artifact that is missing, before the collection can be released to the museum. It is simply legal written proof acknowledging its prior existence in the possession of Mr. Pierce."

"How long will that take?"

"Tomorrow at the earliest. Perhaps we might locate it elsewhere. Safety deposit at the bank?'

"No, and not in the safe, either," said Gerald.

"Is it possible that Mrs. Pierce has it in her possession?"

"Absolutely not. She wanted nothing to do with acquiring any of these."

There was a long pause, and then Wilfred said, "Very well, then, I shall see to the necessary documents, Dr. Fayed, so that the museum can take delivery as soon as possible."

There were murmured words of farewell as Gerald escorted Dr. Fayed out of the apartment. Wilfred would remain behind to telephone his office, he said. The telephone call was short, but afterwards, he did not immediately leave. Rather, I could hear him moving about the room for minutes longer. The sun was setting behind me, the street lamps and marquees were lit along the street. I glanced at my watch, it was nearing five o'clock. I risked peeking through the break in the drapery. His back was to us, and he carried a large rectangular package toward the fireplace. He stopped short, turned, and his eyes traveled across the room. I leaned back into the shadow.

He'd heard a noise, or something that alerted him that he was not alone.

My heart leaped into my throat as I felt the vibration of his footfalls across the room and toward our hiding place. I glanced over at Fred as if in warning. He must have read the dread in my expression, because his eyes were wide with anticipation.

But, rather than throw open the draperies, I heard the sound of Wilfred's footsteps receding into the drawing room. He called out, "Hello," and as there was no reply, reentered the library.

Again, there was the sound of wood creaking, the click of a briefcase, footsteps across the room. A final metallic *clunk* sounded, and then, silence.

We waited for a time, wondering if Wilfred had indeed departed the room and the apartment. Finally, Mr. Benchley popped his head around the panel.

" 'Bout time he left."

I came out to stand behind my friend, and looked around the room.

"I thought I heard him close the library door."

The door stood open.

"You hallucinate, my dear. That's what happens when one is left to one's own devices for hours at a time without libation: 'Idle hands, the Devil's playground,' or something of that sort."

"You misquote; it's 'idle *minds*' that are the Devil's playground."

"I thought it was idle *hands*."

"Well Madame La Farge's hands were never idle, now, were they, and she knit up more trouble . . ."

"I'm confused."

"That's nothing new."

"Nothing a little medicine can't cure. Hey! Do you think there's any more of that imported curative?"

"Let's just get the hell out of here."

"Shall we head out to Tony's?"

"No, I have to get home. I must return to empty Woodrow Wilson. It's five o'clock, and Neysa and Tallulah and FPA are stopping by. Aleck, too."

"Very well, let's free Woodrow Wilson—sounds like a plea for a stay of execution! I have to review Sidney Howard's new play tonight. Want to join me?"

"*They Knew What They Wanted?* Yes, I have to review that, too."

"Then our evening is set. Cocktails at your place, and supper at the Algonquin, the play, and maybe tour a few clubs to finish off the evening."

"An excellent plan, Mr. Benchley."

Tony Soma's Speak

Tallulah Bankhead — *Tallulah, the Femme Fatale.*

Chapter Six

Tallulah arrived promptly at five-thirty with her offering of "White Hearse," my euphemism for God-knows-where-it-came-from rotgut whiskey.

Irving Berlin bounced in humming a catchy tune and lifting our spirits, figuratively as well as literally, with a bottle of Haig & Haig right off the boat.

Room service sent up ice and White Rock, and by five-thirty-five, the party was in full swing.

Aleck arrived with FPA, who brought along Edna Ferber and George Kaufman and a bottle of gin; Neysa and Sherry toted along three artist friends I hadn't seen for a while, who had rooms next to Neysa's studio, and a bottle of Russian Vodka; Harpo and Marc Connolly escorted Ethel Barrymore, who ushered in Frank Morgan, Cliffy (Clifton) Webb, and her brother Jack, carrying a bottle of absinthe and a box of matches. (As suicide was for another day, I kept away from that brew.) Scott and Zelda were in town, briefly, so they popped the corks of three bottles of champagne, while George Arliss brought up the rear with Jeanne Eagles, Sinclair Lewis, Bunny Wilson, Ruth Hale and her husband, Heywood Broun, and a bottle of Canadian rye.

By five-forty-five, three dozen or more friends had descended upon my rooms, and the conversations were high spirited in more ways than one.

There was much talk about the mysterious ailment that was plaguing performers with laryngitis, affording more debuts by understudies this season than combined of several years past. And the question was raised, would there be an Actors Equity strike before Christmas?

Talk and speculation ran rampant about the deaths of RIP and Lucille Montaine. People agreed that the deaths *had* to be related. Who stood to gain? Had there been some sort of lover's triangle? I said, "Perhaps, with all the players involved in the victims' lives, it was a lovers' octagon."

A little before six o'clock there was an unexpected surprise. Wilfred Harrison walked through the door carrying a large rectangular package under his arm. *Aha!* I thought. The package I saw him carrying when I peeked through the curtain panels earlier, at Reggie's place, was my Renoir!

While Mr. Benchley poured him a Scotch and soda, I placed the package aside to unwrap later. Tallulah's radar for especially attractive men must have alerted her of his presence in the room, even though her back was turned, for she pivoted on her toes, and made a bee-line to where we stood, silently begging introduction, which I politely carried out.

Wilfred's disinterest in Tallulah's charms gave me renewed confidence in my own. He came to see and talk with me, and instead found me surrounded with the company of my friends. Mr. Benchley saved the day when he handed Will the drink and swept Miss Bankhead away to talk to Georgie Burns. In fifteen minutes, Tallulah would be performing cartwheels, sans pantaloons.

Will asked if there was somewhere that we might talk.

I looked through the haze of cigarette smoke. The room was packed. In the bedroom, seven people sat on the bed, another three on the radiator cover, a couple on the floor. The bathroom was in use. Several guests were perched on the tub wall, and peeking over their heads, I saw one of Neysa's artist friends passed out in the tub. There was nowhere left to go but the closet. Unfortunately, it was occupied by a romancing couple from the chorus of *The Greenwich Village Follies*.

We plowed through the field of friends and out into the hall.

"I wanted to explain about last evening, at the party, Dorothy."

"What's to explain?"

"My intentions were not to embarrass Miss Fields, but I'm afraid I embarrassed all of us with my silly fabrication."

Who else but a lawyer would substitute for the word "lie" with a word that sounds like it's meant to be cut into a suit!

"What lie?" I asked, making sure he knew I had a good vocabulary for a high school dropout.

"I told you that Miss Fields and I had never met before, but we had, and it was through Mr. Pierce that we had business."

"So she didn't lose the contents of her purse?"

He smiled, making sure I knew that he knew that I knew—well, I think you know.

"In trying to be discreet, I was making everything stand out."

"It's none of my business, Mr. Harrison."

"Oh, please, call me 'Will'?" he said with a pleading look. His dark eyes crinkled in such a sensual way that I—well, never mind that.

"I was talking business with Miss Fields when you chanced upon us in the hall. You see, she could not very well come to Mr. Pierce's funeral."

"It is generally frowned upon for mistresses to make an appearance at such events, yes." I don't know why I was helping him out with his explanations. Was I softening because of his attractive—anyway, I told myself to be quiet. If he was going to trip himself up, let him do it.

"All I can tell you is that Mr. Pierce did not forget Miss Fields."

"It wasn't necessary for you to tell me, Will."

"It was. You see, I thought, perhaps, well . . ."

He was going to ask if he might see me, take me to supper and a moonlight dance, a row in the park's lake, sailing on the Long Island Sound, clamming in the Great South Bay! All right, cut the clamming, but my mind was racing as he blundered along: *Aw, shucks, Honey Lamb, I fancy you!*

And suddenly, reason overrode fantasy when I glimpsed our reflections in a mirror gracing the far wall of the hallway. The bumbling was just *too* out of character for an otherwise suave and polished man to be laying on a little cluck like me. Laid on a vamp like Tallulah, maybe. Not that I'd mind being laid upon by Wilfred Harrison.

"Why don't you ring me up next week sometime," I managed to say, triumphantly, taking the reins of the stampeding horses. And skillfully putting the misunderstanding to bed, I mean, to rest, I extended my hand. "Thanks for delivering the picture, Will, but I should get back in to my guests."

If that was as smooth and as sophisticated as I, Mrs. Parker, had been expected to behave, I did not disappoint. After all, I was the sought-after celebrity, not Wilfred Harrison. Better to put him in the elevator immediately than to let him run amuck inside the apartment where more glamorous women awaited introduction, and would not only equal my playing field, but would topple it. In the future, anything that might develop between us would be on my terms.

Yeah, *sure.*

He took my hand and held it for a moment too long. My pathetic delusion of personal grandeur deflated like a leaky balloon. Harry, the elevator operator, closed the door on him, and I took my first breath in ten minutes.

An hour later, my guests had departed for supper destinations and respective obligations.

Aleck, FPA, Mr. Benchley, and I would go down to the hotel's more formal dining room, the Oak Room, for dinner, and then on to the theatre. But first, Mr. Benchley crossed the street to his rooms to change into his evening suit, as I quickly bathed and powdered and donned a royal-blue, cut-velvet and satin gown, a matching headband, decorated entirely with a swirl of blue feathers, and, because the night was chilly, a black satin wrap, trimmed in marabou. I finished off my toilet with gold watch, strings of jet beads, dangling jet earrings, and a generous splash of Coty's Chypre.

I looked in the mirror and thought, sometime this weekend I would have to finish an article for *Life* magazine, and a short story for *The Smart Set*. Then, I spoke aloud my daily prayer, my writer's mantra: *"Dear God, Don't let me write like a woman; please let me write like a man."*

FPA took Woodrow Wilson out for a pee and in search of a Cuban cigar at the tobacconist's down the street. I had a few minutes alone with Aleck to bring him up to speed on the events of the day. He laughed when I told him of our exile behind the curtain, and our visit to Ralph Chittenham's apartment, and that the mysterious Chinaman was a Cambridge-educated Brit. I told him of Wilfred's brief visit, and the mysterious disappearance of an Egyptian artifact, and that neither Mr. Benchley nor I could decipher what the object was that was missing.

"Why, it must be the birdie-thingy you saw Marion remove from the vase," said Aleck, putting an end to the mystery.

"Of course!" So Marion had taken the most valuable item of the collection! And she took it from a hiding spot: the Ming vase. Who had hidden it there? Had she? Had Reggie?

Marion Fields had some explaining to do.

"Tomorrow we three shall pay Mistress Marion a call," said Aleck, commandingly.

———◆———

Drinking is not unlike falling in love: Flirting leads to the first kiss, and then a move toward heavy petting; soon you find yourself in bed with the boy. One morning you wake up to see a face you hardly know—staring back at you from the bathroom mirror. In the end, when the bloom of romance has faded, you wonder why you can't leave the boy. You no longer love him; it's just that he's so much a part of your life that you can't imagine your days without him. No more love, just need. Drinking is like that sour affair: You flirt with a cocktail or two, soon find yourself guzzling down a shaker or two, and then, when you're very thirsty, you find the bottle is empty, and all that remains is a gripping need and dirty glasses in the sink. Still, one goes back again for the punishment; you can't call it quits. You'd open your arms for love as eagerly as you'd belly up to the bar for a drink. And like a drunk with a hangover, you say, "Never again," but you do it over and over again, because to be without the thing that fills you makes life unbearable. The booze is your hope; hope quells the loneliness. But booze is a mendacious lover, telling you what you know in your heart is untrue: that *someone* will someday really love you, that you *are* loveable, after all.

What delusions we nurture in our hearts.

Eddie Parker was the only man with whom I'd been intimate since our marriage. Even though we lived separate lives for most of the years of our union (first separated because of the War, and later an emotional withdrawal because of his alcoholism and disinterest in almost everything), I remained faithful and committed to my vows. But, his sudden departure, after years of slow retreat from my life, threw me for a loop, and I could no longer deny that anything was amiss. In the few months after my husband left me, I embarked on a rather treacherous affair with a married man. Treacherous for me, it was, not so much at all for the man. The man gone, Eddie gone, I find a degree of comfort in my friends and in my cups.

My friends are clever, precocious children at heart, who find life difficult to cope with much of the time. You wouldn't know it to see them, because they learned that laughter and wit and a good dash of gin makes the best recipe for getting through their unpredictable, harried days. I put on my best face when I am with them, and their company is the best distraction I've found against melancholy. But there comes the hour in every day when I shut the lights and

I am alone. My best face doesn't count for much then; it doesn't serve me well when I am left to linger deep within my loneliness. So I leap at another chance at love when the opportunity presents itself, even though love has not served me well.

Now, Wilfred Harrison was tempting, I'll admit, but I knew the dangers of being with a man like him. Mr. Benchley—my best friend, Fred—knows me well. Although he would never try to instruct me or offer unsolicited advice, he has always been the one person with whom I could be my true self; the friend who shows up at my door, not because I ask for his company, but because he *intuits* my need not to be alone. Ours is an unusual friendship between a man and woman. I think, more than anything, I fear a time when he won't be here.

And as we dined on duck in the Oak Room, I caught his unguarded look of concern when I mentioned Wilfred Harrison's name. That concern made me even more determined to take special care in my dealings with the man.

We were unanimous in our opinion of the new play we attended, and cited our pleasure through our individual reviews. Mr. Benchley and I had taken notes for later reference, as our reviews for magazine deadlines were not due for several days. Aleck's was midnight for the morning edition of the *New York Times*, so he scurried off to the paper's offices, a block away from the theatre, on 44th Street, to dictate its copy with less than an hour to spare. Frank called in the last paragraph of his daily column, *The Conning Tower*, for the *New York Tribune*; we'd all be mentioned in it tomorrow morning, in the column that helped make me and my friends famous.

I sat listening by the telephone booth as Frank called his desk. He looked over at me with a smile, winked, and dictated: "Mrs. Dorothy Parker, comma, a vision in blue velvet, comma, feathers and jewels, comma, was escorted by this modest reporter, comma, the dashingly attired Alexander Woollcott, comma, resplendent in white tie, comma, top hat and extravagant cape, comma, and the ever-humorous Robert Benchley, comma, for a glorious evening at the opening night of Sidney Howard's new play, comma, quote, *They Knew What They Wanted,* period, end-quote. Sid's looking toward a Pulitzer, comma, that's for sure, exclamation mark. And so, comma, off to the Twenty-One Club for a late sup, comma, before cutting the rug uptown at the Savoy, period. What a life, exclamation point."

We lounged at "21" for cocktails while waiting for Aleck. When he arrived, he barreled through the crowd of diners to stand before us, a dour expression on his face.

"Who died?" asked Mr. Benchley.

"You've not heard?"

"What's the big deal, Aleck?"

"What's the story, morning glory?" chimed in a jovial FPA.

"Marion Fields," said Aleck, his voice pitched high and quavering with drama; his eyes, under frowning brows, magnified to bovine proportions by the lenses of his eyeglasses. "She's dead."

FPA leaped to his feet. "Holy moly! Stop the presses!"

———◆———

"I insist that you desist!" shouted Aleck.

His great bulk towered over me, but I knew that his rumbling voice was only for effect. Never could, or would, Aleck be a physical bully; I was safe, as long as he didn't suddenly pass out and topple over to crush me.

"Your meddling in these murders is too dangerous. Someone out there is killing people! Whoever it is might think you know something, even if you don't, and then he'll come after you. And then where will you be?"

"Dead?"

"What would we do without our Mrs. Parker?"

"Mrs. Parker, you can't abandon this world for us to spend all our evenings with Edna Ferber for company," agreed Mr. Benchley, "should the killer knock you off, too."

"If the killer got me, I wouldn't expect you to enjoy your evenings at all," I whispered. "So Edna would ensure your misery."

"Selfish little witch! Aleck's right, you know!" said Mr. Benchley. "He'll just have to tag along with us, like a heavy, to protect his darling Dottie."

We all snorted.

FPA returned to the table. "You kids gone bonkers? What's all this about desisting, and why is Dottie in danger?"

I looked over at him and realized that the man was totally lost in a world of crazy doubletalk that he was unable to decipher. After all, FPA knew nothing of our investigations.

With his promise that everything we were going to tell him had to be kept out of his column, we retraced our movements since the day of Reggie's death.

"So let me get this straight—" said Frank, waving his stogie.

"I sure hope *you* can straighten this whole thing out, Frank," said Mr. Benchley.

FPA looked up at the chandelier as if its crystals held the answers to the mystery. He puffed out a smoke ring, and chewed on his cigar for a long moment, appearing to ruminate on his words before spitting them out:

"This is how I see it: Somebody murdered RIP, and tried to make it look like an accident. That same person killed Lucille, and it sure didn't look like an accident. Now, they find Marion Fields, killed, and it looks like an accident, again, but it's no accident, I'd say, and she is no longer on the list of suspects for murders one and two." He came down from the chandelier to look at each of us in turn. "All I can figure out is that everyone connected to RIP is dropping like flies! I say it's probably best to let the cops try to sort it all out."

"The voice of reason," said Aleck, thumping his fist on the table. "Thank you very much, Frank."

"Yes, Frank," I said, "Thank you for making me totally confused."

"How'd she get it, Aleck?" asked Frank.

"Hit by a car, corner Broadway and 46th," said Aleck.

The Reginald Pierce Theatre was on 46th. I asked if there were any witnesses.

"Rush hour. About fifty witnesses saw it happen."

"So then, maybe it wasn't murder," said Mr. Benchley. "It may just be coincidence."

"Please, you know how I feel about coincidences."

"There aren't any?"

"You know there aren't," I said.

"Witnesses say it looked like she was pushed; only nobody could say who pushed her, or give a description of the pusher."

"Aleck," I said, "Can anybody say where she was coming from, where she might have been going, if she had a companion with her when she was killed, did she—"

"Hold your horses, Dottie!"

"Well? Do you know?"

"Oh, all right! She'd been seen leaving the theatre's lobby."

"The Pierce Theatre? What was she doing there?"

"Don't know. The box office manager saw her leave."

"What time?"

"Rush hour. Five o'clock or thereabouts."

"We were there! At the theatre. In Reggie's apartment when she was killed."

"The thing we have to figure out is what the three victims had in common. What did they *know* or what did they *do* that got them all killed?"

"You mean, whom did they piss-off," I said.

"Who felt threatened enough to knock-off three people?" said Mr. Benchley. "We know," he continued, "at least we think we know, that Mistress Marion may have stolen the bird statue that was considered the most valuable artifact of Reggie's Egyptian collection. Whoever knew she had it might have killed her for it. The motive would be money, and a strong motive it is. It's reason enough for someone to kill Reggie, and if the killer couldn't find the statue because it was hidden in the vase, and he then suspected that Marion had it. . . . But, why kill Lucille? What was her connection? I'm dumbfounded."

"You and me, both, Bub," agreed Frank.

"Maybe the murderer put the bird in the vase for safekeeping, and then Marion found it," said Aleck.

"I don't think it matters at all how the bird got into the vase, except to know that it was hidden, and hidden quickly, just to get it out of sight. It wasn't the most secure of hiding places," I said.

"There's the problem of the gun. Where is it, and who took it, and was it the murder weapon?" asked Mr. Benchley.

"You asking me?" said Frank

"It's rhetoric."

"Oh, sure."

"What if the statue didn't have anything to do with Reggie's murder? Maybe he was killed for some other reason, and the killer learned, after committing the dastardly deed, about the priceless artifact. Somehow the women foiled his plans."

"Could be," considered Aleck.

"We're spinning our wheels," I said, getting up from the table. The three men leapt to their feet. "Oh, sit down boys. It's just that I think better on my feet."

I paced back and forth before our table, the men waiting quietly, expectantly, as if I would present some great solution for their patience. I stopped short, looked at them and said, "Lucille."

"What about her?"

"Marion lobbied Reggie to cast Lucille as the lead in his play, even though she was wrong for the part. It all has to do with Lucille."

I amazed myself! I had no idea how I'd arrived at this breakthrough, but I knew I was onto something. "We have to find out how Lucille got Marion to influence Reggie into giving her the part."

"Find the connection between the two women," said Mr. Benchley.

"Frank?" I said, "Can you find out more about Lucille Montaine and Marion Fields through your paper?"

"Whattcha want to know?"

"Anything in their pasts that might connect them, back before they had a friendship in New York. They may have met long before hitting town."

"Sure. I'll get on it right away."

"And I'll get our *Times* research people to check all of the papers for any mention of either woman," offered Aleck.

"How soon can we start?"

"Get me a telephone," said Frank.

"It's going to take a while," said Aleck.

"Shall we place a little wager on who comes up first with the link connecting the women?"

Aleck and FPA beamed at Mr. Benchley's proposal. As members of the Thanatopsis Literary and Inside Straight Club, they leaped at a bet challenge.

Mr. Benchley sweetened the pot with the suggestion that they broaden the field of players. "We've got the resources of the biggest newspapers and best reporters in the country. Shall we call the boys in?"

He meant, of course, the *World* editor, Herbert Bayard Swope, Marc Connolly, George S. Kaufman, Harold Ross, Heywood Broun— Round Tablers all, and Thanatopsis members.

"Can they be discreet?"

"Are you kidding me?" said Frank.

"Do they have to be?" asked Mr. Benchley.

"Actually, Dottie, dear, I think we'll all be safer if it gets out that every reporter in the city is looking for the murderer, not just you and the police," said Aleck, as Frank raced off to the telephones to start the ball rolling at his *New York Tribune*.

Forgoing the *Savoy*, we four shared a cab to our respective residences.

Woodrow Wilson greeted me with his usual frenzied excitement. I could tell by his lightfooted romp through the apartment that he was ecstatic that I had decided to call it an early evening. I sat on the floor with him, in my blue-velvet splendor. He rolled on his back for a belly rub and then flipped over for a proper petting. I hugged him to me, and he passionately licked off my face powder until I laughed so hard that tears filled my eyes. I couldn't help but admire and envy how little it took for my friend to find instant happiness through my small offerings of affection. Being with Woodrow was a lesson in living the moment with joy. How easy it was for him to find it in a belly rub and a lick!

It would just be the two of us, Woodrow and I, for the rest of the night, and as I fell off into a deep and restful sleep with him under the crook of my arm, I felt comfort from the simple, loving devotion of the best of God's creations. And for now, that love was enough for me.

Woodrow Wilson— *Sketch of Woodrow by my friend,*
illustrator Neysa McMein.

Chapter Seven

Franklin Pierce Adams is not only one of the most widely read columnists, and the highest paid one in the country, but also one of the most influential. Together with Herbert Bayard Swope, they presented a formidable front for information gathering.

The two men met with Aleck, Mr. Benchley, Marc Connelly, George S. Kaufman, Harold Ross, and Heywood Broun in my rooms a little before noon the following day. As New York has a dozen daily newspapers, the purpose of the meeting was to hash out a plan for the dailies to flush out the murderer. And the best way to do that was to dig deep into the backgrounds of not only the victims, but the past lives of all the possible suspects. Hopefully, there would be a link between the victims and suspects, some connection unknown to us now, but a compelling reason for murder. We needed to piece together what we already knew with what the men might uncover in order to nab the culprit. Swope called it "investigative reporting."

With the cooperative use of the newspapers' archives and researchers, and through Swope's editorial, a public discussion about the triple murders might put pressure on the police, but could also produce witnesses who had been afraid to come forward earlier. The autopsy findings on Reginald Pierce's cause of death need not even be revealed, as Aleck had promised Joe. But the cause of death was no longer an issue. By now, everybody knew he was murdered, because the people around him were dropping dead. Someone out there saw something, heard something, something that appeared innocent at the time, yet might shed new light on the crimes. Frank and Aleck would devote columns to the murders, each expressing the belief that a crazed killer was *randomly* choosing his victims from the Broadway theatre community. In that way, the murderer would think that the police didn't believe the crimes were personally motive driven, after all. He might lower his guard.

"Problem is," said Swope, "Every nut case will be calling in to say that they saw the whole thing, and swearing it was George M. Cohan done them in out of professional jealousy."

"Maybe we should offer a reward for information leading to the killer's capture," said Marc Connelly.

"Not a bad idea," agreed Aleck.

"You don't think that'll bring out more loonies?" asked Frank.

"We live in New York City, they're already out," said George.

We all turned to look at Swope, the multi-millionaire whose fabulous estate on Long Island was the setting for extravagant weekend parties that hosted the stars of Broadway and the literati. Scott Fitzgerald intimated to me that he is writing a novel in which the venue is a Swope-like North Shore estate.

"All right, all right! I'll put up five hundred dollars," said Swope, and then, considering the silent stares, added: "Make it a grand, all right already?"

"A good start," said Aleck, knowing that the other papers would up the ante in the attempt to cash in on the publicity.

Before going down to lunch we agreed to meet daily in my rooms to share information. If one reporter had a scoop, the paper for which he worked would publish the initial story, giving that reporter credit. In the end, when the killer was found by means of our common cooperation, all papers would acknowledge the group effort, none touting it was done alone. Such a challenge had never been broached before now. All the men involved are great friends, but they share a competitive streak. Just sit in and watch them on Saturday nights during the Thanatopsis card games. I doubted the competition would hurt any of the friendships of the Round Table.

It looked like a slow news day: no floods, storms, natural disasters; no big political news, as the national election was still over a month away, and candidates hadn't said much worth reporting; there were no scandalous trials or upcoming executions.

We could get started immediately, so that the evening papers and the morning editions could all carry the lead, *The Broadway Murders*.

I spent the afternoon writing up the reviews of three plays for the *Saturday Evening Post*. When I was done being clever and bright, I moved onto a short story I'd been working on for several months, about a man who treats his wife and children with cruelty, and abuses his mistress. Henry Mencken will publish it for his magazine, the *American Mercury*. It's a subject that is close to home. I've entitled it, "Mr. Durant."

I took a break for a late afternoon walk to clear my head of the very personal story I was writing, and to exercise Woodrow Wilson. I'd no plans for the evening, except for the five o'clock rush of traffic through my apartment of friends dropping in for a drink or three. Mr. Benchley had taken an early train home to Outer Mongolia to spend time with Gertrude and the boys; Aleck was off to the theatre with Edna. I thought about telephoning Neysa, to see if she wanted to have supper together, but I decided to let the evening surprise me. She might show up for cocktails; I'd ask her then.

When I'd returned to my rooms, I noticed the package containing the Renoir pastel portrait Wilfred had delivered the previous evening. I untied the string and removed the brown paper wrapping. Crushing the paper into a ball, I threw it at Woodrow. He had a fling jumping on the crunchy paper, flipping it about the apartment as if attacking an adversary, with the occasional bark and growl necessary to intimidate his foe.

I studied the portrait of the young girl. There is a common wide-eyed look about us. She, too, is not as innocent as she wishes to appear. But, there is a certain vulnerability about her, around the mouth. She doesn't smile, and her hair is mussed just enough under a rather punched-down bonnet to give her a gamine appeal. I may have been like her once—five years ago—but I have aged some, mostly through experience.

I lifted the picture to the desk and leaned it against the wall, unsure where best to hang it. I was grateful to Reginald for leaving it to me. I was grateful to have this little token in remembrance of my aunt and uncle.

I sifted through the afternoon mail, throwing the half-dozen bills into the desk drawer, but opening the personal letters. One in particular caught my attention, as it was written on heavy, quality stationery. I tore it open, expecting an invitation to some event, and found instead a note from Wilfred Harrison, expressing his apology for crashing my cocktail party of the night before, and hoping that I would do him the honor of having supper with him on Saturday evening. There was a knock at the door, and as Woodrow barked, "Who goes there?" I slipped the note, along with the letters from friends, into the drawer.

Neysa entered with a gentleman friend, whom she introduced as Martin. He owned an art gallery on the East Side where Neysa was to exhibit her paintings. Within a couple of minutes the apartment was wall-to-wall people looking for a drink.

After calling down to room service for the ice and White Rock, the Marx Brothers, all four of them — *oh-my-God-what-did-I-do-wrong-to-deserve-this?* — barreled in through the door. They were lugging all sorts of junk, which they dropped at my feet. There was no room to stand, even, and people were stepping over all sorts of things. Harpo goosed a guest with a huge pair of deer antlers he carried under his arm before dropping it on the floor in the middle of the room. They wanted me to go off with them to an afternoon tea party they'd been attending. It seems the tea they'd been drinking wasn't as unadulterated as one might think.

Some Mad Hatter at the tea party had the idea of extending the fun into the evening with a scavenger hunt through the city. The "items" the Brothers had to return with were: horse blinders — the horse-drawn ice dray was parked outside; a street-corner sign — people would wonder where 47th Street had gone; an alley cat in a basket — which they'd left down at the front desk so as not to alarm Woodrow Wilson; a NYPD policeman's cap — snatched off the hat rack at Joe Woollcott's precinct house; deer antlers — procured (stolen) from a fish-and-game club on Madison Avenue; and a stuffed fish — Groucho dropped the stuffed marlin while being chased out of the club, so they ordered a stuffed filet of sole to-go from the Gonk's kitchen. From me they demanded ladies' pink underpants, which they insisted I would find in the top left drawer of my bureau. When I demanded to know how they knew in which drawer I kept my panties, Harpo just rolled his eyes to heaven and pursed his lips in cherubic innocence. And last, they had to bring back Dorothy Parker!

Making a bee-line to my bedroom they laid out all the paraphernalia they had gathered on the bed—except the horse, the cat, and the stuffed sole. Groucho was already at my chiffonier about to search for the panties, when I moved him aside to fetch them myself.

"But, you have to be in them," said Zeppo.

"That'd be nice, but I don't know if Mrs. Parker wants to wear pink tonight," said Groucho. "She may be in her blue mood, or maybe she'd prefer red."

"The instructions were," said Harpo, "Dorothy Parker in pink bloomers."

"Chico, give me the list," said Groucho, taking the crumpled paper, adjusting his eyeglasses and reading aloud, "Dorothy Parker *and* pink undies. Not 'in' but 'and'!"

"Oh, well, that's different . . ."

"I'll say it is," said Groucho. "Of course it'd be more fun if she's in them than out of them." He reconsidered. "Wait a minute! It's more fun if she's out of them than in them!"

I ushered them out of my bedroom and closed the door, agreeing to go with them to the party on 35th Street, when my guests were gone. I poured them each a drink, and ten minutes later we left, the prizes in tow, except for the cat, which we had to retrieve, the fish from the kitchen, and eleven guests from my party who wanted to see who won the game and meet the other contestants. We piled into four taxis, the cat in its basket on Neysa's lap, Woodrow Wilson on mine. The ice dray followed. I made Groucho promise to return the cat to its original location, before he and his brothers went on to their 8:30 P.M. performance that evening. He said the cat was not a stray, but belonged to his landlady, but I was not to tell the others.

We had three more items to fetch on the return to the tea party: a book stolen from the public library, a park bench, and a vagrant's shoes.

Needless to say, the cab drivers were not at all pleased by all the stopping, and all the junk the boys had gathered; the fish was stinking up the cab; the cat was clawing at the window. Eventually the cabbies complied when Chico invited them up to "tea" when the mission was complete.

"We've already worked it out, see?" said Groucho. "The New York City Public Library is right next to Bryant Park. I can snatch a book from under the clutches of the librarian, with a little diversion, while you all take a tire iron and pry up a park bench. The party is just a couple blocks away on 35th Street. Harpo and Zeppo, you carry the bench over. There's no more room in the cab."

All the cabs pulled up to a screeching halt in front of the largest marble structure in America, at 5th

Avenue and 42nd Street. Zeppo pulled on his brother's sleeve when Groucho tried to exit the cab.

"Wait! What are we going to do about getting a vagrant's shoes?"

"Since Heywood Broun is out of town, you'll have to pull the shoes off of one of those fellas hanging 'round the park."

"Steal the shoes off a homeless man?" I screeched, appalled.

"She's right. All right, Chico, give the bum your shoes," said Groucho, bounding out of the cab. And with that he was off, running up the long expanse of steps to the library.

"I'm not giving anybody my shoes!" said Chico.

"Give the bum Zeppo's shoes!" said Harpo.

I was appalled. I'd laughed at the reference to Heywood Broun, because the truth be told, the journalist looked like a Skid Row tramp-come-uptown; in fact, recently, while standing outside the Algonquin, a woman passerby handed Broun a dime and told him to buy himself a meal.

But, that they would take shoes from a poor, downtrodden fellow?

People tumbled out of the lined-up cabs to watch the Brothers' handiwork. A few joined Groucho to watch him "borrow" a book; the rest marched after Harpo, Chico, and Zeppo into the park; a cabbie provided a tire iron from his trunk to help pry up a bench.

And on the bench, to their surprise, was the much-sought-after "vagrant."

"You can't take away a poor man's shoes!" I cried.

"Oh, yeah? Watch me," said Chico.

"Dorothy is right, Chico. It would not be nice to take his shoes," agreed Harpo.

"All right, all right!" said Chico. "Zeppo, give the man your shoes."

"Not on your life!" said Zeppo.

"My life has nothing to do with it."

"Chico!" I said.

"All right, all right!" he said. "We'll have to take the shoes with the man *in* them!"

"Two birds with one stone! You're a genius, Chico," said Harpo, slapping his brother on the back.

The rather "frayed around the edges" fellow, cowering on his bench, looked up pleadingly at me. A dozen crazy people had descended upon him from out of nowhere.

"Well," I said to the Brothers, "We should ask this gentleman, politely, if he'd like to come along."

"Would you like to go to a party?" asked Chico, switching from an all-business frown to a slap-happy grin, which was a little scary, if you ask me; it sounded like he was asking a girl out on a date.

"No," said the man, fear in his eyes, as if these crazy people planned to kidnap him and roast him on a spit for supper.

"There'll be food," said Chico, like a spider luring a fly into a web.

"No, please," he pleaded, frantically looking for a means of escape. "I don't want to."

"Why the hell not?" said Chico, offended.

"You scare me," said the man, his voice quivering.

The towering, twenty-three-story American Radiator Company Building frowned darkly down at us.

"Offer him five dollars," I whispered to Zeppo.

Seventeen dollars and fifty cents later we were finally on our way: the Brothers walking down Sixth Avenue carrying a bench, cement footings and all, and our guest, the rather musty-smelling vagrant, whose name was "Mr. Caruthers," with me, Neysa, her friend Martin, Woodrow Wilson, and the cat in the basket in our cab. A few minutes later, the four taxis drove up to the house on 35th Street. The horse blinders were yanked off the work horse, the iceman invited up for a "cup of tea."

I left the party at 7:00 P.M., having munched on leftover tea sandwiches and cake, to go home to do some serious writing. As Bryant Park was on the way, I offered Mr. Caruthers a lift, which he gratefully accepted. Although his bench had been taken, he was quite content, having eaten dozens of tea cakes and sandwiches, as well as having lined his pockets with more of the same. He was seventeen dollars and fifty cents richer, wore a "new" pair of brown alligator boots, a clean, starched dress shirt, suit, tie, and overcoat from the hostess's husband's closet—"He won't mind, he's got dozens to spare," said the hostess—and had my promise to ask Frank Case if there was a job for him in the restaurant's kitchen. He was to stop by in the morning and call me from the lobby.

I stopped at the newsstand on the corner and bought all five evening papers. I wanted to see the first wave of articles about the murders. Before the journalists met at noon tomorrow, the second wave in the morning editions would break. Things should be resolved quickly with this sort of news blitz.

Upon returning to my rooms, I was greeted by a blue florist's box wrapped with gold ribbon. I put the stack of papers on the sofa table and then untied the box. Within lay one perfect long-stemmed red rose. The card read, *One perfect rose deserves another*, and was signed, "Will."

Thoughts raced through my head; why just one perfect rose? Why not a dozen? The florist from whence this came had scads of perfect roses; it was a red rose, and that in itself was presumptuous of the sender. He should have sent pink, white even, but red was bad form coming from a fellow I had yet to see socially. The choice of a rose in itself was unfortunate; lilacs or violets would have been more appropriate to the occasion. I would rather have received a box of Belgium chocolates, or a bottle of Courvoisier, or both! I stuck the offering in a half-empty soda bottle, and went into my bedroom to change out of my street clothes and into a robe.

As the tub filled, I poured myself a scotch, lit a cigarette, and sat on the bed to plan my evening at home. My mind wandered over the events of the past week. I had the feeling that there was something I was overlooking that was central toward identifying the murderer. I knew it was best to just wait it out while the boys investigated. But, patience was never one of my virtues. My eyes fell on the box of papers and photos from Lucille's apartment. I carried it to the living room. After my bath I would look through all the papers again to make sure I hadn't missed anything, and then I would read all the newspaper articles in the evening editions.

I had just gotten out of the tub when there was an insistent knock at the door. Throwing on the robe and wrapping my hair in a towel, I was surprised to find Aleck at my door, Edna at his side, both dressed to the teeth for their evening of Theatre. They had only a few minutes to make the curtain, I knew, for it was after eight o'clock. I thought, if they wanted me to join them, I'd decline as I would never get ready in time, anyway, and I wanted to stay in for the rest of the evening.

I'd barely finished my greeting and was about to plant a kiss on Edna's powdered cheek, when Aleck spat out, "They've arrested Gerald Saches for the murders of Reginald Pierce, Lucille Montaine, and Marion Fields!"

Gerald Saches was front-page news the next day, and I wondered if the boys were still going to show up at my apartment at noon, since the case had been solved. They did show up, though, and each brought with them information they had gathered, including background information on each of the major players of this drama. All took it to heart that the murderer had been found, but thought they might aid in the conviction with the facts they had gathered over the past day.

According to Swope, Maxwell the houseboy had indeed spoken with the police. In his statement, he said that he left RIP's apartment at midnight, right after the arrival of Gerald Saches, who was in a snit about something, Maxwell knew not what.

The police, on a search of Gerry's house, found a gun they believed to be the murder weapon used to kill Lucille. They also found a letter from Reggie that they believed was the motive for his murder.

I asked Swope, "Why would Gerry kill Lucille? If he pushed Marion into traffic, it must be because she suspected he'd killed Reggie. Maybe could even prove it. Gerry left the Pierce Theatre at five o'clock, around the time Marion was killed. . . . But, kill Lucille?"

"Just the fact that he was in possession of the gun is enough to link him to Lucille's murder."

I wasn't convinced.

"Let's say, Gerry didn't kill anybody. Did anyone come up with any information that links the victims to other suspects?" I asked.

The offerings were meager, a risqué photo of Lucille that Marc had discovered, for which she'd posed back around '19, that the men ogled over but was certainly not so compromising as to hurt her career, should she have been blackmailed. "Maybe there are other, more revealing shots," mused Marc. "Then you have blackmail material."

"Yeah, but who blackmailed whom? I don't think there's any connection to the other victims," I said. "So, no two people went to school together, or grew up in the same town or worked for the same business?"

The faces that looked back at me were questioning. Finally, Marc Connelly said, "I don't get it, Dottie. Gerry's the guy. Why don't you buy it?"

"The jury is out on that one, fellas; things don't fit, and we all know Gerry. Here's a man who everyone knows wanted to marry Myrtle, and even though his best friend swept her away, he remained a friend to the man, backing off with dignity. Gerry protected Myrtle from knowing about Reggie's infidelities, and yet considered Reggie his best friend—backed him in every venture as a partner from the time both their fathers were killed. They stuck together, built their businesses together. It doesn't make sense that Gerry would've killed anybody. Certainly not over love, and I very much doubt over money; Gerry is rich. People kill over love or money, when you think about it."

FPA paced the floor, scratching his head, and said, "So you think it don't wash, *hum?* Anybody else feel that way?"

Only Mr. Benchley raised his hand. "It might be a good idea to talk with Gerry," he said, "find out his side of the story."

"He's in jail, and the judge wouldn't set bail because the charge is triple homicide and Gerry might run," said Ross.

"Has anyone spoken with Myrtle?" asked Mr. Benchley. "She might shed light on what Reggie's disagreement was with Gerry."

"She left for Florida the day after the funeral," said Heywood. "Ruth called at the apartment and was told by the housekeeper she'd left for an extended time."

"She might be part of the whole thing, you know," said Ross. "Myrtle knew about the mistress; the wife always knows. And knowing how Gerry was nuts about her, she might have put him up to the murders."

"I'll bet the police have their sights on that angle. I'll bet they plan on arresting Myrtle next," said Marc.

"So, say they were in it together, in cahoots, as they say. It explains killing Reggie and even Marion, but it doesn't explain Lucille's murder," said Mr. Benchley.

"They are not stupid people, you know. Gerry and Myrtle are too smart to commit crimes that so easily point to them," said Aleck. "Wouldn't they have at least tried to make it appear as if someone else had a motive to kill?"

"Right. For instance, if Gerry killed Reggie with malice aforethought, why would he let himself be seen by Reggie's houseboy, who'd say, as he just has said to the police, that Gerry was the last one in the apartment the night of Reggie's murder," said Mr. Benchley.

"I'm telling you all, there was something going on that we don't know about. There's a back story somewhere, in the victims' past. Someone's got to talk with Gerry," I said. "What he tells us, together with what we come up with, might clear him and give us the true killer."

"His lawyer's not going to let any reporter near him, on the chance he further incriminates himself," said Swope.

"I'm not a reporter; I'll go!" I said. "And the more I think about it, I'm sure he's innocent, so maybe he'll talk to me."

———◆———

"Why would I kill my best friend?" Gerry asked me, as we sat across from each other, a screen between us. He looked slightly crazed, as his eyes, red with fatigue, flitted nervously around the room. He had the appearance of a man who'd been yanked out of bed and told to dress quickly to escape a fire: thinning hair, uncombed, disheveled clothing, a day's growth of beard, and that look of panic, as if his foot were caught in the track of an oncoming train.

When I finally got through to Gerry's attorney

and explained that Gerry and I were friends, and that although I was a writer, I was not a reporter in the strict sense of the word, and that anything Gerry told me would not be seen in print the following day unless it would exonerate him of the crimes, and that I hoped to prove the man's innocence, he agreed to let me speak with his client. So when Gerry posed the question, why would he kill his best friend, I told him that that was the very question I had asked myself.

"Gerry, the police found a letter to you from Reggie in your office."

"Yeah, but I still don't see how the letter proves I killed him."

"What was in the letter? What was it about?"

"It had to do with the Egyptian stuff. I found out that the people he had dealings with had shady reputations. He may have bought looted treasure, a solid-gold figure, about eight inches tall, of the goddess Selket. It was suspected of having been smuggled out of Egypt last year after tomb robbers plundered the excavation at Deir el-Bahri. Now, I think most of Reggie's collection had been acquired legally, but even if Reggie wasn't guilty of any deliberate wrongdoing, it didn't mean that the dealers he bought from weren't thieves. He could be in possession of stolen artifacts. I told him of my concern, that since he had borrowed from our production company to purchase several items for investment, and if they were sold to him illegally, he could lose more than just our money. That happened some time back, over a month ago.

"After the first time I spoke to him about it, I made a few more inquiries. I had to be careful, of course; I didn't want to draw attention to Reggie. I put Whipple, our lawyer, on it, and his investigators found out that a small statue had indeed been smuggled out of Egypt last year. The dealer, under investigation by Interpol, was the same dealer from whom Reggie had made purchases. I knew for sure that Reggie had the Golden Selket.

"The day I found out, I went to talk to him, but he had already left town on a business trip. It was urgent that we speak, and although I didn't want to do it over the telephone or send a cable, I called to the hotel where he was staying, and left a message asking him to get in touch with me. But then, I couldn't wait for his call, because I had to get to Philly to see about problems with the new show that was opening there in out-of-town trials. Same show Lucille was in.

"Before I left town, I scribbled out a letter to him and had it posted. I kept the topic vague, in case it fell into unfriendly hands. I referred to the statue as, 'the purchase we discussed recently.' All I said was that things had to be dealt with immediately, or the consequences would be great. If he didn't address the problem, I'd take things into my own hands. I was back in town in a couple of days when I got his reply. It said not to threaten him; he'd do what he wanted to do. That was it, you know, a few lines scrawled out in anger that I tossed in my desk drawer. I tried explaining that to the police, but they think the word 'threaten' had to mean I wanted to hurt him, but the threat I made was that if he didn't return the illegal purchases, I would, as I controlled much of the business's assets. If only they could find the note I sent him, it might help explain everything."

"But, you were at his apartment the night he died. What did you talk about?"

"We were finally both back in town for the show's opening, so I took the opportunity for a private talk with him about the situation, away from the office or public places where we might be overheard. I wanted to protect him from the ramifications of buying stolen goods, and protect myself, financially, as well. Yes, I was upset with him when I first entered the apartment; I'd been worried for weeks about the situation he had gotten us both into, and from all I'd recently learned about the dangerous people he'd been dealing with, but he told me he had returned the money he borrowed from the company for the purchases, and flat out denied that he had the stolen Golden Selket. He wanted to reassure me that he was on the level, and he showed me a figure that was indeed a Selket statuette; it was not made of solid gold, but bronze. And he assured me that had he known about the dealer's reputation, he would never have dealt with the man."

"And his angry note to you?"

"He apologized for it, saying he had been under lots of pressure when he wrote it."

"What kind of pressure?"

"Three shows, all with problems, Marion pressuring him to divorce Myrtle, his sons drifting around doing little or nothing with their lives except getting girls pregnant and gambling away their trust funds. They were always at him to fix their messes."

"The boys?"

"Yes. And he was always bailing them out."

"Had he ever, recently, refused to help them?"

"Not that I know. Oh, I know what you're thinking, but those kids wouldn't have killed their father. They're stupid, not homicidal, believe me."

I decided to let that go. I'm pretty sure there are lots of stupid people who have murder in their hearts and would not hesitate to kill. I changed the subject.

"But why do the police think you killed Marion?"

"I left Reggie's flat around the same time that Marion was killed. I was there to assist in the transfer of the Egyptian collection to the Met. But, I had no reason to kill Marion. I had no reason to shoot Lucille, for that matter."

"Perhaps Lucille saw Reginald's murderer. The police probably think Lucille saw you kill Reginald, or that she knew something that would incriminate you. The police matched the bullet that killed Lucille to a gun found at your home. Tell me about the gun, Gerry."

He smiled, threw up his handcuffed hands, and shook his balding head. "It was a gun I bought for

Myrtle. There were a string of robberies last year at the Dakota, and she was alone most nights, so I bought her the pistol for protection. She was more frightened of the gun than of burglars. She agreed to keep it in her bedside table, however. Then, one day, a few months later, she discovered it missing. She told me about it, but when she asked Reggie if he had taken it, he said it was probably stolen by a servant they had recently dismissed. It was around the time he moved into the apartment above the theatre.

"Was the gun reported stolen?"

"I don't know. Myrtle couldn't be sure for how long it had been missing."

"When the police found the gun this morning, and you recognized it as the one you gave to Myrtle, did you tell the police what you just told me?"

"No, and Dottie, I'll deny telling you what I just said, if it comes to protecting Myrtle. Do you understand that? I have no choice."

I nodded and said, "You *do* have a choice, Gerry, but I understand the choice you have made and why."

"Listen, Dottie, even if they buy my explanation about getting the gun for her protection, it's not going to get me out of trouble. If they think the gun was ever in Myrtle's possession, well, they're sure to think she may have been in it with me."

"So you want to take the fall alone, is that it?"

"They'd think Myrtle killed Reggie and Marion out of jealousy. Or she got me to do it. Better they think it's just me, rather than she."

This was love, all right, and I'd never witnessed such self-sacrifice. I was both touched and appalled. Touched by the devotion of the man, and appalled, if in fact Myrtle had pulled the trigger, that she would let Gerry fry for it!

I knew a place where the gun *had* turned up, in the desk drawer at Reggie's apartment, and I had left my fingerprints on it as well, before it was moved again. If it had been stolen by a servant who worked at Myrtle's Dakota apartment, how'd it get in the secret drawer at Reginald's? How many people knew of the secret drawer in the first place? But, as it would complicate things further, I was not ready to tell Gerry or anyone else about what I suspected at the moment.

"Might she have done it?"

"Killed them? Not Myrtle. She loved Reggie, and she knew what he was like since their first year of marriage. If she cared about his affairs, she didn't wear her heart on her sleeve. And Reggie? He was a complicated guy. He loved Myrtle and was good to her. He just needed lots of women. Never serious about any of them, until Marion. Still, whatever he may have promised the girl, he'd never have divorced Myrtle."

"Have you any idea at all how the gun found its way into your house?"

"How it turned up at my house, under the stairwell, I don't know."

I thought, *not such a great hiding place; it was meant to be discovered.* "Tell me what else you remember of the night of Reggie's murder. You were the last person to see him alive."

"That can't be true, because the murderer saw him last and it wasn't me."

"Did Reggie say that he was expecting anyone to visit that evening?"

"No."

"Did he receive any telephone calls while you were there?"

"No, not that I remember—wait! Yes, there was a call, and it was very short."

"Did you overhear what was said?"

"That's what I mean by short; Reggie said 'Hello,' there was garbling through the receiver, and then, without another word, Reggie hung up."

"While you were with him, was anyone else in the apartment?"

"Just the Chink. He let me in when I rang; but he left for the rest of the night, I think, a little while before I did."

"Maxwell Sing wasn't a live-in?"

"No."

"How long did you stay at the apartment?"

"Maybe fifteen or twenty minutes. Reggie showed me the bronze Selket statue in the display, and then we had a drink in the living room, talked about one of the shows that had opened the evening before, and then there was the phone call. As I said, I left soon after."

"Did you handle the figure?"

"No, Reginald had it behind glass."

"How long was it after the phone call that you left?"

"Soon. I got the impression Reggie needed to head out somewhere, and I was relieved that we'd settled the problem of the collection and the money. I wanted nothing more than to go home, have a late supper, and get into bed with a good book. So I left, walked home because it was a nice warm evening and the walk relaxed me."

"Could it be, though, that Reggie didn't plan to go out, but rather expected to receive someone at his apartment?"

Gerry considered a moment and then said, "He untied the ascot he was wearing, and then untied the sash of his smoking jacket, as I finished my drink. I got the impression he was about to change into evening clothes, and that he intended to go out. . . ." There was another little frown of confusion. "I guess I *assumed* he was going out, as Marion was always calling him a stick-in-the-mud because he preferred staying in nights."

"So, he had plans for seeing Marion that evening?"

"No, I remember now. Marion was not in town. He mentioned it, because when I arrived I was quite upset with the news about the stolen artifacts, and I asked if he was alone. I wanted no one to overhear our conversation. I specifically asked if Marion was there or expected, and he said she was away until the weekend."

"Did he say where she went?"

"If he did, I don't remember; only that she'd be gone for another couple of days."

"Who told you that Reggie was buying stolen artifacts?"

"I wasn't told by anyone. I found out."

I wondered if he was protecting someone else. "There was someone or something that first made you suspicious that he had stolen goods."

"An overheard conversation, and that's all I can tell you, Dorothy."

He looked at his folded hands as if they held answers and he wasn't about to loosen his grip. The man looked spent, and I knew that I had learned a great deal through our talk and I thought it best to let him rest, if he could do so in such a dismal place.

"Gerry, one last thing: The people in your household—could anyone you employ at home have any reason to plant the gun in your home?"

"I have a housekeeper, Henrietta Morgan, who's been with me for fifteen years. She lives in since her husband died of flu in nineteen-eighteen. She'd flinch at the sight of a gun, let alone handle one."

"No one else?"

"No. It's just me. When I have house guests, which is rarely, Henrietta might hire additional staff, usually her sister-in-law and her husband."

"Has anyone come to visit, say, since Tuesday? Workmen, repairmen?"

"I don't know. I'd have to ask Henrietta."

"All right. . . . Gerry? Do you mind if I speak with her? She might be able to tell me if there was anyone out of the ordinary come to the door, or if she went to the front door while the back was open to the garden. You know what I'm getting at?"

"I see. You want to know who planted the gun."

"Yes."

"Then you do believe me." It was a statement, not a question, and his expression looked hopeful for the first time.

"I do. And I'm going to try to get you the hell out of this hole as fast as I can!"

I walked out of the room to reclaim a very happy Woodrow Wilson who was sharing the roast beef sandwich of the precinct's desk sergeant, Joe Woollcott, Aleck's policeman cousin, who started the ball rolling when he called Aleck at lunchtime last week to tell him of RIP's death.

The two men were mirror images of each other, but worlds apart both in personality and in cultural interests. Where Aleck loved the Theatre, Joe loved the Horses. Where Aleck's acerbic wit might smite, Joe's approach to all creatures, especially Woodrow Wilson, was pure gentleness. The only shared interest, other than family ties, was their mutual love of food.

I thanked Joe for doggie-sitting Woodrow, who pulled on his leash, reluctant to leave when there was beef to be had. We went out into the late afternoon sunshine.

Before meeting Aleck and Mr. Benchley at Tony Soma's, as we'd arranged earlier, I walked the few blocks to Gerry's townhouse to speak with Henrietta Morgan.

Mrs. Morgan was not quite the woman I'd imagined. I'd expected an elderly, gray-haired, Irish washerwoman type with red, water-cracked hands, who would answer the door in a blindingly white apron, a wooden spoon in one hand, a dishrag in the other. But the woman who came to the door could not have been older than thirty-five, had a head of luxurious black hair, eyes lined with long fringes of thick lashes that set off compelling blue eyes. Her figure was tall, slim, and rivaled any model's. She wore a simple and impeccably tailored cashmere dress that gave her an aristocratic air. I wondered why such a beauty as Mrs. Morgan had come to take a position as housekeeper when the world outside the door would lay its riches before her, should she so venture off the threshold.

She knew who I was, and after leading me into the parlor, said that my timing was perfect: She'd be right back with tea and scones right out of the oven. Woodrow, belly full of Joe's roast beef sandwich, laid down at the foot of my chair.

When we had settled, the tea poured, I told Mrs. Morgan that I had just come from seeing Gerry, and of my mission to ask her about the traffic in and out of the house between Tuesday and the arrest. From my purse I took out my little notebook and pencil to jot down the names of a dozen people — the cleaning lady, delivery boys, repairmen, couriers, production company personnel, secretaries, accountants, lawyers, a petitioner, and Gerry's bootlegger. The milk, post, ice, vegetable, and soda men were the usual fellows. Mrs. Morgan was adamant in her insistence that the front and back doors were always kept locked, as were the windows, and only she and Gerry had keys.

I asked if she had left any of the visitors alone, for any reason, in the reception hall; had she gone to fetch a pen to sign for a delivery, that sort of thing. Even a few moments away may have given someone the opportunity to plant the weapon. She recalled taking the accountant's hat, coat, and stick, but leading him into the study; the courier had arrived to pick up a package; she left him alone for less than a minute to retrieve it from Gerry's study. Marion had stopped by to see him as well, but Gerry had just left the house for a dinner meeting with a new playwright. "Let's see . . . she was writing Gerry a note over at the console table—"

"That table by the stairway?"

"Yes, but I never left her alone—wait, the soda man arrived and rang the front bell because I didn't hear the kitchen bell. But I only turned my back to open the door. Could she have planted the gun?"

I shrugged my shoulders and shook my head, for I didn't know. I suspected it was Marion, but it might have been the courier, or the accountant. She said she would think hard for any other times someone might have had the opportunity to slip the gun in the cubby under the stairs.

I sipped my tea, and scarfed down the fabulous warm scones, which I loaded up with huge dabs of clotted cream and strawberry jam, as we continued to talk. She began to reveal more and more of her personal distress that Gerry was accused of the murders. I told her point-blank that I believed him innocent. That seemed to comfort her a little, as I could see the lines of tension around her mouth and forehead smooth a bit.

Her pride in the home she had made for Gerry was obvious; for looking around the beautifully appointed room there was evidence of her care. I asked, brazenly, if the décor had been the work of her hand. She was at first reluctant to take credit, but said, "Yes."

She was very forthcoming in telling me that she had once been a decorator, but had given it up years ago to marry. Her husband went to fight in Europe in '18, and came back wounded in body and in spirit. I understood how difficult it must have been for her, as it was for her husband, as my own Eddie has not fully recovered from the war wounds to his soul.

It had been necessary for her to return to work, but decorating did not offer enough to support them, so she took a housekeeping job with Mr. Saches. When her husband died of flu during the epidemic, Gerry offered her a live-in position.

Through Gerry's generosity, she began to build a modest career in interior decorating once again, but continued to keep her rooms in the townhouse, as well as overseeing the daily running of the house. The gratitude she displayed was touching, really, and I became determined to do what I could in the future to move her career along. I knew lots of very rich people with very bad taste who would benefit from Mrs. Morgan's sense of style. I liked Henrietta Morgan; she had style and grace, but most of all I admired her loyalty to Gerry. She loved him in the same way I loved my friends. I wouldn't be surprised if she were *in* love with him but had too much class to throw herself at his head.

I left the house with new information and details on who had entered the house over the past few days and may have planted the gun since I'd held it last.

I didn't want to be late meeting the boys, and as it was the evening rush hour, I employed Woodrow Wilson to distract a dandy hailing the cab that had just turned off the avenue.

"Hail a cab, Woodrow!" I ordered as the taxi slowed to a stop, and he sprang into his routine of a nip on the trouser cuff and a fast reversal to draw the fellow's attention to his feet, left and then right. I opened the door, slid in, tugged the leash, and in hopped my best boy.

Woodrow and I taxied down to Tony's; the sun was setting over the Hudson River after falling behind the tall buildings of midtown. The traffic grew heavier, and at times, to a standstill. I took out my notebook and looked over my list of suspects. I crossed out

Marion Fields's name, and then, after a hesitation, I crossed out Gerry Saches's, too.

So now there remained Myrtle, who had the most to gain; Reginald's sons, because either one of them may have had more to gain in his father's death than when he was alive; and an Egyptian antiquities dealer—whoever he was I had to find out, because Reggie's murder may have been committed to protect that dealer from prosecution for theft.

And where and how did Maxwell Sing fit into events? I had watched as he snuck into Reggie's desk, into the hidden drawer. What had he taken from that hiding place? What was it about the gloves he wore that day at Ralph Chittenham's that bothered me so? The pretentiousness of a servant wearing gloves when not serving dinner, was that it? No. He was hiding something, but what? And did Maxwell Sing have a more sinister association with Ralph Chittenham, other than finding immediate employment with the critic after Reggie died?

Chitty's apartment abutted Myrtle's.

According to Gerry, the gun had been stolen from Myrtle's bedside table about the same time that a servant had been fired. Who was the servant? Maxwell Sing had not been fired; he had simply left work at the Dakota apartment to work for Reginald when the couple separated. Had Max stolen the gun, and not the dismissed servant? The time of the theft was unclear. Who better to blame than a disgruntled employee? Had the Pierces, after all, notified the police of the theft? If not, why not? Had anything else been taken?

Then there was Chitty. What was Ralph Chittenham's connection to the three murdered people?

My mind was racing to fit the pieces together.

I thought back to the seemingly clandestine meeting of Marion Fields and Wilfred Harrison at the Waldorf the other night. How had Marion been "taken care of" by Reggie, as she was not named in the will? I would ask Wilfred. As Marion was dead, murdered, her financial situation was no longer private and would be open to scrutiny, I presumed. He shouldn't hesitate to tell me.

Marion had taken a bird figure from a vase . . .

Perhaps what I thought I saw was not what I *really* saw.

It wasn't a bird. It was the Golden Selket!

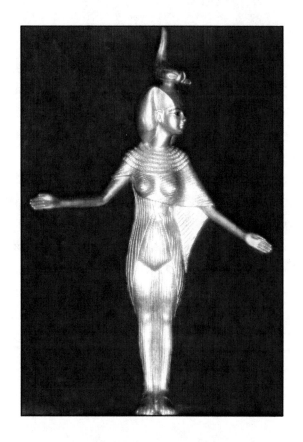

The Golden Selket—
The goddess Selket protects one from the deadly bites of scorpions. She wears one atop her head.

Chapter Eight

As soon as I got to Tony Soma's, I made for the telephone and dialed up the offices of Whipple, Conrad and Townsend and asked to speak with Wilfred Harrison. His secretary said that he had left the office at five o'clock for the evening, but that she would call around and let him know that I had telephoned.

I ambled over to a corner table to wait for the arrival of my friends. The waiter brought our beverages to the table, an orange blossom for me, a bowl of water for Woodrow Wilson; a chunk of cheddar and crackers for me, steak scraps and fried potatoes for Woodrow. My boy was eating well today!

Aleck and Mr. Benchley stormed into the speakeasy trailed by FPA, and we all had news to share.

The men put in their drink orders, and then Aleck looked at me and said, "Ladies first."

"You can wait, Aleck," ribbed FPA, who immediately received a series of verbal expletives from my big friend that cannot be printed here.

So I told them the details of my visits with Gerry

and Mrs. Morgan, and that I'd put in a telephone call to Wilfred Harrison to find out more about RIP's separate bequest to Marion.

"Well, Mrs. Parker," began Frank, "I got a couple of interesting telephone calls. First one came in from an elevator operator at the residential hotel where Marion Fields had been shacking-up since last March at the expense of Reginald Ignatius Pierce. It seems Mistress Marion had a couple of regular visitors."

"Pray tell, who?" said Aleck, pouring cream and a jigger of brandy into a shaker.

"A gent and a dame."

"Proceed." He added the crème de cacao into the mixture and threw in some ice.

"His description of the dame sounded a lot like Lucille Montaine, so I showed him a press photo of the dead star, and hot dog, that was her, he said, came by once a week. The last time was last Wednesday morning."

"The last day anyone saw Lucille alive," I said. "I wonder how long Lucille and Marion knew one another before Marion got involved with Reggie?"

"Could Marion have played any part in Lucille's murder?"

"We'll never know," said Mr. Benchley. "We've been told that it was Marion who wanted Reggie to give Lucille the star part in the show, so we know they were friendly for some time, if Marion was willing to go out on a limb for her."

"Hold your horses!" said Frank. "The elevator boy said they didn't act so friendly."

"Whatchasayin'?" asked Aleck, stirring up a froth in the shaker.

"I asked the same thing, and he said it was the way they looked at each other wasn't too nice. You see, the elevator opens on Marion's floor across from her door. The boy would see Marion open the door to Lucille, and it wasn't the 'howya doin' hugs-and-kisses kind of greetings dames do." He took a Cuban from his inside coat pocket and proceeded with the ritual of removing its wrapper, running it under his nose, rolling it at his ear, clipping the end.

I thought about what Frank had told us. When does one answer the door to a person one knows and expects, but is not necessarily happy to greet? "They had business, then," I said.

"Maybe," said Frank.

"Did he notice anything else unusual about Lucille when she'd go to visit?"

"Good question," said Frank. "You'd make almost as good a reporter as I, for, dear Dottie, I asked that very question."

"Cut the crap, Frank!" piped in Aleck, while handing Mr. Benchley a cup of his concoction to sample, "Was she peculiar or not?"

Frank struck a match, and, cheeks puffed out like a blowfish, fired up the smelly thing. He leaned back in his chair and blew the smoke to the ceiling, where it swirled around before dispersing. He would not be rushed. "No."

Mr. Benchley took a moment to comment that

the color of the drink Aleck had concocted was reminiscent of "Calvin Coolidge's winter complexion," and suggested a healthier countenance might be achieved with an additional jigger of crème de cacao. Aleck told him where to put it.

"Children!" I admonished in a tone not unlike that of Sister Mary Immaculate at the Academy. "Mind you, pay attention! Now, Frank, what about the man the elevator boy saw?"

"Wore a blue messenger's uniform from Achilles Messenger Service, 'cept for the shoes, he said. He noticed the shoes first time the guy showed. They were the good kind, a buffed shine, expensive, too expensive looking for a fellow who ran around the city all day. He stopped by Marion's place couple times a week."

"Did the boy talk with him?"

"The guy wasn't the chatty type, but it was kind of strange, you see; he'd stay in the apartment an awful long time for a courier. I showed him photos from Lucille's show; I showed him pictures of Reggie and his sons: nothing. Not Gerald Saches, either. The guy always wore a cap, hid his face. Maybe Marion had a guy on the side, from the way the boy talked.

"See, one day, after the elevator boy had dropped the courier at Marion's floor, he had to come right back up with another resident of the floor. When the elevator door opened, he saw the guy using a key to get into Marion's apartment. That's when he thought things smelled fishy."

"Any other visitors?"

"Just delivery people, the usual. And lots of dinners being sent up from a couple of restaurants down the block."

Mr. Benchley noted, "You said you got a couple of telephone tips."

"Oh, yeah, I did," said Frank. "The other was a woman, telephoned that she saw Myrtle Pierce in the company of Marion Fields having lunch together in a little Bavarian restaurant last Thursday."

"What?" bellowed Aleck. "If that was so, you've held the big story for last, you sonofabitch!"

"I tell my stories in the order I so choice, fat boy!" returned Frank, used to Aleck's bluster. He took a dainty sip from his cup of gin and tonic, his pinkie finger extended affectedly, then waved for the waiter to bring him another.

"As you were saying before you were rudely interrupted, turkey neck," said Mr. Benchley in an attempt to further lighten the mood.

Frank ran a finger under his heavily starched shirt collar and then straightened his tie. "The woman in question—"

"Which one?" demanded Aleck. "Marion, Myrtle, or the caller?"

"The caller, and please do not interrupt me when I am on a roll or I will hurt you, Aleck."

"Get rough and I shall sit on you; see how that feels, you fawn's ass."

"Boys!"

I was used to their affectionate verbal wrestling, though it got silly at times. Had Harold Ross been with us, the two would have abused him, instead, as the brunt of their jokes and adolescent name-calling. As it was they only had each other to push around.

"Mrs. Parker doesn't approve, duck lips."

"Oh, all right, then, carry-on, pogo stick."

"Thank you, lard-head."

I may have said that each, in his own right, was brilliant, but I never said they were mature.

"Very well. The caller informed me that she is the lunchtime waitress at this place on the east side, and that she immediately recognized Myrtle, because this waitress, see, is an aspiring thespian—"

"We don't care what her sexual preferences are, old boy," said Mr. Benchley.

"Quite hysterical, Bob; you need a new gag man. Anyway, she'd seen Myrtle on stage before she gave it all up and married Reggie. The other woman with Myrtle, she didn't know, but thought she looked an awful lot like Mary Astor."

"Holy kamoly!" said Mr. Benchley.

"Language, Mr. Benchley!" I couldn't help myself.

"It wasn't until she saw Marion's pix in the paper this morning that she knew for sure that the girl wasn't Mary Astor, but she was the same girl she served lunch to last week, last Thursday, she said." Frank flicked his cigar ash, and sat back in his chair, a self-satisfied grin slapped over his face.

"The last day of Marion's life," said Mr. Benchley.

"She was murdered later that night," said Aleck.

"Now we've got that established, what did they talk about, did she hear anything?" I asked.

"They were talking business. Talking big money," said Frank. "The waitress said they came in at about two-fifteen, after the lunch rush. The waitress remembered, because she thought she was done with any more luncheon customers, and she wanted to make it cross-town to an audition for the new Ziegfeld show, and there was only one diner left, finishing up his lunch, when the women came in, the older one first, and a few minutes later, Mary Astor. Because the place was empty, she could hear snippets of their conversation.

"And?"

"She said they sounded like they were negotiating the price of something. Whatever they were referring to, one of them said, it was 'cheap at that price.'"

"So, we know that Marion was a busy girl last Thursday," said Mr. Benchley. "She was visited by Lucille in the morning, and had lunch with her lover's wife mid-afternoon."

"We've got to question Myrtle!" I said, leaping from my chair, startling Woodrow Wilson, who'd been lying in a food stupor at my feet. I picked him up and held him on my lap. "Has the waitress gone to the police with her story?"

"She's afraid to go. She saw my column and decided to telephone me, but I have to keep things off the record until they catch the culprit who murdered Marion. I can understand she's scared. Three people are dead, and she's worried that she'll be next if the killer is Myrtle, and she finds out that there's a witness who overheard the conversation."

"It was Myrtle who killed Reggie and the ladies?"

"Her alibi's firm. And she certainly couldn't have strangled Reginald on her own. She's—what? Five feet tall and ninety pounds? Reggie was a lot more than twice her weight," said Aleck.

"That's like Mrs. Parker trying to strangle you, Aleck," said Frank.

"Believe me," I said, "I've tried too many a time and failed."

They laughed. Then, Mr. Benchley suggested: "Perhaps, Mrs. Parker, if you dropped drugs into Aleck's drinks, and then laid the pillow over his face, and pressed your entire weight against it—"

"Don't give Dottie any ideas, Bob!"

I ignored the nonsense, but in truth, it was a way a small woman could overtake a man as big as Reginald Pierce. And, the coroner found a feather in his hair.

"Myrtle might have done just that, Mr. Benchley—I must go see Myrtle."

"Not alone, Mrs. Parker. You're two inches shorter than she, and she might overtake you."

"*Shit!* I can't see her."

"I'm glad you see reason, then."

I threw Mr. Benchley my usual acid glare accusing him of idiocy.

"It's nothing about reason at all! I can't see her. I just remembered. She's left town until Godknowswhen!"

"I'll mark that date on my calendar and we'll meet her train," said Mr. Benchley.

"Do you think she knows we're on to her?" asked Frank.

"How could she possibly think that, you dip-stick!" said Aleck.

"Dip-stick? You're calling me a dip-stick?" said Frank, scrunching up his face.

"Stop it right now!" I hated playing teacher. Where was my yardstick?

"I can't buy it," said Frank. "There's no murder in Myrtle's heart."

Aleck came back with, "When have *you* looked into anyone's heart? There's murder in everyone's."

"I suppose we are all capable of killing," said Mr. Benchley, suddenly serious. "And it's true that Myrtle had the most to gain from Reginald's death. But, it stacks up too nicely to come to the conclusion that she planned the murder of three people. Anyway, she has a tight alibi for Reggie's."

"She may have hired someone to do him in," posed Aleck.

"And leaving town makes her look even more guilty, if she'd done it," said Frank.

Aleck looked over the tops of his frames at FPA, and the glare was in his eyes this time and not just reflections in his glasses. "How can someone be *more* guilty?" corrected Aleck. "She's guilty or she's not; you can't be more or less or a little or a lot guilty! It's like being pregnant, you are or you're not! Or dead! You can't be a little dead, or more dead, than other dead people."

"Unless you're Buster Keaton, that is," said Mr. Benchley to me.

"*Awww*, shut up, you gas bag," said Frank to Aleck with a straight face.

Tonight these two were like a bad marriage and had to be ignored. I said, "Let's keep Myrtle as a suspect as she may have gotten around her alibi. I'll put her at the top of the list."

"Does anyone want to know what I found out?"

"Please, Mr. Benchley, do tell," I said, glad for a change of focus.

"Maxwell Sing is Ralph Chittenham's son."

"Holy moly!" said Frank.

"No crap?"

"Shit!"

They all turned to me like a chorus of cackling jackals: "Language, Mrs. Parker!"

———◆———

Aleck and Mr. Benchley both had prior dinner invitations, but we agreed to meet again at my rooms at the Gonk at midnight. Frank wouldn't be joining us, and although he didn't say it outright, we all knew that his wife, Ruth, was getting annoyed with his many late nights; he needed to spend an evening by hearth and home, especially since Frank intended to join the Thanatopsis Literary and Inside Straight Club for their Saturday night poker game. FPA's way of life could sure put a strain on a marriage.

We left Tony's to go our separate ways. It was a brisk evening, though cold for October, but the fresh air was reviving. A stiff wind off the Hudson worked to clear off the acrid coal smoke spent from newly fired furnaces. Both Woodrow Wilson and I needed the exercise, so I refused Aleck's offer of a cab ride to walk the short distance home. I had lots to think about.

After Mr. Benchley told us about Chitty's and Max's relationship, he went on to say that he began poking around into Number One Son's background for the very same reason I had given credence to the possibility of his active involvement in the murders: Maxwell *knew* about the secret drawer in Reggie's desk. Also, Maxwell was in one way or another involved with all the major players.

The key to unlocking Maxwell Sing's past was to look into Ralph Chittenham's. That Chitty's apartment was next door to Reggie's and Myrtle's was coincidence, as was the employment of a common servant. (People were always trying to steal good staff from their friends, but the coincidence raised a red flag.)

Mr. Benchley took to heart my belief that there were no coincidences and began his search.

From Chitty's own newspaper, he'd dug up a biography that amounted to little more than the columns readied by an obituary writer for publication should Ralph drop dead tomorrow. So he called Bob Sherwood at *Vanity Fair*, and the two spent the afternoon searching through issues of the magazine for any mention of Ralph Chittenham, his social and organizational activities. Sherry even telephoned around in the guise of doing a story on the critic. And they came up with some interesting information.

Ralph Chittenham was born in Philadelphia in 1888 to Henry and Alice Porter Chittenham. His father was heir to a fortune from coalmining. One of six children, Ralph was educated at Exeter, and received a degree from Harvard, after which he went on to study Greco-Roman Art History at Oxford. He remained in England for three years, working in London at the British Museum under the tutelage of the curator of Greek antiquities. Ralph needn't have worked a day in his life, for his parents had always proudly indulged the whims of their son, who was the one exceptionally brilliant child from a brood of unimpressive offspring. It was an age when to be idle and rich was viewed as the great American success, and the family fortune had never grown so expansively as when Ralph's father, Henry, bought and converted two textile mills for the manufacturing of weapons on speculation that America would join the War in Europe. Ralph could pretty much do as he liked. He cringed at the idea of ever returning to the Philadelphia he'd left behind when he went off to school, but he returned to the States when England joined the fight in '14, and secured a position at the Metropolitan Museum of Art in our fair city, where he spent the next year researching 12th-century Benedictine illuminations. But soon, not content in his work, the young man sought escape from the bowels of the Met's laboratories, and through a family friend, the publisher of a now-defunct newspaper, he secured the job of art critic for that publication. When the paper closed down in 1920, he left the country and traveled through Europe and the Middle East for more than a year.

It is known that during that time he secured passage to Alexandria. What he did and where he went from there may only be told by Ralph, as it is at that point that the trail runs cold until his return to New York and his employment as Arts Editor at the *Morning Star Messenger* in '22.

And whom was he in company with when he returned by ship to New York? None other than Maxwell Sing, claiming to be Ralph Chittenham's son. By my calculations, Chitty had to have been 16 when he fathered the boy, and it was obvious the lady in question had to have been of the Chinese persuasion.

Maxwell Sing. Houseboy, my arse!

Chitty had some explaining to do.

Maxwell Sing polishing silver

Chapter Nine

I hardly expected to see Wilfred Harrison sitting in the lobby of the Algonquin, dressed in evening clothes and reading an evening paper, when Woodrow Wilson and I arrived home. He stood up to greet us, and I led him to a quiet corner.

He made me nervous, or should I say, he *unnerved* me. I couldn't help but stare at the man, for his Apollonian good looks were not so much pretty as they were of perfect proportion, flawless, really, and although his dress suit was impeccably tailored to show the broadness of his shoulders and the long, lean line of his back, I found myself mesmerized by the way the individual black hairs of his eyebrows formed such perfectly bent arches, how the cleft of his chin was like the blessed kiss of God upon His creation, how the closely trimmed fringe of his hair echoed the clean, curved wonder of his sculpted ear. I swayed, literally, *swayed* from side to side, as I stood next to him, breathing in his clean earthiness, like a cedar forest after the rain. His voice—his warmtimbred baritone, like the rustle of sheets—soothed, calmed, and did easily seduce a nervous type like me. I felt myself unraveling, slowly, willingly. I was coming undone.

He was so very beautiful that I had to force myself to actually listen to what he was saying, to ignore the hypnotic tone of his voice and concentrate on the words.

Although he may have thought I had telephoned for personal, romantic reasons, my real agenda was to question him about Marion Fields and anything he might tell me that would find her killer. I had to come clean, tell him about my suspicions, but before I did, I wanted him to know that I really was interested in getting to know him for more personal reasons. And as I am often shy around men when I have a notion of romantic interest, I tend to speak sentences rife with acerbic adjectives in iambic pentameter. Words are my shields, and sometimes, my enemies.

But, did I want such a man in my life? I know it was crazy, but falling in love with such a man as Will could be dangerous in so many ways. A catch like Will would ultimately cost me dearly, I knew that. It couldn't last. When he got to know me, he'd want to leave me; when I got to know him, I'd find him not so beautiful, not so perfect, and I would behave so badly that he would *have* to leave me. I am small and sweet-looking perhaps, but even with my brilliant career, my sought-after presence, I am not enough for such a man. And because he will find me lacking in so many ways, and for all that I am not, he would be the end of me.

I straightened my spine as I reconciled my fantasy with my reality. I melted a bit when he told me that he had left a dinner given by a partner in his firm just to see me. It was not the best political move to do so, I figured, though he was loath to suggest or in any way imply concern over it. He suggested dinner, if I was available, and we might go wherever I wanted. I grabbed at the invitation, but wisely left him in the lobby while I went up to my rooms to change into evening clothes and to settle my little man, Woodrow Wilson, in for the night.

Twenty-five minutes later, I returned to the lobby bathed, face restored, dressed in an Aberdeen crêpe-de-chine gown, cut on the bias, dripping with nine strands of fully faceted pale-amber-toned crystal beads, circling in layers like dancing lights from my bare neck to my hips; the same amber crystals dangled from my ears; a chic wide band of gold lamé embroidered with a peacock feather motif wrapped my bobbed hair. A cape of honey-colored dyed muskrat, fringed with red fox, draped my shoulders; strapped heels were on my feet and my favorite Worth evening purse dangled from my fingers. If I say so, myself, I looked smashing for a little cluck.

And all the while, as I dressed, as I came down the elevator from my rooms, as I crossed the lobby to where he sat so elegantly, languidly, waiting for me, I knew very well that I was sticking my fork in the toaster.

But, my bun was stuck and I was very hungry.

I made two or three restaurant suggestions, and left the final decision to Will. The Algonquin night doorman, Peter, whom we all called St. Peter as he guards the entry gates of our "final resting place of the evening," hailed us a cab and we were off to Pierre's, one of the finest French restaurants in New York.

If you took great care, and had the cash, any booze could be had for the asking, and at Pierre's, the Chateauneuf-du-Pape flowed freely.

I do love champagne. Oh, how I love champagne! I was damned from the moment I first saw Will waiting for me to return home. And now, sensual pleasures compounding: champagne.

From the anticipation of uncorking the dark-green bottle, and the dread of losing too many precious ounces as the liquid bursts forth, to the cheerful burbling as it pours into the glass, and the wonderful golden shimmer of the liquid when you raise your glass to the candlelight. The foam grows to the top of the flute like a living thing; the toast, the electric crackle at the lips like a first kiss, the breath of alcohol that assaults the nose, the bracing sting as the magic fluid dances over the tongue, and the cold shock to the throat that instantly warms the chest with unhurried and tranquil comfort: All these assaults to the senses make it a sublime indulgence.

And after two bottles with five courses, I felt sublimely indulged.

The musicians on violin and accordion

transported us to Paris in the spring, and Paris in the spring is certainly sublime. I pushed aside my crème brûlée, fully sated, ready for love.

But nagging at me were questions, for my intellect would not submit. I had to regain some semblance of clarity to present them to Will.

Throughout dinner our conversation was centered on the cultural benefits of living in the city, and people we knew. We spoke very little of that which was personal in nature, other than relating the basic facts of our lives. I grew up on the West Side of Manhattan, my mother died when I was a child, my stepmother, before I turned ten; the Academy, *Vogue*, *Vanity Fair*, freelancing, the Theatre. For some strange reason, I could not speak of Mr. Benchley. I suppose I couldn't have him there in the room with us, even though he was always with me, even when he was far away.

Will, the third son of factory workers in Detroit, a scholarship to Yale, Skull and Bones, Rowing Club, law school, boxing, baseball—how about that Babe Ruth!—his love of jazz—we'd head up to Harlem and the Cotton Club next time, I told him. There would be a next time, surely.

Could he sit in on the Thanatopsis poker game some Saturday night? I assured him my friends would love to take his money as soon as anyone else's; I'd arrange it, I said. I wanted my friends, Jane especially, to give him their seal of approval. Mr. Benchley, too. But, we didn't talk about how or what we felt or thought or wanted, not about anything of importance in life.

It was simply a match game of I like, he likes, that sort of impersonal exchange. That's all that should be covered for the first time out.

But, I took a really good look at him, beyond the handsome profile and elegant wardrobe, and I really liked the rather quiet, measured and thoughtful way he spoke. I liked his genuine interest in me, not so much the celebrity me, but the woman me. I'd see him again, if he asked me, that's for sure. An unpretentious man in my world comes along once in a blue moon.

Broaching the subject of Marion Fields was not as difficult as I thought it would be, as Will gave me the opening I needed to get started when he asked if I was enjoying my Renoir. I told him I was, indeed, happy to have it, and grateful that Reggie had remembered me so extravagantly. I told him the story of my interest in the picture, about my aunt's and uncle's fateful voyage on the *Titanic*, and about how Reginald and I had both attended the same auction when the Renoir came up for sale years later, and how he had far more money than I to buy it.

And then, "So you were you Marion Fields's attorney as well as Reginald Pierce's?"

"Not either's. Mr. Pierce was a client of one of the law firm's partners, who fell ill the day before the funeral. I was asked to read the will on his behalf. As for Miss Fields, she isn't my client."

"You were unable to tell me any details about the gift Reggie arranged for Marion, outside of his will. But now that she's . . . dead, is it something that can be discussed?"

"Some money in trust," he said, "not a lot." He looked up at me and his eyes narrowed and softened. I thought he was going to add something more about Marion, but instead he said, "Do you know that you have the softest brown eyes. They're the color of fine cognac." He reached across the table to take my hand in his. "I'm so glad that you called me, Dorothy. Oh, my, Dorothy, you're grand!"

Shit! This is not good. Turn back now, said a voice in my head, not unlike Mr. Benchley's. It couldn't have been him, though; my friend did not use four-letter words. I would not listen. I told him to shut up.

"This probably strikes you as corny when I say it," continued Will, "but a woman such as you, why, to have you on my arm, it's a dream come true.

"Gee, I'm a little crazy about you—" he went on, uninterrupted, because I was speechless by now, "—more than a little, and if you don't think it's too forward of me to say so, I've had a little crush on you for a long time, from afar. I've read everything you've written, and I've always felt that behind that biting prose was a soft heart. I can see your heart through those lovely eyes."

God, help me! Make him stop, because I can't speak. My tongue is wrapped like a pretzel around my throat.

"And, now, when I'm finally lucky enough to meet the most charming woman, she allows me to escort her to dinner. It's true what they say: You are the toast of New York."

So what if his lovemaking was corny; it was

oh, so wonderful to hear. I unfurled my tongue, and managed to croak out, "Thank you."

"I have a confession to make."

Crap, you're married.

"I hope you won't be angry."

Only if you're married.

"I haven't been honest with you."

You didn't tell me you're married.

"Well, you see, when Mr. Whipple at the firm, Mr. Pierce's attorney, fell ill, well, I asked to represent him at the reading of the will. You see, another partner of the firm was going to do it, and I knew he was very busy, and I convinced him, you see . . ."

"Well, at least it isn't like you're—" I stopped, abruptly, as I was about to say "married." I threw in a fast substitute: "—a murderer, or something!"

"You see, I wanted to meet you. I knew you were named in the will, and it was my chance, you see."

"Well," I fluttered, "I couldn't be more . . . flattered, really."

"Gee, you're swell," he said, dreamily, kneading my hand, gazing deeply into my eyes.

After he signaled the waiter for the bill, he leaned in closer and said, "May I see you again? Please say, 'yes.'"

I didn't have to say anything because it was written on my face like bright red-letters on a billboard, so he continued with, "I'd love to paint the town red with you, Dorothy, but it'll have to wait. I have to be in court first thing in the morning, and I have a couple of hours of work to do before I call it a night."

I made an inane comment about the trials and tribulations of the hard-working attorney, but I felt a little crushed at the abrupt ending to our evening, all the same. I had been prepared to take him to my rooms and leave messages for Aleck and Mr. Benchley to call up from the lobby before they stormed my place. It had also crossed my mind, too, that Wilfred might be able to help us with our investigation into the murders, but that was the last thing I wanted to discuss with him tonight, anyway. Right now, I was enjoying a romantic evening with a man I hoped to get to know better.

In the cab he wrapped his arms around me, and by the time we turned off the avenue and onto my street, his lips were on mine. I felt my heart beating wildly in my chest, and a fluttering in my belly that had nothing to do with the digestion of the cassoulet from dinner.

He asked the driver to wait as he saw me up the elevator to my rooms. Woodrow Wilson yelped excitedly on the other side of the door. After turning the key in the lock, he once again took me in his arms for a longer kiss. I managed to gurgle, "Good night," and slipped in through the doorway to the adoring kisses of my little man, Woodrow Wilson. Delightful, but not quite knee-buckling.

Within the hour Aleck and Mr. Benchley would arrive, and I had little to tell them. I took Woodrow

Wilson for a short stroll down the street so that he could attend to business and I could cool down a little bit. I stopped at the corner newsstand and bought the late editions. The night had gotten colder, or was it that I was no longer basking in the warm glow of Mr. Perfect, Wilfred Harrison? I wrapped my fur more snugly around me as I headed home.

I threw off my shoes and settled in to read the headlines, but there were no new leads on the Broadway Murders. The police had their man, Gerald Saches, so that manhunt was over. But on the obituary page of the *World* were Marion Fields's photograph and the short story of her life:

Born 1899 in Ann Arbor, Michigan, she was the only child of Harold (deceased) and Brenda McEnerny (survives her daughter). Star of her high school's plays, she came to New York for a career in Theatre. There followed a short list of shows in which she appeared in the chorus.

An idea struck me. I called down to the desk and asked the operator to place a call to Brenda McEnerny in Ann Arbor, Michigan.

I had just hung up the receiver when Aleck and Mr. Benchley arrived at my door, sending Woodrow Wilson into a frenzy of excitement. When my friends arrived at this hour they usually brought an offering of sorts for me, and always a morsel for Woodrow. I settled the men in with drinks, and laid out the dozen petitfours pocketed in a linen napkin from Aleck's dinner party. Mr. Benchley's marzipan was wrapped in brown paper and string, and had been purchased at a sweetshop around the corner.

"I just got off the telephone with Brenda McEnerny."

"Costume designer for Belasco?" asked Aleck.

"No"

"Am I supposed to know this McEnerny person?"

"Not at all. She's Marion Fields's mother. Just spoke with her. She is boarding a sleeper out of Ann Arbor for New York, arriving Grand Central tomorrow afternoon. She's coming to see about Marion's belongings. I told her I'd meet her train and take her to the apartment."

"Ah," said Mr. Benchley, "she might shed some light on who may have killed her daughter."

"I hope so. But she hasn't seen Marion since she ran off in 'nineteen. She didn't know she'd changed her name." (It hadn't yet occurred to her that Marion had taken the name Fields as a stage name rather than retain the ponderous-sounding McEnerney.) "She didn't know Marion had come to New York, not until this morning when she saw her daughter's face on the front page of her newspaper."

"Well, it's time we take a closer look at Ralph Chittenham," said Mr. Benchley. "Pay him a visit."

"To what end?" asked Aleck. "The man and his son have no motive for killing any of the three victims."

"Yes," I agreed, "I don't know how anyone can tie him to any of the murders."

"Things don't stack right, though. Think about it. He's an arts critic with degrees in ancient art history up the wazoo. Reggie has a collection of Egyptian artifacts, some of which Gerry feared may have been looted from the Deir el-Bahri excavations. That was a Metropolitan Museum dig, dintchaknow? Ralph was with the museum during that time, and not too long after leaving his post he booked passage to Alexandria. We don't know where he went from there; we can only guess."

"You think he was Reggie's dealer, is that it?"

"Perhaps," said Mr. Benchley, weighing his words, careful not to jump to false conclusions. "Or, he may have found out that Reggie's collection did indeed include the looted Golden Selket. We need to find out if, during the months that his movements were unaccounted for, he was at the dig."

"You think he stole the Golden Selket from the site and then sold it to Reggie?"

"Maybe. But I think he may have some direct connection to the statue."

"He may have killed Reggie for it," I said, nodding, because it made sense.

"Or, perhaps he tried to steal it from Reggie's collection, and when Reggie caught him in the act Ralph killed him; and then Lucille knew or saw something, so she had to die. It's all speculation, of course."

"Ralph didn't kill anybody," said Aleck. "He's not the sort."

Mr. Benchley said: "I didn't know there was 'a sort,' Aleck. Everyone is capable of murder: Mothers kill to protect their children, men to protect their land, and throughout history, in the name of God, for God's sake! Anyway, Gerry told Mrs. Parker that Reggie received a telephone call the night of his death. Maybe Ralph was the caller who telephoned Reggie to say they had to meet, and things proceeded, with or without the initial intent to kill—"

The memory of a conversation at the Waldorf the other evening popped into my head. "Wait a minute! I don't think he was even in town that night. He was in Boston reviewing a show. That's right, he was reviewing *Grounds for Divorce*, Ina Claire's new play. I've heard good things about its out-of-town runs. She's supposed to be marvelous in it. It opens here next week. I remember the conversation because I have to review the opening night. He couldn't have killed Reggie or Lucille. He was hundreds of miles away."

"Where was I during this conversation?" asked Aleck.

"Fussing over Fanny Brice."

"Oh, yes. But, dintchaknow?" said Aleck. "Last week's performances of *Grounds for Divorce* were canceled. Ina and half the cast fell sick with that illness that's been going around. The Boston opening was delayed a week. Opens tomorrow, but with Ina's understudy. She's got pneumonia and is in the hospital. Read about it in *Variety* this afternoon."

Mr. Benchley said, "So if Chitty said he saw the play in Boston last Wednesday he was lying."

"He was giving himself an alibi, but didn't realize the one he chose would blow up in his face!" said Aleck, a little too happily.

"I wouldn't be surprised if Maxwell was his spy in the Dakota household, and then, later, at Reggie's apartment. If he wasn't the dealer who sold Reggie the statue, then perhaps he was trying to steal the Golden Selket!" said Mr. Benchley.

"Do you think the statue was hidden in plain sight in the Ming vase all that time?" I asked.

"Marion knew where it was," said Mr. Benchley.

"Or guessed. She obviously knew its value. Ralph may have figured that she knew where it was hidden, and that she had stolen it from the apartment. I wonder if Ralph has the statue now."

"Should we tell the police what we've discovered?"

"Not yet," said Mr. Benchley.

"Bob is right," said Aleck. "Just because his alibi doesn't wash, it may just mean he was cheating at writing the review, heard or read other notices and didn't want to bother making a trip to Boston. Perhaps he was somewhere else instead, not necessarily murdering Reginald Pierce."

"And to play devil's advocate, even if he had something to do with the statue, it doesn't mean for sure he'd kill for it. Let's sleep on it," said Mr.

Benchley. "I can't see us racing over there at this hour to confront him. Tomorrow I'll check at the museum. See if he ventured to the Deir el-Bahri excavations."

"I'll meet Marion's mother's train after lunch, and while we're at the apartment, maybe I'll learn something."

The boys left me a little while later with lots to think about. I had a restless sleep with Wilfred Harrison dominating my dreams.

———◆———

I spent the later hours of the next morning delivering long-overdue articles to the offices of magazine publishers, as I desperately needed the commissions. Flush once more, I popped into several shops to settle bills, and then spent half an hour deciding whether or not to buy a lovely little number in midnight-blue lace. Woodrow Wilson was my voice of reason when he barked his disapproval and headed for the shop's entrance, turning his back toward me to face the street, indicating he wished to leave the premises. I know he had to pee, but sometimes I really do think he's trying to tell me not to be an ass. I was weeks behind in my rent, and although I knew the Gonk's management, Frank Case in particular, was glad to have me as a tenant, as my celebrity brought in lots of business, I knew I had to settle that bill, too.

Dress poor, and soon to be once again penniless, or nearly, off we trooped for home and our one o'clock luncheon with the boys.

And how nice to receive a telephone call from Will a couple of minutes after my return, thanking me for spending last evening with him, and saying that he was looking forward to seeing me on Saturday night.

At twelve-thirty the newsmen of the Round Table met in my rooms to share information they'd gathered over the past twenty-four hours. There were lots of new leads and descriptions of the killer from unreliable sources, all differing: The killer had been seen entering the Chinese restaurant across the street from the Reginald Pierce Theatre the night of Reggie's murder. He was tall, blond, and had a scar across his left cheek. At the same time, a bald, mustached midget from the circus at the Hippodrome was seen running from the back-stage alley of the Pierce Theatre. A third witness bumped into a cloaked figure wearing a top hat. He had a limp and sported a handlebar moustache, etc., etc.

One of the witnesses to Marion's murder, who had been interviewed by the police, spoke with Swope. He said a tall, dark, and handsome man, around thirty years old, rushed through the crowd at the curb and pushed Marion. Of course, when you looked at the fact that on any Broadway street, within an hour of the final curtains of six-dozen matinees, one is likely to see tall, dark, and handsome men, actors all, more than anywhere else in Manhattan, finding such an individual fellow would be close to impossible!

And then there were the crazies, among them

religious fanatics who spoke of evil-doers and the moral decay of our culture, of the damage the Broadway Theatre was doing to the souls of the American people. To these nuts the murders were committed by God's messenger to rid our country of the depravity that was corrupting our children, and it was only a matter of time before God would finally kill us all, as He had done to Sodom and Gomorrah.

On that note, we went down to lunch.

The New York Public Library at 42nd Street— *Groucho stopped here to snatch a book for a scavenger hunt. Up he ran the long flight of steps flanked with grand, carved marble lions facing 5th Avenue. Behind the Library is Bryant Park, where we fetched a park bench—and a vagrant. Down the side street to the left of the library is 40th Street. In this picture, which is ten years old, there is airspace where the American Radiator Company Building now stands.*

The Marx Brothers—
These fools are as crazy off-stage as they are on-stage, but what fun!

Chapter Ten

After lunch, Mr. Benchley, Aleck, and I went our separate ways: Mr. Benchley, uptown to Fifth Avenue and 80th Street where stands the Metropolitan Museum of Art, with the hope of learning more about Ralph Chittenham; Aleck, two avenues over to the *New York Times* newsroom, in an effort to contact, by telephone or telegram, the missing Myrtle Pierce; and I, to Grand Central Terminal and Track 26 to meet the 3:10 from Ann Arbor.

The streets were congested with traffic, as I walked the few blocks to Vanderbilt Avenue. There was construction in every direction I looked. The Park Avenue skyline was changing once again, as residential apartments and hotels were claiming air rights, and the tall skyscrapers were rising taller every week. The heights were startling! The Metropolitan Life Tower had already soared to 50 stories, and the Woolworth Building, the world's tallest, to the magnificent height of 57 stories. These miraculous feats of engineering threatened to block out all sunlight!

Grand Central Terminal, with its great stone eagles, their wings spanning the exterior frieze, sat atop the sweeping gesture that was Park Avenue at 42nd Street. As I approached the building from its northwest side along Vanderbilt Avenue I passed the Biltmore Hotel. I was immediately brought back to the evening Mr. Benchley and I "visited" Lucille Montaine's apartment, and the impression on notepaper we'd found on which had been scribbled "Biltmore 11:30."

By my wristwatch, I was early to meet the train, so I stopped short to look into a shop window, much to the displeasure of a gentleman walking close to my heels. He barely missed crashing into me for the gaining tide of pedestrians. He double-stepped to avoid impact, tripped, and that sent his bowler flying into the air. I retrieved the hat, apologized, and handed it back to him. "My hat's off to you, Madame," he said, his initial annoyance melting into a flirty, dimpled smile, before he bobbed onward in the sea of floating black hats.

As I crossed the street through strings of motorcars, one of those new Chrysler 6 automobiles zipped round me like a shiny bright bluebird. Entering the lobby of the Biltmore Hotel, I looked at the bronze clock, the clock under which lovers meet.

That was it! Lucille was meeting her lover! But who was he? Could he have been a resident of the hotel? Did he work close by? Or was it simply the ordinary meeting place? Perhaps, though, there was nothing clandestine about the meeting. Perhaps she was just meeting a girlfriend for lunch or shopping.

It was all such a guessing game! But it would have been unusual for an attractive woman like Lucille not to have had a lover. Why hadn't we even considered her death as an act of vengeful passion by a lover? It didn't have to tie in with Reginald's murder at all. If it did, though, perhaps it was her lover who'd done them both in. I vowed to pursue the identity of such a man, but for now, I had to meet a train.

———◆———

Mrs. McEnerny said that she would be wearing a gray herringbone traveling suit and a distinguishing gray hat with feather, so as the hoard of passengers poured off the train and walked up the ramp with porters in tow, it was anyone's guess as to which of fifty-odd women, dressed in gray suits and topped with feathered caps, was my girl. I'd just have to keep my ground until she approached me. And she did.

"Oh, Mrs. Parker," said Brenda McEnerny, "you've found me."

If she wished to see it that way, I'd not tell her differently.

The woman who stood before me was a head taller than I and looked not too many years older than her daughter. Some women are like that; they retain a youthful look well into old age. Her auburn hair showed no gray, and the skin around her eyes was tight, not bagged. I refrained from asking her age.

"I recognized you from your photographs, Mrs. Parker."

"Please call me 'Dorothy.'"

"Brenda."

"Yes, then, Brenda," I said shaking her hand. "I am so sorry about Marion. I can't know what you've been going through." I picked up one of the two small valises she had set on the floor, and turned to lead the way toward the street.

The Beaux Arts interior of Grand Central occupies a vast space, its vaulted ceiling one-hundred and twenty-five feet high, and its marble floors gleaming, in spite of the constant foot traffic. One cannot help but look up at the magnificent ceiling, and is never disappointed by the celestial mural painted in gold leaf over cerulean blue depicting constellations that are lit with electric light bulbs. The grand staircase looms to the left of the main entrance, and was modeled after the one in the Paris Opera House. Melon-shaped, gold chandeliers light the hall, and sixty-foot-tall windows flank each end, making one feel quite tiny under the great expansive dome. I turned to glimpse the wonder of it all in Brenda McEnerny's face. I suggested three things for her to remember during her visit to the city: First, if she wished a few moments to look at the sights around her, it was best to stand still and let the crowds flow around her while holding tightly onto her purse, and second, when crossing the streets at the corners, she should move with the crowd and never make direct eye contact with the drivers wishing to turn into her path. Eye-to-eye gives a driver license to cut you off. And third, if lost, get into a cab and tell the driver to take you to Mrs. Parker's at the Algonquin. In the meantime, she needed to stick close to me.

Once out the doors, she stopped dead to take in the marvel that was Midtown Manhattan. She'd applied her lesson well, but I'd failed to inform her to let me know when she intended to gawk, so that I wouldn't leave her trailing behind a block or more. I raised my free hand, and a cab pulled to the curb.

I asked Brenda if she'd like to stop for some refreshment before we headed up to Marion's apartment, but she said she was anxious to go there right away. I gave the driver the address and we were off on a short tour of Manhattan.

Brenda was silent throughout the ride, her eyes drinking in the sights outside the window. At one point, while stopped in a knot of traffic, she looked over at me and smiled. "I suspect Marion loved the excitement. It sure looks like an exciting place." It was said wistfully, and I could see the mist forming over her eyes.

"It can be very exciting, yes."

"And sometimes dangerous, too."

"Yes."

I felt an acute rush of sadness for this woman who emanated the pain of loss long before the news of Marion's death had reached her. And not only loss; there was something else about her that showed through her stoic smile. I recognized it as a longing for something that she knew she could never come to possess. Such resignation in her face! Such a bleeding vulnerability! Loss and longing together can be unbearable, can turn your spirit into iron after a while. She was not iron, yet, but I could see by the way her mouth worked and her shoulders slumped that too much more pain would turn this sweet soul bitter.

I wanted to hug her to me, or pat her hand at least, to reassure her that it would all turn out all right, but I knew that was a lie; to tell her such things, however heartfelt in the moment, would only serve me, not her. To make me feel better for not really caring too much or thinking too much or mourning at all the death of her daughter, a rich, married man's mistress, a young woman not so very unlike me. I feared if I made a gesture, I'd only embarrass her. I feared, too, that I might make a bit of a scene, complete with tears — tears shed that would not really be shed for the loss of Marion, but for my own pathetic circumstances. Oh, miserable, selfish creature that I am! I pretended to look out of the window beyond her, and said nonsensically, "Marion lived in a very lovely residential hotel. There it is now."

Brenda offered to pay for the cab, but I objected and took care of the driver, and then, valises in care of the doorman, who handed her keys to the apartment, we rode the elevator up to the fourth floor. I wondered if the elevator boy was the very same one that FPA had spoken with. Arrived at the door, Brenda unlocked it and turned the knob.

As if she were gripped by a strangling hand, a gasp escaped her throat.

The living room, still bright in the westering autumn light, had been ransacked, and I doubted it had been the police who'd conducted this search. I knew immediately what the thief had been after.

Brenda walked slowly into the bedroom. More of the same.

But there was violence, here, for items were not simply strewn about haphazardly, but ripped and smashed and thrown across the room. A murderer did this, someone with hatred in his heart, not the police.

"You're coming with me," I said simply, but firmly, touching her arm. I couldn't in all conscience let Brenda remain in the apartment alone that night. "You won't stay here. You'll be my guest in a room at the Algonquin, where I live."

She didn't argue with me; the state of the apartment had so confused and distressed her. But, the predominating emotion of the moment was fear. By the very violence with which someone had torn up her daughter's belongings, I could see that she suddenly knew that her daughter's death had not been an accident.

I became so incensed that I wanted to scream, to spew out a string of obscenities, but I couldn't, because I knew it would only make it worse for her. She didn't say a word; she didn't cry or swear. The only indication of turmoil was the blank, paling, wide-eyed stare as she took in the room. I thought she may have gone into shock.

Before we left the bedroom, Brenda picked up from the floor a little book. The pocket volume of Shakespeare's *As You Like It* had been Brenda's gift to Marion, years back when she starred in the play in her high school's production, she said. The inscription was personal, and I did not ask to read it. Her expression looked strained, tears welled in her eyes, and then she turned in a rush to bolt toward the bathroom. I heard the retching, and then the sound of water running in the sink.

As I waited for Brenda to collect herself, I leaned against the bedroom door glumly surveying the miserable state of the apartment. That's when I glanced across at the fireplace, and my sights rested on the charred-edged remains of newsprint atop a stack of unburned logs: papers not just thrown in the trash, but meant to burn to ash. But whoever it was who'd decided to burn the newspaper, Marion herself perhaps, had not bothered to see it burned completely through. The logs beneath were barely scorched. I gingerly lifted the brittle papers—news clippings!—off the logs, and placed them flatly between the pages of a copy of *Vanity Fair* magazine I picked up from the floor.

Within an hour we were home and Frank Case settled Brenda into a pleasant room two doors from mine. I suggested dinner in the Oak Room, but Brenda declined, saying she was tired and wanted to rest, as tomorrow she had many things to attend to, the worst of which was making arrangements to take her daughter's body home.

Woodrow Wilson greeted me at my door, and then ran to sit beside Mr. Benchley, napping on the sofa. He opened his eyes, sat up, stretched, and adjusted his tie.

"Don't you have a bed?" I asked.

"'Cross the street."

"How inconvenient."

"Yes." He patted an attentive Woodrow Wilson on the head, and proceeded to put on and then tie his shoes. "And dreary."

"You could get some furniture."

"It would be wasteful. I'm rarely there," he said, standing and waiting for me to say something.

"Drink?" I said.

"Thought you'd never ask. There's soda and ice, there. Oh, and I took Woodrow Wilson for a spin around the block."

I thanked him. "I've news."

"Me, too."

"Ladies first."

"Aleck's not here."

"Pearls before swine."

"Which am I?"

"I meant that I'll go first," I said, ending the stalemate.

When I had finished telling him about Brenda McEnerny's arrival and the destruction of Marion's apartment, Mr. Benchley smiled and announced, "Ralph Chittenham was indeed in Egypt back in twenty-two; specifically, he visited the Deir el-Bahri dig. It was not an unusual thing to do, for a scholar to be interested in seeing the progress that was being made, even though he wasn't representing the museum in any official capacity. His years at the British Museum and at the Met yielded him many friends in the field of archeology."

"But now we've linked him to the Golden Selket!"

"That's just it. There is no link, not really. I tried to speak with Dr. Fayed, whom we spied from behind our favorite drapery panel the other day, but he was not available."

I took his glass, and as I refilled it he explained.

"There is a problem, you see: Several people have said that they had seen a Selket statue in the burial chamber they were excavating. But it was never catalogued."

"Are you saying that the chamber may have been looted after it had been opened, and before all the treasure was catalogued?"

"There's just no firm evidence either way," he said. "But, I did get a chance to stop in and browse through one of the galleries where artifacts from that Deir el-Bahri site were on display, and while I was there, wouldn'tchaknow, the curator happened to be working on an installation of sarcophagi in the adjoining room, and I got to speak with him for a couple of minutes.

"He was at the site when Ralph, who said he was traveling through, agreed to pitch in when several native diggers refused to work because of the rumor of a mummy's curse, or some such nonsense, that was supposedly the reason several members of the company fell seriously ill. This curator and Ralph were working to free the entrance stones leading into what was believed to be a burial chamber. When it appeared that enough progress had been made to open the chamber, our curator sent word to fetch the director."

"So, he left Ralph alone with an opened tomb holding scads of golden icons?"

"No."

"I don't get it, then."

"The entrance was guarded until the director's arrival. The director arrived, but Ralph had left by that time. Ralph had been suffering from stomach pain for some time, and it appears that his appendix chose that day to rupture. This coincidence sent many more native workers to flee the dig. Ralph was taken to a hospital and was still in surgery when the chamber was finally opened."

"Did he ever have access to the chamber?"

"That's just it, he didn't. He was never through the entrance. Not that first afternoon, nor any day afterward. He was not part of any team that did the cataloging or photographing of the artifacts. So if we might have been secretly harboring suspicions that he stole that statue, there is no evidence that he did, or that such a statue was ever in that tomb."

"Wait a minute! Is there or is there not such a thing as a Golden Selket?"

"Oh, yes, of course. The goddess Selket was a female goddess who donned a huge scorpion on her head, reminiscent of some rather Victorian, avian monstrosities that I recall my aunt wearing during my youth . . ."

"Goddess of what, exactly?"

"She protected the Great Queen Isis, wife of King Horus of the afterworld — of whom the pharaohs were incarnate — from insect bites, scorpions in particular, and a statue representing her would stand guard over the dead in a tomb. And although it was very likely that there was such a figure entombed at Deir el-Bahri, only a few witnesses claim to have actually seen it."

"We need to talk with Chitty."

"I think we do. But, I think, too, that we should let the police know what we suspect."

"What exactly do we suspect?"

"That perhaps Ralph, ruptured appendix notwithstanding, may have aided in the theft of an Egyptian treasure."

I considered his last statement as I fed Woodrow Wilson a biscuit. I sat down next to Mr. Benchley on the sofa, slipped out of my shoes, and put my stocking feet on his lap. Mr. Benchley gave excellent foot massages.

I said, "And *what* else do we suspect? Do we think Ralph killed Reginald Pierce, Lucille Montaine, and Marion Fields to get his hands on a statue that we're unsure ever existed? Or do we suspect that he was the dealer who sold the Golden Selket to Reginald in the first place?"

"I think we simply inform the police that we have reason to believe that Ralph Chittenham may have information leading to the arrest of the murderer, and that they may consider checking him out, alibi and all."

"But they have Gerald Saches. To them it's a closed case." I closed my eyes and said, "Bless you, dear Fred, my arches were killing me."

"At your service, Madame," said Mr. Benchley, kneading the underside of my right foot with his able fingers. "Did you report the ransacking at Marion's apartment?"

"No. The police would say burglars hit it after they saw her obit in the papers."

"Then, let's just ring up Joe Woollcott and let him know we're going to pay a visit to Ralph later tonight, just in case we wind up dead and they want to know who done it."

"That's encouraging. I'll make the call. Hand over the telephone, please."

He did, and I asked the hotel operator to connect me to the 20th Precinct. As I held the line I asked, "Where's Aleck tonight?"

"With Frank. Dinner at Jane's and Ross's."

"Did they track down Myrtle?"

"Dunno. But Jane rang up while you were out, and I picked up. She said, if you weren't busy she'd like for you to join them for dinner, and since I'd picked up, she invited me, too. Eight o'clock."

"You'd make a very excellent houseboy, now, wouldn't you? Answering telephones, arranging dinners, napping on the sofa while the mistress of the house is out . . ."

"Masseur and dog walker, confidant and dinner escort. Should my literary career stall, I may take it up. But I don't come cheap."

I reclaimed my foot, and went into the bedroom to change into a modest dinner dress. An hour later we were in a taxi heading for numbers 412 & 414 West 46th Street.

Last year, my close friend, Jane Grant, and her husband Harold Ross, a founding Round Tabler, bought two brownstone houses in Hell's Kitchen, just west of Broadway. The idea had been to break through the common wall attaching the houses to create one large house. It proved to be a bit too big for the couple, who had no children, and had no plans for any, and Ross's big idea of starting his magazine and using some of the space for the publication's offices had not yet germinated.

Aleck, who had a hand in the lives of all his friends, suggested renting out apartments on the third floor. Each of two more apartments on the second floor would be occupied by himself, and another friend, Hawley Truax. The two men would buy into the venture.

On the first floor were rooms for Jane and Ross, along with a kitchen and dining room. It was in this dining room that plans were made for Ross's new magazine, *The New Yorker.* The space doubled as a general gathering place for the home's residents, and on Saturday nights the table was cleared for cards, cash, cigars, and cocktails, when the members of the Thanatopsis Literary and Inside Straight Club met for poker.

Jane, my fervent suffragette friend, women's activist and journalist, had, upon her marriage to Harold Ross, declared she would retain her maiden name as claim to her singular identity. Jane, who then cut off her long dark tresses, not in the conventional bob of modern protest, but a shockingly severe man's cut, parted at the side and slicked black behind her ears, the model of feminine modernity in every way publicly, reverted to domestic servitude upon entering through the portals of 412 & 414 West 46th Street, where she cooked, served, emptied ashtrays, picked up, washed up, and swept up after the half-dozen or more men flicking cigar ash, spilling drinks, missing the toilet, and generally stinking up her home.

All of her striving for women's equality to men, which she had worked so hard toward achieving for her generation, could be reduced to little more than inconsequential rhetoric should her sisters of the cause ever see her on any given Saturday night. I wondered for how many more weekends she could play inden-tured servant before she became a lunatic?

I was looking forward to Jane's fine home cook-ing, which was rivaled only by Bea Kaufman's.

In the cab Mr. Benchley and I discussed how we might approach Chittenham when we went to his apartment later that evening. We couldn't just storm in affecting an accusatory tone. If he were the murderer, we would be risking our lives. If he weren't, it would just be plain-old bad form. New York is a small town in some ways, and everybody in the newspaper business, and in the Theatre, and in book and magazine publishing knows everybody else, especially the big players. We were big players, as was Ralph Chittenham. He may not have been my cup of tea, but Chitty was respected, sometimes loved, often feared, was exceptionally accomplished, and had enough money to sue the pants off Mr. Benchley. (As I had no assets, other than my talent and a couple twenties, he'd not come after me.)

We decided to tell Chitty all that we had found out about him. Lay the cards on the table, and hope that he didn't have a gun in his smoking jacket.

The cab crawled across the congested traffic where Broadway and Seventh Avenue bottlenecked at Times Square, and then onward to Eighth Avenue, past brilliantly lit marquees and the crowds of anxious theatregoers. When we turned north toward 46th, we were stalled once again by a stream of limousines, motorcars, and the crossing masses, guided by a traffic cop. If my feet hadn't felt so painful from my day of racing around town on foot, we'd have popped out of the cab and walked the long avenues to Jane's. I was hungry, too, having eaten little at lunch, and the day was far from over. I leaned back against the seat, and turned to look out the window at people from all walks of life happily anticipating the excitement of seeing a show. Mr. Benchley chatted on.

It was then that I glimpsed a familiar form. I knew it was he before I ever saw his face. His pace was faster than anyone else's as he zig-zagged through the crowds. He turned the corner from Eighth Avenue onto 46th.

"We'll get off here," I said.

"We're just a few blocks—I thought your feet hurt."

"They do, but I just saw Maxwell Sing and I think he's headed toward the Pierce Theatre."

Mr. Benchley handed the driver his fare, and off we went, cutting east through the northerly moving tide, where, as if caught in a steady river current, we bobbed along. As we neared the theatre, progress was stalled in a jam-up of people piling into the lobby. There was no sight of the houseboy.

Logic had it that he was headed for the side entrance to Reginald Pierce's apartment. But, when we arrived, the door was locked. Mr. Benchley and I stayed fixed to the alley, trying to figure out to where the young man had disappeared.

Several cast members in costume had gathered

outside the stage door to chat and smoke. Mr. Benchley asked if they had seen a young Chinaman pass by.

"Are you looking for Max Sing, Mr. Benchley?" asked one of the actors. Robert Benchley was not only a famous writer, critic, and social commentator; he was a Broadway star, since last season's Music Box Revue. Every young actor in New York knew who he was.

"Yes," said Mr. Benchley.

"He went through to the back, to the apartment entrance."

We thanked the kid and continued on, where Bobby the Burglar worked his magic. We had to take the elevator, and would have to risk the noise of the cables creaking and echoing in the shaft announcing our arrival, but there was no other way up.

The elevator door opened onto the foyer, across from the apartment door that stood ajar. From within we could hear the sound of voices in rapid, animated conversation. We edged closer to the door, a column of light from the salon guiding our way.

A huge, shadowy figure cast its dark form along the wall. I recognized the cultured voice that spoke, and although it would have made good sense to knock on the door to announce our presence, neither of us moved, so transfixed were we by the conversation.

"It's done."

"I made the call."

"And do you think they'll get it?"

"When the money is paid."

"The ship leaves at nine, there's not much time."

"What's the telephone number?"

A telephone was being dialed.

The sudden cranking and whir of the elevator startled us, and I gave a little cry. The shadow grew larger, and then morphed into Ralph Chittenham, smaller, but no less frightening, who widened the gap of the doorway to stand frowning at our fully illuminated selves.

Light glinted on gunmetal. Ralph Chittenham pointed a weapon at us. The elevator clunked to a stop and the door was pushed open to reveal a rangy, sandy-haired man in his forties, tanned to a dark mahogany color, his face ruggedly craggy.

"Dr. Fayed," said Chittenham. "Come in, please."

"What's going on? Who are these people?"

"They are of no consequence to us, Dr. Fayed. But they must be dealt with. I shall be with you momentarily."

Maxwell Sing led the guest into the apartment, while Ralph Chittenham motioned at us with the gun to enter the salon.

"Well, you might as well come on in," he said, leading us into the library, the gun at our backs. The room was empty of art and the collections, specifically all of the Egyptian artifacts.

"Stand over there," he said, pointing to a corner. "I've got business to take care of first. I'll take care of you two in a minute."

"What did he mean by that?" I whispered to Mr. Benchley.

"He's going to kill us, like he did the others."

"What was that? You look sick, Dorothy," said Chittenham, leaning in to look into my eyes.

"Leave her alone," said Mr. Benchley, moving between Chittenham and myself.

"What's going on, Benchley?"

"I could ask you the same thing."

"What the hell are you doing here?"

"I could ask you the same thing!"

Chittenham realized that he was waving the gun; he returned it to his pocket. "I thought you were—"

Something clicked in my head and I said, "Did you call that man 'Dr. Fayed'?"

"What about it?"

"Dr. Amir Fayed from the Met?"

"Yes, what about him? And what are you doing here?"

"I could ask you the same thing!"

"Shut up, Bob, you keep repeating yourself."

"That man is not Dr. Fayed!" I said.

"I most certainly am," said the weathered face, indignantly. "Really, Ralph, we have little time. We must go find—"

"Quiet!" yelled Chittenham, and then, "Sorry, Doctor, but these people, they are not part of this, so the less said—"

"Ah, I understand," said the doctor, "they just happened to get in the way, is that it?"

"Something like that."

"But, I saw him, Fred. That is not the man we saw the other day."

"He is not Dr. Fayed," said Mr. Benchley. "Dr. Fayed is shorter and dark-haired and—"

"Wait just a minute, Benchley!" ordered Chittenham. His eyes lit up with new understanding. "This man you believe to be Dr. Fayed, when did you meet him?"

"The day before yesterday."

"Where?"

Fred and I looked at each other.

"Well? Look, you two, I don't have time for these games—"

He was reaching into his pocket.

"Here. We saw him here," I said.

And before we could get the confusion settled, the telephone rang and Chittenham pounced to pick up the receiver. "Let's go," he said, and then he, Maxwell Sing, and the fraudulent doctor were out of the room, disappearing through the bookcase at the side of the fireplace.

A secret entrance!

Mr. Benchley and I leaped into action.

Fred tried to find the release mechanism for the hidden door, while I pondered whether or not to call the police. But, what would I tell them? That we knew the person responsible for the Broadway Murders, and he was on the run, somewhere in the city? We had no idea where these men were going or what-fresh-hell they were up to.

"Got it!" said Mr. Benchley, and in a second we found ourselves racing down a spiral staircase that opened into the theatre's office, next to the box office in the lobby. At the opposite end of the room a door stood ajar, an open invitation to follow, and we found ourselves in a long corridor, at the end of which we caught sight of Ralph Chittenham's coattails. Racing onward along the corridor, we soon arrived on the upper-level dressing rooms, a backstage area of the proscenium. Below us, as I looked over the steel railing to the bottom of a flight of stairs, I glimpsed the heads of the three scoundrels, pushing aside a gaggle of costumed actors that was making its way from off the stage.

We weaved down through a flock of performers climbing up to their dressing rooms, Mr. Benchley nodding and smiling pleasantly as he acknowledged their greetings. As we passed the stage manager calling the next scene curtain, I nearly careened into the scrim that was suddenly hoisted down to block my path. We avoided catastrophe and started a new route along the back wall of the stage.

Angry whispers from a stagehand trying to prevent the three men from crossing the stage alerted us that we were close on the heels of our quarry, and as they pushed ahead, so did we, just as another stagehand turned to stop our progress. Ignoring many pleas, we zigzagged around the various obstructions.

The scrim rose up, and we were blinded by light. Suddenly, our silhouettes could be seen by the audience as we crossed stage right to left. There was a sprinkling of laughter.

The actor and actress on stage were in the middle of a love scene and were as yet to understand the commotion behind them. Cooing, locked in an embrace, extolling the joys of their wooded retreat, they continued their dialogue:

"—to be alone with you at last, my darling, away from the glare of millions of eyes—"

The three culprits burst onto the set as they bounded right through the cabin's door.

"—They'll never find us here, my love!"

Maxwell Sing knocked over a lamp as he tripped over the head of a bearskin rug. The lovers turned, and although momentarily unglued from the distraction, resumed their lines.

Dr. Fayed ran around the sofa, toward the footlights, tripping on a table leg, spinning a vase filled with flowers to teetering imbalance. He performed a little sidestep, arms flailing, in his efforts to prevent it from falling to the floor.

"It's so quiet here—"

The vase hit the floor with a loud crash.

"—away from the hustle-bustle of town—"

The stage manager, having seen us start our cross, lost his place in his cue script and mis-cued the lighting technician and a grip. Up came the lights, and then up came the backdrop, the interior wall of the Adirondack Cabin, with wooded landscape behind it, exposing me and Mr. Benchley against a brightly lit cityscape of Manhattan.

"Not a soul for miles and miles—"

The audience reaction was thunderous.

Although I felt really awful at causing the interruption, I knew from having seen the dreadful play that this was going to be the biggest laugh of the evening. I was wrong; it was only the beginning of what was to become uproarious.

And what clinched it were the actors' dumbfounded expressions, as they stupidly, haltingly, tried to carry on the dialogue. It served only to feed the audience's furor, for the couple pretended that we were not there; the laughter became all the more hysterical.

Mr. Benchley and I stood blinded by the stage lights for a few moments, as Maxwell, Chittenham, and the doc stumbled over each other and the furniture, before making a break toward the orchestra pit.

It was then that Chittenham, dragging an electrical cord that had wrapped around his ankle, tripped, crashed through a storefront window of the Manhattan street scene, and landed, like a Yankee slugger sliding into home plate, at the feet of the lovers on the sofa.

"I beg your pardon," he said, politely.

The audience roared.

At this point the lovers decided they should carry through with improvisation, including us in their dialogue. According to their revised script, we became the couple next door and the town council, come to welcome the lovers, or some such nonsense. The actors offered us refreshments, which was even more ridiculous. At this point, we were in touching distance, Chittenham on all fours.

Mr. Benchley grabbed at his coattail and there began a struggle, not unlike a rodeo bronco and his steadfast cowboy, as Ralph tried to throw him off his back. He was successful at last, and Mr. Benchley lay prone and winded on the bear rug.

Chittenham made it to his feet, and when asked by the actress if he'd prefer tea or cocoa, Mr. Benchley reached up and once again grabbed at his coattails, causing Ralph to lose his balance. On his way down, Chitty landed on the actress's lap.

I broke a vase over the doc's head, and then Maxwell Sing, coming up behind me to stop my flailing arm's momentum, got one in the eye, instead. The audience stamped, whistled, yelled, and cheered, and Mr. Benchley stood up and took a bow.

Chitty and his gang of thieves bolted off the stage, and Fred and I gave chase down the aisle and toward the lobby doors.

Eardrum-bursting hoots and screams of laughter followed us out through the lobby doors and into the street.

Ahead, a cab door slammed, and as it pulled away from the curb Mr. Benchley turned his attention up the street and whistled. Within seconds, from half a block away, three cabs made hay to reach the finish line. The winner cut in to the curb.

We hopped in and the driver asked, "Where to?"

"Follow that cab!" we both yelled at his back. So fierce we must have sounded that the cabbie took off, tires screeching, the clutch released with a force that threw us violently back in our seats.

Traffic had lightened up by now, as all 180 shows in Manhattan were in performance. Chittenham's cab was heading west, and after a minute, I realized we were headed toward the docks on the Hudson. The bits of conversation that we'd heard confirmed that: "The ship leaves at nine," he'd said.

The two cabs made bee-lines across 46th Street, past brownstones, then tenements, across rail tracks and further on warehouses lining the docks of Hell's Kitchen. I could hear the deep bassoon sounding of a ship's horn, and in response, the high-pitched toots of its tugboat.

Our cab pulled up alongside the pier, and Mr. Benchley pitched a dollar bill at the driver, who beamed his pleasure when Fred told him to keep the change. Mr. Benchley helped me out of the cab, and we ran toward the pilings, where there was a great commotion of autos, police cars, and officers storming the gangplank onto the freighter that, tonight, would not be departing on time.

Hotel Biltmore

Grand Central Terminal— *with its celestial ceiling and gold-plated chandeliers.*

Chapter Eleven

It was ten o'clock before the police allowed us to leave. And when Mr. Benchley and I finally departed the shipping pier's offices we did so with friends.

Aleck, FPA, and Jane and Ross had arrived at the pier a short time after Mr. Benchley and I had been threatened with arrest for obstructing an investigation. Aleck's cousin, Joe Woollcott, vouched for us, and then called our friends just as they were about to sit down to a dinner of roasted leg of lamb. Needless to say, Aleck did not appear in the best of moods for forfeiting the hot meal.

And as we marched east, across the long avenues to 412 & 414 46th Street, we resembled a disgruntled, windblown, downtrodden party that had seen a good time gone bad; I, worst of all, looked like a trampled taxi dancer at three in the morning: My feet were *killing* me.

And what was most humiliating was the addition of Ralph Chittenham, Maxwell Sing, and the real Dr. Fayed, all of whom were invited by Jane to come for cold lamb, a bit of potent libation, and full disclosure of events leading up to our arrival at the pier. By the time we reached Tenth Avenue, I was lagging behind the troops. Mr. Benchley took pity and scooped me up to carry me the final blocks to the house.

We collapsed on sofas and chairs around the sitting room, as Ross did the honors with a bottle of Haig & Haig. Jane took me into her bathroom, where I freshened up and combed my hair, and slipped into a pair of her soft slippers, before rejoining the others.

The men had gathered around the dining room table like starved alleycats waiting for fish heads to be tossed their way.

Aleck, in particular, was looking wan, and actually rose to join Jane in the kitchen to assist in a timely delivery of the roast and all its accoutrements to the dinner table.

Maxwell Sing was put to work placing the additional dinnerware at the table and opening bottles of wine on the sideboard. Little was said during the initial feeding frenzy that followed, but when the shoveling slowed, people began to speak.

Jane, who hadn't the foggiest idea what the fuss had been about, wanted explanations. FPA wanted clarification. Ross demanded additional information, and Aleck just wanted dessert.

"We thought you were the murderer, Ralph," said Aleck.

I explained. "You see, Chitty, it was a series of things pointing your way. Your apartment is next to

Myrtle's and Reggie's. Max worked for Reggie, and then you hired him. And then there was your lie."

"Oh?"

"You lied about being in Boston the night of Reginald's murder. You said you reviewed Ina Claire's new show, but the show was dark that night because half the cast got that dreadful disease that's been doing the circuit."

"And then," added Mr. Benchley, "Dottie wanted to pin it on you because she thinks you're the worst Theatre critic she's ever known."

I cringed.

Chitty threw back his head and gave out a hearty laugh. "I probably deserve that, but I had to get in Reginald's good graces. He was suspicious of critics, and I needed to soften him up a bit, make him think me a fool. I knew Dottie didn't like me, as Dottie doesn't suffer fools lightly."

I said, "With the exception of Mr. Benchley."

"And then you were in Deir el-Bahri at the time of the initial theft of the Golden Selket," said Aleck.

"And your education, and the fact that you had worked at the Met: All those things added up and made you the likely suspect," said Mr. Benchley. "Oh, and I almost forgot: Maxwell's white gloves."

"How so?" asked Maxwell.

"You were wearing them."

"Was I?"

"Gave you away, far as Mrs. Parker could tell."

"Really? How so?"

I didn't comment on the wordage. "I thought you were hiding something."

"I was going to polish the silver, and I always wear gloves to do that."

Now we understood that Ralph Chittenham was one of the good guys.

We wanted to know more about Maxwell Sing and Chitty's relationship with him.

"Max is my adopted son," replied Chitty to Frank's question. "My wife, Cassandra, an archeologist from Greece, whom I met while working at the British Museum, was in China at the time of the Republican Revolution and the overthrow of the Qing Dynasty in nineteen-eleven. Max was the son of her assistant, who was killed. She searched, but there was no family with which to leave the child. Cassie didn't want to place him in the local orphanage, as conditions were horrible, and she felt responsible for him. She kept Max with her, and returned with him to England. He was ten years old at the time. A few years later, when I was at the British Museum, Cassie and I met and married in seventeen, and I adopted Max. A year later Max went off to university.

"The War ended, and I came back to the States, while Cassie went home to Greece for a visit and to see about an exploratory mission for future excavations of the Alexandria region. But, I was never to see her again because Cassie died of blood poisoning from a scratch on her leg while on a dig. We'd been apart for only a few months when the news came of her death.

"In twenty-one, I sailed to Greece to visit her grave and to finally meet her parents. I traveled on to Egypt. The Met was digging in Deir el-Bahri on the Nile. I stopped there for a time before going back to England for Maxwell's graduation ceremonies from Cambridge. He sailed home with me.

"For the past two years Max has assisted me in my work. To look at him, no one would guess his educational background, that is, as long as he plays the coolie halfway convincingly, which is a role our society is most willing for him to play. People of color tend to be ignored if they present a servile front. They are rarely coaxed into sharing their histories or thoughts or ideas or feelings, as it is believed they haven't any. And for that reason, Maxwell was the perfect plant."

"So how long is it you've been investigating the theft of the Golden Selket?" asked FPA.

"Not long after the *second* tomb had been opened at Deir el-Bahri. It had yet to be cataloged, but people remember seeing it."

"But, what led you to Reginald?" asked Mr. Benchley. "What was the evidence that he ever had the Golden Selket?"

"We followed the dealer who was likely to have trafficked in stolen treasures."

"The short, dark, middle-eastern man who'd identified himself to Gerald Saches, and to the estate lawyer, Wilfred Harrison, as Dr. Fayed," I added.

"Yes," said the real Dr. Fayed. "He was posing as me! Which is quite brazen, actually, for we look nothing alike. I am tall and handsome, and people often mistake me for Lawrence—"

Dear Lord, I thought, *this fellow's full of himself!*

"The man you spied is Shahram Ali," interjected Chitty, "and he has been slipping out of the hands of the authorities for quite some time. It's believed he's responsible for the theft of numerous paintings and sculptures from collections in Europe during the War. Interpol, a new organization that was founded last year in Vienna to assist in the cooperation of international police forces, asked me to investigate when it was suspected that a Golden Selket had been sold to a buyer in the United States.

"I was back in New York, and had taken the position of Arts Editor at the paper, coincidentally, often reviewing shows offered by Reginald Pierce, the suspected buyer."

Perhaps there were coincidences, after all, I thought.

"And Maxwell was the perfect spy," I said.

"Yes, pretending that he spoke little English gave him an advantage. People would speak freely around him."

"I gently insinuated myself into the household," added Max.

"We saw you go into the secret drawer of the desk in Reggie's library."

"Yes, I know."

"What do you mean, you *know*?" asked Mr. Benchley.

"I saw your feet. Your shiny dress patents sticking out from behind the window curtain. When I counted three sets of shoes, I turned off the light and fled down the hidden passage. I didn't see more than the shoes, but I feared you might have been Mr. Pierce's murderers returned to the scene of the crime."

"What did you put in the desk, in the secret compartment?" asked Aleck.

"Nothing. I took my money. Mr. Pierce owed me three weeks' pay, and that's where he kept a 'stash' as they call it here."

"Wait a minute!" cut in Ross. "Is this man, the fake Dr. Fayed, this Shahram Ali character, is he the murderer?"

"I'd say he is," said Chittenham. "But, I wouldn't be surprised if he was in cahoots with others."

"There's that word again," said Aleck. "*Cahoots!*"

"And he wasn't found hiding on the freighter trying to make his getaway," said Mr. Benchley.

"And neither was the Golden Selket."

"That means he's still out there," said Jane, a worried look on her face.

I could tell what she was thinking, but before I could reassure her that he wouldn't be killing anyone else, Aleck cut in.

"You're right to worry, Jane. Bob and Dottie can identify him. We'll have to keep them in our sights until he is captured."

"Wilfred Harrison and Gerald Saches can identify him as well," I said. "They, too, were taken in by his act. As a matter of fact, Wilfred was supposed to have had Ali sign papers today for the release of the collection to the museum. I should have guessed something smelled fishy when the fake doctor said there was a *bronze* statuette missing!"

"That's right," said Mr. Benchley. "He could have signed off on the rest of the collection and made off with what was there, but he was still hoping the Golden Selket would show up, that perhaps Wilfred Harrison or Gerry might locate it for him! He wanted to delay the release, and Wilfred was unwittingly used as a pawn. He believed Ali was Dr. Fayed!"

"Outrageous!" rumbled the real Fayed. "Stand us side by side, and—"

What a bore.

"So everything, all the collections were packed up and trucked out. But the truck went to the docks, not the museum," said Mr. Benchley.

"This Ali character must *have* the Golden Selket. Ali must have figured, *before* he met with Wilfred and Gerry, that Marion had the statue. Maybe he'd already arranged to meet her at the corner, and he killed her, pushing her into traffic. Then he went to Marion's hotel and tore through the place looking for the Selket. I'll bet he found it, and is probably far away from here by now." I looked over at the worried expression on Jane's pretty face, and added, "There's no reason for him to bother to come back to harm anyone. I'd say the mystery is solved if not a murderer caught."

"We figured Marion took the statue from a hiding place in the vase, but how did she know it was more valuable than anything else in the room? How did she know where to look?" said Aleck.

"Do you think she was working for Ali?" asked Ross.

"She might have killed Lucille. But why? What'd Lucille have to do with anything?" said Mr. Benchley.

"I don't understand about the gun," I said. "Who hid the gun in the drawer?" I looked at Max and asked, "Did she know about the secret drawer?"

"Perhaps. Although I never saw her in the desk. But, Mr. Pierce may have shown it to her."

So many ideas were chasing each other in my head that I was becoming dizzy keeping track of them all.

"So this Shahram Ali killed Reginald, Lucille, and Marion for the Golden Selket," said FPA. "What a scoop!" He rose from the table and went into the living room to use the telephone.

Chittenham called out to him. Frank stopped midway, turned, and addressed Chittenham.

"I'm calling the story in to my paper. There's still time to make the deadline for the morning edition. I'm gonna tell the humdinger of a story of what happened tonight."

"No, Frank," said Chitty, "you cannot use my name at all. It would expose me and the work I am doing. And lots of people watched as the five of us trashed a set and nearly closed down a show this evening. If you mention my name it will only bring Dottie, Bob, and Max into the picture."

"What about me!" said Dr. Fayed. Self-righteous ass.

"You, too."

"But, it's the Show Business story of the year!"

"And it'll be all yours, Frank," said Chittenham. "But, not quite yet."

"Why not yet?" asked Ross.

"We have to wait until the ship we unloaded this evening docks at its destination. When the now-empty crates are delivered we may be able to arrest Ali. That's five days from now."

"So you think Ali isn't wise that the shipment was discovered?"

"I'll bet he left town long before the truck arrived to deliver the goods to the freighter. But rest assured, he'll be at the delivery drop to collect his money. That's when the authorities will pick him up."

The pout on Frank's face only accentuated the moose-like aspects of his features.

Chitty felt for him, and added, "You can say the killer is known by the police, and it is not Gerald Saches. Whatever you do, *don't say that you know the killer's name.* Matter of fact, say the police are withholding the identity of the murderer."

"Will I ever be able to tell the real story?"

"Soon, a week or so, Frank, but Max and I will be portrayed merely as innocent bystanders in your story, understand?"

"Gotcha!" From the next room we could hear Frank shout into the phone. "This is Frank Adams Pierce! Now give me the city desk editor! Stop the presses, Jack! Bury the lead! Have I got a scoop!"

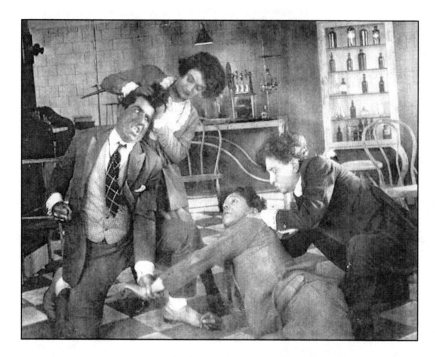

On-stage fight— *Somebody in the audience snapped this picture when we stormed the stage in pursuit of our suspects. That's me pulling Ralph's hair; on the floor is the actor in the play, Joseph Brown, and the real Dr. Fayed on the right. Mr. Benchley, Maxwell Sing, and the actress understudying Lucille Montaine's role, Rosemary Willard, are too far stage right and out of the picture.*

Chapter Twelve

I thought it only right, as I had taken Brenda McEnerny under my wing, to at least invite her to breakfast before she went to Wilfred's offices to see about Marion's bequest from Reggie.

"If it is enough to pay for her funeral, I'll be glad enough for it."

I put Brenda in a cab and took Woodrow Wilson for a walk up Fifth Avenue.

So much had happened over the past week. Three people were murdered for a five-thousand-year-old relic that, for that many years, no one knew even existed. I'm not a materialistic person. I travel lightly, owning little more than a few books and my dog. Books and Woodrow Wilson give me joy. It strikes me as an awful burden to rely on things to bring one happiness.

I was tired from the escapades of the evening before, and it was much too early for me to be walking around the city. We headed back home.

When I walked into the lobby, James, the desk

clerk, handed me several telephone messages. FPA had
called to say he'd had new information about the true
identity of the fraudulent Dr. Fayed. He and Aleck
would come see me before lunch. Gerald Saches had
called, and the message was short and heartwarm-
ing: "Thanks, my darling Dottie. You're swell." And
my sister Helen telephoned, could I come to Sunday
dinner? Bunny Wilson sent a wire to cancel an evening
we'd planned the following week, as he had to go out
of town last minute. But the message I was most
interested in was from Wilfred Harrison: "Supper
Saturday night at Le Petit Maison?" He'd not be in the
office today as he had to be in court, then a meeting
with clients. Would I call him this evening at home?
He'd left his home number. I pocketed the message
notes, and took the lift to my rooms.

I lay down on the bed. Oddly, I was not sleepy,
just a little world-weary, I suppose. I'd only slept a
couple of hours after returning home from Jane's and
Ross's. But it was sadness that tired me out, when I
should have felt invigorated and glad—glad that it was
all over, happy that the murders were solved and that
Gerry would be cleared and was being released this
morning, and that Myrtle was no longer a suspect.
And through all of this, one good thing had come to
me from the tragedies: I'd met a most lovely man who
helped me to believe I *was* lovable.

My disappointment in love during the past year
had left me feeling small and inconsequential, unattractive and bitter; it was nice to feel wanted. I smiled

at the thought, but in spite of my smile, I was still profoundly sad. I was crying, but why? Why couldn't I be just plain-old-happy?

I knew what it was. It was the ghosts.

If I thought I was hard-skinned enough to let it roll off my back, I wasn't so tough, after all. Reggie and I had never been close, and I had never even met Marion before the party at the Waldorf; Lucille, although a terrible actress, was flesh and blood and human, cut down at the prime of her life. I knew so little, really, about them. For all their faults, they didn't deserve to die. But they were dead, these people who'd walked the city only a few days ago. They had had hopes and dreams and ambitions, and people who loved them, and those things were gone, now, with their lives.

I looked at the wreck of my life. I, who had not respected enough the gift of life within myself, who had tried to end my life not so long ago, was somehow privileged enough to go on living. It made no sense to me.

I cried for Reginald, Lucille, and Marion.

And, I cried for me.

Woodrow Wilson whined and hopped up on the bed to lick away the salty tears. I wiped my eyes and breathed deeply, my doggie at my side.

The room was bright with sunlight, and a rectangle of it flooded onto the box I had taken from Lucille's closet. Here was my opportunity to learn more about the life of the young woman I had so casually disregarded.

When I'd first looked over her letters and scrap-book, her reviews of out-of-town runs, I was looking for facts, trying to find connections between her and Reginald's murder. Now, as I brought the box to the bed, the box containing clues to the life of Lucille Montaine, I decided to look at everything differently. I wanted to know the person, the living, breathing Lucille, the young woman with aspirations of a career on the stage. I thought her lacking in talent, but in a few years, with maturity, she might have earned a place of respect on the stage. Did I feel guilt about panning her performance in Reginald's show? I did, and yet, I knew it was not only my job to be truthful, but when the truth is told, my audience expects a lethal dose of deadly droll. So the bodies pile up, so to speak. Selfishly, I was glad she had escaped my direct chilling notice. Reviewing the audience, however, was, I tried to convince myself, my way of being kind.

I opened the scrapbook. The glue had dried and become brittle, and many news clippings fell off the pages. Half a dozen clippings fell onto the bedcovers, as did a couple of letters that I had carelessly failed to re-tie in the ribbon they were bound with, along with the scrap sheet that Mr. Benchley had pinched from her living room telephone table and had later shaded over with a pencil to reveal a message of place and time.

Out of my odd sense of respect, I would put every thing back in order; I would re-glue the no-tices in the book. It was a small gesture, but it was something to do, and I needed to do something to keep my thoughts off my own problems.

I went into the sitting room and got a pot of glue from my desk. Back in the bedroom I spread out the rectangles of newsprint across the counterpane and proceeded to arrange the sheets chronologically, by the dates printed or noted by pen. I then arranged them on the scrapbook page before applying the glue. Before me lay the life story of Lucille Montaine, aka Ethel Herring. I was suddenly determined to see that her parents received these personal items of their daughter.

I was about to paste the edges of a review from the *Detroit Register*, when I saw it. I more closely scrutinized the page, and quickly fetched a magnifying glass from the desk. The orange spots from the glue did not totally obscure the newsprint. Of course, the trick of the reverse point of view held true in murder cases as well as in comedy. But in this case, quite literally: Flipping things over, looking at things upside down, brought new discoveries.

I pulled the cables and telephone messages from my purse, and retrieved the fragile, brittle charred newsprint I'd taken from the ashes of Marion's fireplace and had slipped into the copy of *Vanity Fair*.

Suddenly, everything made sense.

I went to the telephone and asked the hotel operator to connect me with Mr. Benchley.

Will had asked me to supper for tonight, Saturday night. I remembered his interest in the Thanatopsis poker game, so I asked the boys at lunch if Will could sit in for a few hands; I thought I'd surprise him after we'd eaten with the suggestion that we stop by. I'd chat with Jane while he played, and maybe I'd even bring him luck.

The result of my discovery had been draining for me, and I, as suggested by William Cullen Bryant, in his poem, *Thanatopsis*, would face my impending doom with as much courage as I could muster. And that took good food and drink.

I wouldn't talk about any of it, I decided. It was too depressing. Yesterday, arrangements had been made for the dispersal of Marion's belongings to various charitable organizations, and the coroner had signed a release of her body, allowing Brenda to take her daughter home after the weekend. I packed up Lucille's box of memories and sent them off to her family in Des Moines, with a little note expressing my sadness at her death.

I was spent.

My exhaustion and the accompanying sick stomach was the result of the dread I felt. I wanted to nap, but was too restless. I was hungry as I hadn't eaten at all, but I couldn't swallow more than a bite of the sandwich that room service had sent up. So this is how Helen Hayes feels when her debilitating stage fright strikes, and I wondered how she, and all actors who suffer it, managed to pull themselves together each night to walk out onto the stage knowing they might be trampled by critics.

The weather had turned. The warm days and brisk evenings of early October had given way to the damp, shorter ones of impending winter. Saturday morning had dawned foggy, as the mists from both rivers bracing Manhattan converged to spread a low, gloomy blanket over the city. By evening the atmosphere felt denser, as the usual westerly winds that sweep across the island had stalled; the fog hovered, pierced through by the towers of new skyscrapers risen from the grid.

Tonight, I thought—when there was a knock at my door—Wilfred would hold my hand across the table, he'd put his arms around me in the cab, kiss me, and perhaps, if the mood was right, he'd want to come back with me to my rooms. I was nervous about it. I'd been so hurt in the past, and now, here again had entered an attractive, seemingly lovable man into my life, and I was just not ready, nor, I feared, strong enough, for what was to come.

He stood there with a luscious bouquet of orchids for me, and a tasty portion of boned roasted chicken for Woodrow Wilson. I offered him a drink before putting the flowers in an old milk bottle, and then fetched my coat and purse from the bedroom.

The telephone rang, and it was Mr. Benchley, calling to say that he had not gone home to Cancun, to Gertrude and the children this weekend, but had remained in town.

As we went down the lift, Will slipped his arm around my waist, and I tried to relax my posture in spite of an instinctive stiffening of my spine.

I stopped by the desk to ask if Jimmy the bellboy could take Woodrow Wilson out for a spin before midnight. Frank Case nodded at me as I bade him goodnight while walking through the lobby and out onto the street. The doorman hailed us a cab. Frank Case lit his cigarette, and as our cab pulled away from the curb, I watched as his figure faded in the mist; only the light of his cigarette remained until we were close to the avenue.

The restaurant was busy with diners when we arrived, but although most of the tables were filled it retained its quiet, romantic atmosphere. The restaurant was composed of several dining rooms, with curtained alcoves off the central room, designated for customers like ourselves: couples seeking more private settings. The lights were low; candles flickered, washing the red-damasked walls with shadows and dancing upon the silverware and crystal; roses adorned the tables and the waiters moved and served with silent deliberation.

We didn't speak much during supper. I found it difficult to find things to say. I wasn't feeling very well, and whenever I looked over at Will, he'd be studying me with those gorgeous, sultry dark eyes. Rather than melting, and because I felt a bit shaky, I was feeling self-conscious.

It was sometime between the Coquille St.

Jacques and the Beouf Bourguignon that I began feeling oddly ill. Voices echoed, and then deafened, my equilibrium unsteadied by a carousel of moving objects. I felt myself losing consciousness, and then a few seconds later I'd become alert for a moment, before falling back into a dreamlike state.

I can remember trying to rise from my chair in an effort to go to the ladies' lounge, but the struggle was too much, and after a time, I gave up the idea. People hovered around me. I heard the words, Will's voice, smooth and mellow at my ear: "taking her home" and then, "hospital," and then, "allergy." Wilfred wrapped me in my coat. I was in his arms, floating through the room.

Somehow, I'd been put into a cab, and I heard a loud horn blast, which broke through my dreams, and within a few minutes the "spell" subsided and things came into sharp focus again. I looked up into the eyes of the man who held me close to his chest, as the cab seemed to fly along the streets; the constant bumping in my head, as its tires smacked over potholes, provoked nausea.

Oh, no! I thought. *It wasn't supposed to be like this.*

We were to have supper, and then I would surprise Wilfred with the invitation to sit in at the poker game. But, now everything had gone wrong. All the careful planning was undone. And those thoughts of ruined plans were more daunting than the possibility that I was sick enough to be dying.

The two men were talking, the cabbie and Wilfred, and there was something familiar about the cabbie's voice. The shock of discovery shot adrenalin through my veins, and I was brought back to my wits again, if only for a few moments. I said that I was going to be sick, and when the cabbie turned and looked at me, I knew for sure who he was. He must have believed me because when I started to gag Wilfred told him to pull over. Wilfred opened the door and I started to wretch. Wilfred loosened his grip so that I might lean out farther, and that's when I made my break. He pulled on my arm, and I slipped out of the coat sleeve.

The fog was still thick, and the droplets of condensation soaked through my dress. All I knew was that I had to run away.

I had no sense of direction because I could barely see more than a couple of yards ahead, and in my confusion I made a bad turn.

The screech of tires and the blast of a car horn sent me flying onward into the street.

Horns squawked, shattering the shell that muffled my brain. The squeal of breaks, and then metal crushing metal in repetition, were like a chorus of quarreling crows circling my head. I ripped through, somehow, unscathed.

My feet were no longer on cement. I was running over soft, soggy earth. Suddenly, I felt the world flip out from under me. Landing on my rump, my hands grasped wet grass. The impact of the fall shook me to my senses.

I sat there for a moment, the wet earth a stronghold, knowing that I could not be seen, aware that I was in a park, or the grounds of a big house, and that I was still in the city, because of the sounds of traffic and honking car horns. I could see the faint glow of lamplight when I looked above me. I wanted to lie down, to feel the cool grass along my face, to close my eyes and sleep.

I rose to my feet.

It was too dangerous for me to make a sound, for I couldn't know for sure if Wilfred and the cabbie—the fake Dr. Fayed, the man named Shahram Ali—were closing in on me.

Was I in Central Park, I wondered, listening for the sounds of the city around me, trying to gage distance from the street? Did the sound of passing cars indicate a brisker pace, as might be heard from the winding thoroughfares through Central Park or along Riverside Park? I knew those parks like the back of my hand, having grown up on their lawns and meadows and woods and knolls and bridges and paths.

Not Central Park; at least, not deep into the park. Not Riverside, for I could not smell the briny Hudson.

I didn't believe we'd traveled very far from the restaurant when I'd made my escape. Which parks were near the restaurant?

The plunk and patter of hard rain plummeting down gave way to the steady drumroll of a heavy downpour, and soon I was dripping wet. But the violent rain brought a clearing through the fog, and along with it, a clear vision of my surroundings: Bryant Park.

On such a night, there was little chance of help, of anyone to be wandering about. Forty-Second Street bordered the park's north side, and it must have been there that I'd escaped the taxi. To my east, a couple hundred yards away, was the New York City Public Library. At best, I might hide along its shadowed walls, protected from immediate view by the trunks of trees surrounding it. But, there, too, I might be trapped.

The rapid, repeated splatter of footfalls along the path grew sharper, and I sensed that they were closing in on me. At one point, the fog thinned, and I glimpsed the indistinguishable suggestion of a figure, like an apparition, floating in the soft glow of lamp-light. The rain beat down the fog.

I held my breath as the footsteps resumed their ominous tapping, growing louder and louder until I thought he'd made me out, while I stood rigid alongside a tree trunk. I strained to see, waited for a hand to reach out from the mist to grab hold of me. My heart tore at my chest, my pulse so loud in my ears that I could barely hear the subtle shift of pitch as the footsteps receded. I was certain that if it had not been for the noise of the downpour, he would have heard the rushing of the blood through my veins.

I knew enough to avoid the paths, as the click of my heels would give me away, but I was afraid to move in any direction because Shahram Ali could be close by, too.

But, if I couldn't see them, I realized, they could not see me, at least not until the rain had totally obliterated the fog. I had no time to just hold my ground; I had to move on toward safety, toward people, toward help. And that's when my attention was guided to the closest retreat, and I groped my way in the direction of its tower beacon, a pulsing red orb in the fog.

The American Radiator Company Building facing the park's south side was nearing completion, and no doubt there would be a night watchman guarding the site who might help me.

The fog parted like a stage curtain as I neared the building. I looked up along its incredible height. I felt so insignificant and helpless before its dark, foreboding façade, the mist swirling around, lending an almost menacing, supernatural aspect to the structure. But I knew it was my haven and I had to enter, and fast, because if the fog that hovered low to the ground finally lifted I would be revealed.

I crossed the street, empty at this time of night, and then the expanse of concrete sidewalk, until finally, slick black marble was underfoot. I moved as gingerly as I could, trying not to make too much noise, staying in the shadows; I feared slipping on the wet marble, and cursed my foolish satin shoes.

I arrived unscathed, but the big brass-and-glass doors would not open. I pounded, more afraid of being seen than heard, praying for a guard to appear in the meager light that glowed within.

I soon gave up and looked around me. The

street was now visible, as the fog had given way. Traffic on the avenue was now my best recourse. I might find a brownstone's front doors open, inhabitants willing to let me in to call the police.

I bolted like a scared rabbit when I heard him, and then saw him coming at me through hedges that lined the park. Shahram Ali was faster than I, and he grabbed the skirt of my dress, bringing me down to my knees. We were in a deep shadow cast by a streetlamp. The man rolled atop me and pinned my arms.

I screamed and he released one wrist to cover my mouth.

I bit his finger and he pulled away, so I screamed again; one arm free, I poked my fingers in his eyes and tried to push him off me.

All at once his weight went dead atop me, and then he rolled off to lie, as if asleep, beside me.

I was brought to my feet, expecting another struggle, but it was not Wilfred Harrison's face I saw, but another, familiar one that I looked into.

Mr. Caruthers stood before me, surprise registering on his face, for he recognized me, too. In his hand he held a metal pipe.

"Are you all right?" he asked.

"Yes," I whispered, "but there's another man after me."

"Come on," he said, grabbing my hand and pulling me toward the rear of the building. I could see a deep shadow along the black brick wall. It was the well of a door.

But before we reached the safety of the building, Wilfred Harrison leaped violently down upon my rescuer. I screamed as he punched Mr. Caruthers across the jaw, and watched the poor man fall lifeless to the ground. I screamed again, and then made a run for the door.

But, Wilfred was determined to get me. I knew it was my end when I felt his arms wrap me from behind, lifting me off the ground, so that no matter how I struggled I'd remain flailing and locked in his grasp.

"Shut up, Dorothy, or I'll kill you now!"

I shut up.

He carried me into the shadowy door well, and pushed me up against the wall as he opened the door. Pulling me into the semi-darkness beyond, he pushed me to the cement floor. My eyes slowly became accustomed to the dimly lit room; from a distance I could discern a bare light bulb.

"It wasn't supposed to end this way, Mrs. Parker," said Wilfred, leaning over me, the available light giving his face a ghoulish cast, and so close I could feel his hot breath on mine.

"That's what they all say." I found that he was no longer very attractive at all.

He ignored my little quip. "You've really screwed things up for me!"

"I suppose you think this is a song and dance for me."

"Shut up with your wisecracks. I want to know

how much you know and who else knows it," he said, grabbing me by the shoulders.

"Why should I tell you anything, if you're going to kill me after I tell you?"

He shook me hard. My teeth rattled.

"What makes you think that I suspect anything about you?"

"All those questions about Marion. You never even knew her."

"Curiosity," I said. "Why did you drug me?"

"It was easier that way. You'd become ill in a public place; I'd make it look like you were despondent that I'd just dumped you during supper; I'd take you home, and tomorrow morning you'd be found dead of an overdose of pills."

"They'd never believe it was suicide."

"Do I have to remind you? You've got a track record, Mrs. Parker."

"What's with the formality, Will? I thought we were on a first-name basis."

"And then you sent that woman to see me, Marion's mother."

"She went to see you at your office because you told me Marion had a trust from Reginald Pierce. How was I to know it was all a pack of lies?" I foolishly couldn't help adding, "Did you duck out the back way when you saw her coming? Brenda McEnerny, your mother-in-law."

"How did you find out?"

"Lucille Montaine."

"She told you?"

"Posthumously. A marriage notice. There was a photograph of you and Marion at a nightclub on the back of a press clipping of a play she was touring with that she'd cut from the *Detroit Register.* She was blackmailing you and Marion, wasn't she? That's how she got the part in Reginald's show. She knew you and Marion were married, and she threatened to tell Reginald, didn't she? I'll bet you had some plan to steal a lot more than the Golden Selket."

"We never intended to steal any of that Egyptian stuff."

"What was the plan, then?"

"Once he married Marion, Reginald would have rewritten his will, leaving her his fortune. But, he was just stringing her along."

"He told Marion he was divorcing his wife, and then Lucille wanted more than a part in a play, she wanted a cut, too. So Reginald found out about what you and Marion were planning, and that's why you killed him."

"That's not why. He knew nothing, that stupid old man. He was just at the wrong place at the wrong time."

"I don't get it."

"He saw me with Lucille. Carrying her body after I'd killed her."

"What was Lucille doing in the apartment anyway?"

"I killed her in the hidden passageway. After the show. After everyone had left the theatre."

"Lucille went to see Marion at her hotel earlier that day."

"As she did every week to get the money. But Marion told her she didn't have it, that she was going out of town, and that she would leave the money in the passageway, so she could get it later after the show."

"The money wasn't waiting for her, but you were."

"Reginald wasn't supposed to be in the apartment at that hour. He was supposed to be away; he was supposed to meet Marion. He heard the gunshot."

It made sense, now. The phone call Gerry Saches said Reg had received during his visit was from Marion, calling on some pretext to get him to leave the apartment. Gerry's unanticipated visit had delayed Reginald's departure, keeping him in the apartment long after he should have been on his way. He heard the gunshot.

"I had to take care of him, too."

"You didn't shoot him. Why didn't you shoot him? Why the cherry tomato lodged in his throat?"

"Why do you think? I smothered him. I wanted it to look like he choked. I went as far as setting out a tray with the leftover food from the play, the food they put out for the banquet scene, to make it look like he was eating a late supper. Marion said he often ate the roast and salad. I set the scene, even tied his tie."

"But, he knew never to eat a tomato!"

"Yeah, well, I didn't know that."

"Why hide the gun?"

"Hiding the gun was Marion's idea: Place the gun in Reginald's hand for fingerprints, then hide the gun to be found later, when Lucille's body was found. Make it look like Reginald had shot her before he choked. We figured someone would find the gun, but nobody did."

I didn't tell him that I found the gun. "Marion was there?" I said.

"She arrived . . . unexpectedly. After I rammed the tomato in his throat."

"She didn't know about his allergy? That's hard to believe."

"Yeah, well, she knew, but she never told me, and I didn't tell her I stuffed the tomato in his throat until the next day. I was pissed. But, that night we had to play it by ear, you see. She hid the gun in the drawer for the time being. But the police never found it. Later, when it looked like Gerry would take the fall, I planted it in his house."

"Ah, yes, the courier. You are the man, the courier, seen at Marion's, and then you got into Gerry's house, easily, past the housekeeper. But why did you kill Marion? Why, if she was your partner? I don't get it."

"She double-crossed me. When we found out how valuable the Golden Selket was, she pretended she didn't know where it was. She stole it before I could find it and was making off with it."

"But it was in plain view."

"Was it?"

"Covered in black shoe polish to give it a bronze cast."

He laughed and bared his teeth.

"You don't have it, do you? I'll find it."

"It's already been found, Wilfred."

"Where is it?" He tightened his grip on my arms.

"I'm supposed to tell you? That would be stupid of me. I tell you; you kill me."

"Don't mess around with me, Dorothy."

"We're back to cozy first names, I see."

He didn't see it coming, the pipe smashing across his back. Wilfred crumpled to his knees, his eyes rolling closed, and nearly took me along with him to the floor.

A swollen, bloody face looked down at me as I whimpered, unable to cry out. Mr. Caruthers gently lifted me up and away from the murderer, taking me into his arms to steady me.

From a distance, I could hear voices, police sirens, and whistles. And as we emerged from the building, limping along, holding each other up, I could see that the rain had cleared away the fog; the sky was visible through the trees, and running toward us were Mr. Benchley, Aleck, and FPA along with the rest of the Thanatopsis Literary and Inside Straight Club.

Bryant Park is cheerful in the daytime.

The American Radiator Company Building—
The showdown.

The Final Chapter

The Thanatopsis Literary and Inside Straight Poker Club took its name from the poem, *Thanatopsis*, by William Cullen Bryant.

The Unitarian assurance that all creatures great and small will eventually return to the embrace of vernal nature, interred *in the narrow house*, goes on to challenge the reader to conquer inevitable death with courage.

A lot of hooey, if you ask me, and obviously composed by someone who had never been challenged to a duel, gone "over the top" from the trenches, been pushed out of a window, or been gripped at the throat by a murderer. After all, Bryant was only seventeen years old when he picked up his pen, mildly depressed, and reading Wordsworth. When he wrote the verses he was safely "embraced" in a chair by a flaming hearth. What could he possibly know of death, except that he feared it? I suppose the bravado expressed in the poem might be beautiful in its naiveté, but conversely, might challenge one's sense of the ridiculous.

For the boys of the Round Table it was a bit of both, I'd say, for here was an odd assemblage of exceptionally bright, terribly arrogant, and singularly unattractive young men who had, together and individually, somehow, against all odds, challenged and then conquered the greatest city in the world, with the beauty of energy and the arrogance of youth, garnering for each the admiration of their generation.

But it was Saturday night, and Saturday night meant poker.

I'd recovered, if not emotionally, then physically, from my ordeal of the previous Saturday night. The best way to get over a romantic disappointment, I mused, was to have the object of one's affection threaten to kill you. I'd found comfort through my friends, old and new, as well as my little man, Woodrow Wilson, all of whom showed me how fortunate I was to be loved and cared for.

Jane fed us dinner before the game began, and as we lingered over dessert, I felt, more than ever, that we are all a family. And through the ordeal we forged an even stronger bond. Cynics though we appear to be to the world outside, we relish each other's approval and affection.

Ralph Chittenham and Maxwell Sing joined us this evening for supper and cards. Jane and I will play bridge with them, as we four are not poker players, although we do excel in bluffing in real life, when necessary, to fulfill our missions.

Mr. Caruthers, whose Christian name is

Zachariah, turns out to be an accountant whose wife ran off with his client. Worse, the client also took all of Zachariah's money, leaving him penniless and living in Bryant Park. On inclement nights, he found shelter in the American Radiator Company Building's construction site, courtesy of a kindly night watchman, with whom he could commiserate, as the watchman's wife had recently run off with his sister.

Aleck did a little research on my rescuer. It seems that he has a doctorate in economics from Princeton, accompanied the American delegation from the United States to Paris for the negotiations of the Treaty of Versailles in '19, serving as one of Woodrow Wilson's (the President, that is) secretaries, and upon his return took a professorship at Columbia. His extravagant wife had put him into debt, so for extra income he moonlighted the books of several business accounts. When his wife ran off with his client and money, he had a nervous breakdown. But the events of the last week have proven that he is a man to be reckoned with. Before me sits quite a different man from the fellow I first encountered on a park bench when the Marx Brothers took the shoes off his feet, as well as the bench from under his seat—the bench facing the American Radiator Company Building.

Mr. Caruthers has cleaned up rather well, in fact, as Jane's good cooking, a daily shave, and new clothes from Aleck's tailor (he is a generous soul!) have done wonders.

Zachariah plays banker this evening, even

though Aleck has offered to bankroll his game. Thanks to his heroism, FPA's column, and numerous feature stories about his plight and his bravery in nabbing the *Broadway Murderer*, he's the new toast of the town, having received a key to the city from the mayor (a key to an apartment would've been better, but is forthcoming as Jane and Ross and Aleck had offered him a permanent room at 412 & 414 where he's been recuperating from his injuries), and a reward from Swope's paper of one thousand dollars.

I don't know what frightened the man more, Chico Marx trying to take his shoes or all the attention he's been getting from the press.

We were all helping to clear away the dishes, doing obeisance to the new edict from Jane, a requirement of all attending Saturday night dinner and poker, when the doorbell rang. Woodrow Wilson raced to the door.

Ross invited Myrtle Price Pierce in through the foyer where everyone joined them in the parlor. She looked at the expectant faces with trepidation, and then smiled, shyly, as Jane greeted her and took her coat and gloves before offering her the chair beside the fire.

The silence did nothing to put her at ease, nor did the brooding lot of hovering masculinity, as she settled into the wing chair. I cut through the wall of hulking men to sit across from Myrtle.

I said, "Guard" to Woodrow Wilson, and he nodded.

Woodrow Wilson leaped onto Myrtle's lap. The surprise of the Boston terrier sitting squarely, looking directly into her eyes, as he moved his head from side to side, lightened the mood, and Myrtle burst out laughing. She rustled his wiry fur, and then at my command, my little man jumped down to sit at my feet.

Jane offered pie and coffee, and Ross something more spirited, but she declined. "I'd just come back to town, when I heard that everyone, the police mostly, had been looking for me. I drove halfway across the country, just to get away from all the horrible things that have been happening. When I saw a headline in an out-of-town paper that said Marion Fields had been murdered—the very day I had lunch with her—and that Gerry had been arrested for the three murders, I knew I had to return home. The police told me all that's happened.

"Dorothy, they told me at your hotel that you were here, but I didn't expect to see you here, Ralph."

"I don't care for poker, but I play a mean hand of bridge."

Myrtle lifted her large purse from beside her chair, and removed a cylindrical package wrapped in white fabric. She rose and walked over to Chitty.

"You've been looking for this," she said, handing it to him.

Ralph's eyes grew large and his face lifted with a smile. "Is it . . . ?"

"The Golden Selket, yes."

"You've had it?"

"Marion gave it to me." The look of confusion on all of our faces prompted her to continue.

"You see, she called me the morning she died— was killed. We met at a little restaurant in a neighborhood where no one would know us if they saw us together."

I didn't say a word.

"She told me only that she was sorry about Reginald, that she knew who the murderer was, and that he had killed Lucille, too. She feared he would come after her for the small statue she had in her purse, a statue that was part of Reginald's collection, was valuable, and the reason behind all the trouble.

"She wanted to go to the police to tell what she knew, but was afraid they would arrest her, too. She wanted to go away, into hiding, so the murderer wouldn't find her. I got the impression that it was a man she was afraid of. Someone she loved. She wouldn't tell me who he was, only that he was dangerous, and that he would never guess that she had given the statue to me, Reginald's wife, of all people.

"She was in tears at first, and then turned very brave, but I couldn't get the name of the murderer from her. She believed that knowing who it was would put me in danger, too! She said she'd alert the police as soon as she was somewhere safe.

"I gave her a check for a thousand dollars, to help her get away. When she believed the police had their man, she would place an ad in the *Times* with an address so that I might contact her through the mail. She would testify against him. I trusted her. I don't know why. She tried to take my husband and his fortune, and yet I believed what she told me, that she had no part in murder and would try to make amends somehow.

"And then when I came back and heard that it was you, Dorothy, that the fiend was after, that you with the help of a street person—"

"It was Mr. Caruthers, Myrtle." I said, indicating the neatly put-together gentleman resting on the arm of the sofa.

"Beg your pardon, Sir," said Myrtle, "I was misinformed."

Mr. Caruthers and I shared a glance and a smile.

"And don't forget the rest of us who came to the rescue!" said Aleck, rolling his *r*'s.

"You'll make sure she won't, Aleck," said Mr. Benchley.

"And there was Frank Case, the Algonquin's manager, keeping an eye out for trouble," I added. "He followed us to the restaurant and called out the troops when he lost us in the fog."

"We should be nicer to Frank," said a repentant Aleck, of the man who tolerated so much abuse from our club.

"All right, I thank *all* who helped catch the man who killed my husband, but especially Dorothy. She remembered the story I told about Reginald's allergy to tomatoes. And when she finally knew who the murderer was, she put herself out there, alone in the night with the devil!"

With tears welling in her eyes she took my hand in hers. "It was swell of you, Dorothy. If there is anything I can ever do for you. . . ."

There was, and there would be, starting with Zachariah Caruthers. Believe it or not, I saw a flash of—something—when they made eye contact upon meeting.

And then there was Gerry Saches. I knew he loved Myrtle, but when I spoke with him soon after his release from jail, he told me there was nothing romantic about his commitment to her. That was over, twenty years ago. For the past five years he'd been in love with his housekeeper, Mrs. Morgan, but as she was so much younger than he, he was afraid she would reject him, and might even leave his employ and her rooms at his house should she object to his advances. I informed him that he was wrong; she was crazy about him. Yesterday, when they were seen dancing at the Savoy, they informed the press, most notably, FPA, of their engagement.

I thought that perhaps Myrtle might help promote Henrietta's decorating career with a few introductions into the homes of her wealthy friends.

And then there was that sweet young girl, Joan Crawford, the waitress-cum-actress who served lunch to Myrtle and Marion. FPA said she was quite a beauty, who claimed to sing and dance. Perhaps Myrtle might find a spot in the chorus for her in one of Reginald's musicals.

And not to forget Brenda McEnerny, home in Ann Arbor, who had buried her daughter last week. It was as if Myrtle had read my mind, for she said, "Marion's mother, Dorothy. She came to claim her daughter's body. I know you helped her. What can I do to put her mind to rest that her daughter tried to do the right thing at the end?"

I told Myrtle we'd talk tomorrow, as I had a few ideas.

"Dorothy," she said, "how was it you knew it was Reginald's lawyer who killed him?"

"Well, Wilfred took over the reading of Reginald's will from Reggie's attorney, Richard Whipple, one of the law firm's partners. Mr. Whipple became deathly ill the night before the reading, thanks to the poison administered in his coffee by Wilfred Harrison. That's how Wilfred got direct and open access to Reginald's effects. I put the pieces together when Brenda McEnerney came back to the hotel to tell me Wilfred was not in the office, and that there was never a private bequest for Marion, as Wilfred had told me, so I made a few calls.

"But then I found a photo on the glued backside of one of Lucille's press clippings, and in Marion's apartment I found a partially burned newspaper clipping as well. The attempt to destroy it failed, you see. It was an announcement of her marriage to Wilfred, complete with a photograph of the happy couple. The names were changed, but I was almost certain the man with Marion was Wilfred. On the reverse side was the review of the tour that Lucille had appeared in in Ann Arbor. I wanted to be wrong about Wilfred, but . . .

"You see, each woman had copies of the same clipping for different reasons. It was the same clipping that connected the two women, and Lucille used the knowledge of the marriage as blackmail to make Marion get her the lead in Reggie's play."

"Coincidence," mused Myrtle.

"I don't believe in coincidence."

The disappointment I felt upon the discovery of Will's treachery swept over me again, but when I looked around the room at all my friends, I rallied.

"But the thing that made me certain that the faces on the back of the clipping were not simply look-a-likes of Wilfred and Marion, was a clue on a notepad that Mr. Benchley and I found in Lucille's apartment. It was the one thing that connected Wilfred to Lucille, whom he had supposedly never met. The message Wilfred had left for me at the Algonquin asked that I call him at his hotel: "Ring room 1130." You see, he had rooms at the *Biltmore, room 1130.*

"Biltmore 1130," said Mr. Benchley, "had been scribbled on a notepad in Lucille's apartment. We thought, perhaps, it was a meeting place and time, but it was Wilfred's room number, after all.

"But, Mrs. Parker," continued Mr. Benchley, "you have yet to explain your miscalculation of Maxwell's white gloves."

"Shoe polish, of course. Black shoe polish staining his fingers. I could smell the woody scent of it when he answered the door. I always associate the smell with my father. He liked to shine up his shoes, himself, every morning."

"I *had* been polishing my father's boots, earlier, but the gloves were really for polishing the silver service."

"That's where I was mistaken, Max, forgive me; I never saw your stained fingers, only caught a whiff of the shoe polish. But I realized that a bronze finish could be achieved if black shoe polish was smeared over gold—hence, a less valuable bronze Selket, like the one that Reggie showed to Gerald Saches to deliberately mislead his business partner. A perfect way to disguise the valuable golden one. I smelled shoe polish, but I mistook the silver tarnish on your white gloves as being the shoe polish that my imagination made me suspect you were removing from the statue. I didn't know that Marion had the statue. We thought Ralph was the thief, and you were in—"

"Cahoots!" said Aleck.

"Yes, I thought, well, we all thought you were in 'cahoots' with a murderer."

It was over. Three people were dead, the murderer and the art dealer in jail, a stolen artifact recovered, lives shook up, and new beginnings ahead for the survivors. It had been one hell of a week.

The boys were getting antsy for the games to begin, and although Myrtle was invited to stay for the games, she thanked us all again and said she had to be on her way.

Mr. Caruthers helped her on with her coat, and walked her down to the street where he hailed a cab for her. Jane and I looked out the window and watched as the two stood in conversation alongside the waiting taxi. Finally, Mr. Caruthers sent the cabbie on his way. Offering his arm to Myrtle, the two walked briskly down the sidewalk and out of view.

Jane and I looked at each other and laughed.

The End

Wonder City— I love this postcard of Times Square
looking from the Times tower up toward 46th Street.
This is my City, my playground. . . .

Yours Truly

Poetic License

I have taken poetic license in the *Mrs. Parker Mysteries* quite often, but with great care. I have tried to be historically accurate with dates and times when my characters were really roaming the streets, theatres, and speakeasies of Manhattan during the 1920s. I've taken a few liberties, which will, no doubt, raise the proverbial red flags before the eyes of the purists and Round Table devotees. For instance, Dorothy Parker's rooms at the Algonquin did not face the 44th Street front entrance of the hotel as I have placed them, but toward the back of the building on the eleventh floor, overlooking the rear façades of buildings along the south side of 45th Street. At one time, she had a room on the second floor. So it is, too, with Robert Benchley's rooms at the Royalton, the bachelor residence directly across the street from the Algonquin. His rooms were at the rear, not facing 44th Street. He kept those rooms for sixteen years, but for some time lived on Madison Avenue with Charles MacArthur, as well as at the Algonquin. He did not take the Royalton rooms until 1929. Aleck Woollcott did share a residence on West 47th street with Jane Grant and Harold Ross, but that situation lasted only a few years. He bought an apartment on 52nd Street facing the East River, dubbed "Wit's End" by Dottie Parker.

And for the sake of action, I have occasionally

placed an alleyway where there never was one, or invented a church or a theatre that never existed, that sort of thing.

Officer Joe Woollcott of the NYPD is a figment of my imagination. But it is not unlikely that Aleck would have had such a down-to-earth cousin. Aleck was his family's anomaly.

At different times throughout the 1920s, Alexander Woollcott, Robert Benchley, Heywood Broun, Marc Connolly, and Robert Sherwood wrote for, or were editors of, many different publications. To avoid confusion, and finding the changes in employment of no consequence to the storylines of my books, I have kept them on the staffs of only one or two papers or magazines.

Woodrow Wilson, our lovable Boston terrier, was one of a long line of dogs embraced by Dorothy Parker, including Robinson, a dachshund, and two poodles, each named Cliché. But, I chose Woodrow, and have kept him alive years longer than was actually the case.

I do not refer to Dorothy Parker's real-life romantic attachments, nor include those gentlemen in any of my stories, except for her husband, Eddie, and he is mentioned only to give the reader an understanding of her circumstances and the effects of World War I on her life and times.

While researching, I have encountered many

conflicting accounts of events involving my leading characters. It usually has to do with who said/did what to whom, and as these biographers/sources are sincere and unquestionably creditable, and as most of the stories in question are hearsay, or second- or third-generation accounts that these sources are retelling, situations that might not even have happened, these differences are of little importance, really, so forgive me my trespasses, please. First-hand accounts might have been embellished to enhance entertainment effect. (For example, Hemingway credited himself with several clever lines that were quipped by others, but were good enough for him to claim as his own.) I still cannot definitely attribute the line, "Let's get out of these wet clothes and into a dry martini," to Robert Benchley. Some suggest it was a press agent or Aleck Woollcott who actually said the words. Lots of people claim credit. As nearly a century has passed, these retold events might be assigned to folklore. (I wasn't there; you weren't there; so we'll never know for sure what really occurred.) Also, famous quotes once spoken by these famous people were not always spoken at the time and place at which I have put them in my novels.

Praise for *The Broadway Murders*

Those of us who since childhood had wished there was a time machine that could let us experience and enjoy life in other periods, should read Agata Stanford's "Dorothy Parker Mysteries" series. They wonderfully recreate the atmosphere and spirit of the literary and artistic crowd at the Algonquin Round Table in the 1920s, and bring back to life the wit, habits, foibles, and escapades of Dorothy Parker, Robert Benchley, and Alexander Woollcott, as well as of the multitude of their friends and even their pets, both human and animal.

— *Anatole Konstantin*
    Author of *A Red Boyhood: Growing Up Under Stalin*

Oh, boy! I just read *The Broadway Murders*! Agata Stanford's Dorothy Parker Mysteries is destined to become a classic series. It's an addictive cocktail for the avid mystery reader. It has it all: murder, mystery, and Marx Brothers' mayhem. You'll see, once you've taken Manhattan with the Parker/Benchley crowd. Dorothy Parker wins! Move over, Nick and Nora.

— *Elizabeth Fuller*
    Author of *Me and Jezebel*

About the Author

Agata Stanford is an actress, director, and playwright who grew up in New York City. While attending the School of Performing Arts, she'd often walk past the Algonquin Hotel, which sparked her early interest in the legendary Algonquin Round Table.

CPSIA information can be obtained at www.ICGtesting.com
Printed in the USA
LVOW06s0430180813

348392LV00001B/161/P

9 780982 754207